The Marriage Bed

REGINA McBRIDE

A TOUCHSTONE BOOK

PUBLISHED BY SIMON & SCHUSTER

NEW YORK   LONDON   TORONTO   SYDNEY

TOUCHSTONE
Rockefeller Center
1230 Avenue of the Americas
New York, NY 10020

TOUCHSTONE and colophon are registered trademarks
of Simon & Schuster, Inc.

Designed by Jan Pisciotta

Manufactured in the United States of America

10   9   8   7   6   5   4   3   2   1

Library of Congress Cataloging-in-Publication Data

McBride, Regina, 1956–
The marriage bed / Regina McBride.
p. cm.
"A Touchstone book."
ISBN 0-7432-5497-X
1. Women—Ireland—Fiction. 2. Mothers and daughters—Fiction. 3. Separation (Psychology)—Fiction. 4. Married women—Fiction. 5. Teenage girls—Fiction. 6. Ireland—Fiction. I. Title.

PS3563.C333628M37 2004
813'.54—dc22   2003067294

For information regarding special discounts for bulk purchases,
please contact Simon & Schuster Special Sales at 1-800-456-6798
or business@simonandschuster.com

for my parents

I love you

CONTENTS

PART THREE
The Torment of Metals

PART FOUR
Aqua Mirifica

My childhood bends beside me,
secrets weary of their tyranny.

—*James Joyce*

PART ONE

In Ancestral Sleep

The created world began with a separation of opposites. The sun became distinct from the moon. A single vapor divided into four elements.

—MEDIEVAL ALCHEMICAL TEXT

ONE

1910

Merrion Square
Dublin

My husband's mother had decorated the little room at the back of the house with me in mind. It was a room meant for solitude, for revery and prayer, because the face I had presented then, fifteen years before, had suggested a contemplative girl, a girl given to intercourse with the saints. To her I was an unassuming girl, a kind of empty vessel like the Virgin Mary, who would carry holiness in her womb. They were an ecclesiastical family; she wanted her son to father a priest.

A fortnight or two after we were married, and before Manus and

I left Kenmare in the west, Mrs. O'Breen came to Dublin on her own and furnished this old Georgian house for us. It was then that in a surge of generosity toward me she had the walls of this little room painted sea green and scallop shells impressed into fresh plasterwork. She said that she'd been concerned that I would miss the Atlantic. In fact, after having been cloistered at Enfant de Marie, so far inland, I had grown to find the smell and sound of the waves diminishing.

But I never expressed such truths to Mrs. O'Breen. As I never expressed them to Manus.

I was up at dawn this January morning, though it was a Sunday, attempting to draw a blue vase that I'd brought in with me from the dining room.

The night before, Manus and our two daughters, Maighread, fourteen, and Caitlin, thirteen, were speaking in low voices at the dining room table. I'd come in and they'd gone quiet. When I asked them what they'd been speaking about, Manus evaded the question and began describing a horse he'd seen earlier that day on Grafton Street, decked out in ribbons and bells. There was a winter fair in Phoenix Park, and the city had been adrift with gypsies.

I struggled now to draw the likeness of the vase, but my mind was not on it. I'd had it before me for over an hour, yet I had only drawn a few faint lines. I was fixed, instead, on the static representations of water along the wainscotting.

Mrs. O'Breen saw decorative potential in all representations of the sea. Here they were, trimming the very room in controlled waves.

In spite of the plasterwork, the room she had bequeathed me was stark. The barest in the house, furnished with only a dresser and a draftsman's table more suitable for a child than an adult. The table faced the dresser upon which I placed the objects of my still lifes: flowers, fruit, bottles, and jars. When I'd finish drawing them I always cleared away the objects and replaced them with those that Mrs. O'Breen kept there: a marble statue of praying hands, and to either side of it, two separate pairs of gloves, lying palm up. They were the white novice gloves that I had been wearing the day I'd come to marry Manus in the house in Kenmare-by-the-Sea and the nuns' black gloves I would have worn if I'd taken my vows as I had been close to doing before Manus's proposal. But this morning a rebellious humor flickered in me, and I toyed with the idea of rearranging everything, and relegating the gloves and praying hands to some dim cabinet.

In the center of one bare wall hung a painting of the Annunciation in a heavy frame with fading gold leaf. There was nothing grand about this particular Annunciation. No lilies or terra-cotta floors. No sunlit cypress trees out the window. In this representation, only an empty, boggy field and an Irish sky with clouds inclined to thunder.

The angel, human looking, wore gray, one muscular knee and calf apparent as he knelt. He was earthbound, without a trace of divinity about him, except perhaps for his wings, which, in the tension of the moment, appeared slightly flexed, and, though his upper body did not lean toward the Virgin in the manner of a Botticelli angel or di Paolo's, he appeared attentive of her.

Over the years I had thought of asking Mrs. O'Breen about the painting, but in her presence my natural impulse was to be silent.

As she had selected everything else in this house, she had also selected me. I was only seventeen when she saw Manus staring in my direction at Mass at Enfant de Marie. I was a novice then, as she had been a novice when her own husband had proposed marriage to her. My quiet, careful demeanor appealed to her. I had come from a wild, windswept place, the Great Blasket Island. She'd liked the idea that I was an islander and probably thought, as many did, that islanders were more backward even than tinkers. I would be out of my element in her family, dependent, compliant.

The face I wore then suggested stillness and grace. Before my wedding night, Mrs. O'Breen had given me tea in a room with a sea view, filled with statues of female martyrs. Agnes, Lucy, Cecilia. I was at the height of my saintly persona, managing it so well that I had felt myself radiating light. Mrs. O'Breen could not take her eyes off me. For a while there was gratification in being this girl, but the young are in love with the moment, and disappointment had been inevitable. Even I knew that it would come.

I gazed at the face of the Virgin in the painting, expressionless except for the little squeezed mouth and the trace of mistrust in the eyes at the intrusion of the angel.

In retrospect, I marvel that Mrs. O'Breen had once believed so fully in me. Over the years I had found that seeing Mrs. O'Breen in the flesh, her real presence, was easier than feeling the darker spirit of her that made dim susurrations in the walls of this house.

I picked up my pencil and, with a series of quick, curved lines, struggled a last time to draw the dark blue vase. But when I heard the girls' footsteps above, my heart began to throb and I stopped drawing again.

As I ascended the stairs, I heard them talking softly. They startled as I appeared in the doorway. Sitting close together on Caitlin's bed, they were looking at a pamphlet of some kind.

"What is it you have?" I asked them softly.

They exchanged a wary look. Then, gathering her resolve, Maighread stood. "We're going to boarding school in September," she said.

"You're not," I said. "You're both registered for another year at St. Alban's."

Caitlin looked down at her lap, having thrown the pamphlet off to the side. She rubbed her fingers together nervously.

A few months back we had talked about boarding school, one in particular where a number of their friends were going—St. Lucretia's in Wicklow. Pressured by Maighread's appeals, I had almost given in, only because it was a short train ride from Dublin, and because I had had little to support me in my fight against it. It was simply what girls of their age and social class did.

But in the end I'd said no. I had tried to hide the desperation I'd felt at the idea of their going from me, and I'd believed that if they had known how hard leaving home would be, they would not have wanted it. It had, I told them, only been the novelty of it they'd been bucking for.

"I'll not send you unmoored into the world," I had said as my final word.

"It's you who would be unmoored in the world," Maighread had spat back. I'd been stunned at how clearly she could see me.

Now, standing defiant before me, she said, "We're going to Kilorglin in the west. To Enfant de Marie!"

I let out a little, incredulous laugh. "You don't want to go to that nightmare of a place," I said.

"We're going," Maighread said defiantly.

"First of all, it's a terrible place! Girls die there of consumption!"

"That was ages ago, Mammy. Things are different now!"

"It's on the other side of Ireland! Do you think I'd let you go that far away?"

"Nanny's already registered us. We're going," Maighread said. Caitlin shifted uncomfortably on the bed. Maighread watched my face carefully as she always did when she confronted me.

"No one's consulted me about this," I said.

"We all knew what you would say."

I paused. "I'm sure Caitlin doesn't want to go that far away," I said, waiting for her to meet my eyes. "Do you, lamb?"

"She does!" Maighread said coming closer to me, almost as tall as I was, her chest high in a glory of forthrightness.

"Let her tell me herself," I said.

I felt Caitlin softening as she stared at her hands on her lap.

"Mammy," she said tenderly, and Maighread let go an infuriated sigh.

Caitlin shot her a confused look and then said quickly, "We'll not be far from Nanny! You shouldn't worry over us."

I brushed past Maighread to Caitlin. I touched her shoulder. "I don't want you to go," I said.

She breathed hard and set her mouth. "I want to go!"

The room swayed around me. She watched me now like Maighread did, her eyes softer but resolved.

"You never let us do the things the other girls are able to do. You're always afraid about everything."

I sat on the edge of the bed. "The wind there in the west is fierce," I uttered, reaching now for anything.

"What are you on about the wind for?" Maighread asked, holding my eyes.

Manus was at the door then. I was uncertain when he'd come.

"Let them out from under you, Deirdre," he said.

The three of them looked at me, and an expression of pity came into Caitlin's face. She averted her eyes.

"Your mother registered them at Enfant de Marie?" I asked him, rising to my feet.

"Yes. All the arrangements have been made," Manus said. "And September is still far off. You've plenty of time to get used to the idea."

"But I've registered them for school here in Dublin for September. I've paid the installments."

"I notified them. I got the money back."

I stood a few moments without moving, then took a deep breath and walked vacantly downstairs to my little room at the back of the house.

I was fourteen years old, Maighread's age, when I first crossed the bay to Ventry Harbour. Until then I'd resisted the sea, afraid of its moods, its lack of pity, the black boil of it at night. My grandmother and I were leaving Great Blasket Island for good, moving to her sister's house near Ballyferriter, the place she had originally come from before she'd married into island people and the place where she would remain until her death.

I remember the pattern around the rim of a cracked teacup, dark green curlicues snaking this way and that, small, fierce-looking male heads in profile woven into the design. My great-aunt's cold, rough hands grasped the cup as she told me that such designs were called "Celtic knotwork." She spoke an unsettling combination of Irish and English, a disagreeable warble to her voice. The memory brings a heartsore feeling, my parents newly dead, my fate undecided as it was, the alien language deepening in me an uncertainty of the world.

The waves slapped inconsolably at the rocks below my great-aunt's house, throwing white sparks into the air. My grandmother was too old, she said, to care for me properly. My own mother had been born to her when she was fifty. "An old cow's calf," my grandmother had called her. Even after she was dead, my grandmother shook her head when she spoke of my mother. "Never with a lick o' sense."

The last time I would see my grandmother was when she came to Kenmare after my wedding to Manus. She got tipsy, and I was ashamed over her toothless, windbeaten face and the way she regaled Mrs. O'Breen with what a mad thing I'd been as a child; a regular faery like my mother, taking off barefoot in the icy gales, destined to the madhouse with the queer ways I had. And wasn't it a great thing she'd done bringing me to the Poor Maries, and weren't they the miracle workers? Look at me now, with the radiant face of God's lamb.

She had left me at Enfant de Marie with worn shoes and a coat without buttons. One nun told another that I was a filthy, windburned creature and looked like I'd been walking the roads of Ireland for weeks. But it had been the crossing of the sea and standing in the boat crying, my face leaning into the bluster, and the wiping of those tears that had reddened my skin and made the sleeves of my coat taste like salt. I was attached to that coat and its old smell reminiscent of the Blasket, a smell of black turf from the field near the Way of the Dead, different from mainland turf. It was a darker, wetter fragrance like the mud that keeps to new-dug potatoes.

My last name, O'Coigligh, was Quigley in English, and one nun laughed that it suited me because it meant "untidy or unkempt hair." She said I was a trembly girl and grew impatient with my wincing when she tried to comb through my tangles.

Through intense monotony the Irish was driven back from the forefront of my tongue, into my throat. I lived a period of my life underneath language, words rising and moving above me on air, but I hadn't a mouth to speak them. I understood the English quickly, but I resisted it now. Though certain beautiful phrases of it taunted me.

My Beloved is mine, and I am his: he feedeth amongst
the lilies.

I liked the look of it on the page, but I pronounced the vowels wrong, which made me hesitate to speak it aloud. Sister Dymphna shamed me. "You can hear the mud slides of the Blasket in your vowels," she said, insisting there was an ignorance to the Irish spoken on the Blasket. My gut and throat contracted when I tried to speak, and I felt her ruler across my tongue. The tongue, with its quivering will and form amorphous enough to slip and contract and reshape itself, sustained little of the blow, yet it was crippled with indignity. And with the banished language any sense of who I may have been retreated, and I became a blank, white page. They called me Deirdre from the Blasket rather than Deirdre Quigley, to make allowances for my backwardness and my muteness.

Though I don't think I was ever denied food, I was afflicted with the ache of an empty stomach. I tried to soothe it with porridge or bread and bacon. But the extra food did not fill me, and closing my eyes in my cot each night I feared the hunger would make an end of me in my sleep. I dreamt of standing knee deep in the unruly tide off the western strand, gathering limpets and winkles, filling my apron with "sea fruit" as my grandmother called them, the wind lashing my hair against my face, my wet dress slapping at my legs. Seeing a soft light over Woman's Island west of the strand, I heard behind the noise of the wind a tinny, hardly audible music, the melody of Donal na Grainne. In my dreams, my mother and father danced, embracing each other in the private sweetness between them. That is how I saw them, set that way. I could barely recall them at all, except as the two mythic figures, my father's back articulated with muscles and my mother's head gracefully reposing on his chest. Hopeless that they would take their eyes off each other and see me, I'd travel back up to the empty cottage, struggling to cook the limpets and winkles. The low, single flame from the cresset's wick, which floated in its little vessel of seal oil was so dull and oily and low it barely cooked the bit of flesh scraped out of the shell.

Two

In the morning I stood outside the gates of St. Alban's. Sometimes the girls lingered in groups on the steps, laughing and talking, but I never left until the bell sounded and I saw both of my daughters in procession with the others, go in, and the monitoring nun close and bolt the iron doors behind them. A few minutes passed, and I saw the line of girls going by the windows along the second-floor corridor. As she did most days, Maighread looked down at me with disapproval, my anxiety over her and her sister a point of ever intensifying agitation between us. I blinked and looked away.

I had difficulty making myself leave this morning. I waited a while, staring up at the windows. When the girls were small, there had been days when I would look up for hours at the windows of their classrooms. I had been visited back then by a memory, one I could not place in time, in which I saw a woman in a wild helter-skelter run along a pier. As a boat retreated on the water, the woman flailed inconsolably and looked as if she might throw herself into the sea. Two men descended suddenly from the shadow of a hill, rushed her, and held her by the arms.

"Panic" I called the lady in the memory, though I would not identify her. That is the lady who possessed me those early days when I was forced to break with my girls for long hours of the day.

She was there again now, more real than the other things I saw around me.

I closed my eyes. Why did Mrs. O'Breen want the girls at Enfant de Marie? She had no designs on making my daughters into nuns. Though she often sent them rosaries and chapel veils and little figurines of the saints, she had told me once that nuns meant little in the grand scheme of things. She had never hidden from me her single-minded desire that Manus and I have a son. The idea of working to inspire a vocation in either of my daughters was a distraction from her central purpose.

We saw little of her while the girls were infants. When Maighread was six and Caitlin, five, we had visited Kenmare. She had watched them distantly, as if childhood were an inscrutable condition she did not quite know how to penetrate. It had felt horrible to me that she'd never tried to kiss or cuddle them. They'd felt her indifference and answered it back with the same.

Mrs. O'Breen had watched, amazed, at how animated Manus had become in the presence of his daughters; at the pleasure he'd felt fetching them up in his arms and the patience with which he'd participated in their games, obeying their commands. One day they'd covered him in sand and surrounded him with bits of driftwood, decorating him with ribbons of kelp.

During that same visit I'd looked through the window that faced the beach and had seen Mrs. O'Breen walking toward Manus, extending to him an Aran sweater as he'd stood on the foreshore in the wind.

He'd smiled sheepishly at her as she'd helped him into it. She'd pressed a palm to his cheek and looked to be saying tender words to him, and he'd bowed his head slightly in a pleased and familiar surrender, his face lit up at her adulation. She felt such love for him, I'd thought. Why didn't she feel it for his daughters?

But the older the girls got, the more comfortable she became with them. She knew how to court them, giving them opulent gifts. But I could feel the suppressed chill in her, and the enduring disappointment that they had not been born boys.

Why did she want them at Enfant de Marie? She wanted them far away from me and closer to her for some reason. What was she engineering?

A girl from Maighread's class looked out a third-floor window, and that broke my trance. I turned quickly and walked away, knowing the furious embarrassment Maighread would feel if the girl told her I was still there.

It was Monday, the day of my life drawing class at the National Gallery, so I took the coach back along Nassau Street.

There was no human model that day, just a carefully arranged still life: a teakettle, three oranges, a raveled brocade tablecloth. I worked distractedly at my easel, using rough charcoal and newsprint. I reminded myself that September was far off, and that things could still change.

Afterward I went for coffee with Sarah Dooley, the mother of one of Maighread's classmates.

We had been out to coffee a few other times previously, and I wondered if I might try to talk to her about the girls' going away; if I might trust her to be sympathetic, even though I'd heard her speak happily about her own daughter's acceptance to St. Lucretia's for September.

But she had a lot to talk about herself, having just had a row that morning with her daughter. "She's got a mouth on her like a fishwife! I don't know where she's learning it! Always looking for a way to insult me." She took a sip of her coffee, then lifted her head dramatically and said, "From fear of being humiliated, deliver me!"

"Oh!" I said. "I just let Maighread do that."

"What?" she asked, confused.

"I let her humiliate me."

She looked at me hard, at first incredulously, then disapprovingly. I felt myself shrinking under the look.

"You shouldn't," she said.

"Well, I just don't fight back when she tries to rile me up."

"Why not?" she asked.

I shook my head, at a loss to explain it.

"Maybe she needs a fight out of you. She doesn't really want to humiliate you. It's your job not to let her," Sarah said.

"But your daughter continues to try to humiliate you, even though you fight with her."

"It doesn't matter," Sarah snapped, irritated by my challenge. "She's better off because I stand up to her. She respects me for it."

Sarah changed the subject, talking about the class we'd just come from, complaining that there'd been no live model; that we'd paid to draw live models, and that the instructor himself should have taken off his clothes and let us draw him. She looked for a laugh from me, but I could only muster a smile, and a belated one at that. I had the distinct feeling that she did not like me.

When we parted that day on Westmoreland Street I walked in the opposite direction from home, where the buildings were tall and cobbled and gray. The air was damp, the skies pewtered, and soon snow began to fall. I kept thinking I should turn back, but I moved farther and farther away from Merrion Square, gazing absently into the windows of unassuming shops as I passed them. I stopped before a window, stunned to see words in Irish floating on the glass: RÉIDH LE CAITHEAMH. *Ready to wear.* The Irish belonged to the old and abandoned world. What was it doing here?

I peered into the dark interior of the shop and saw a rack of coats in a shadow, and deeper inside, a headless figure in a plain-cut dress.

On two different occasions over the past months, while walking on a crowded Dublin street, I had heard phrases spoken in Irish. The first time had been at the Baggot Street Market.

"Má tá sé I do bhríste." *If you've got the guts.* A challenge issued in a soft, bawdy female voice.

I had stopped dead still, then turned slowly, searching for the woman who had spoken, but no one had stood out to me in the various groups of people. I'd heard the words again in my mind and imagined a young island woman wearing battered woolens and an apron.

A few weeks later I had just gotten off the tram at Inchicore. The streets had been crowded as I'd walked south toward Stephen's Green. A man's voice in close proximity behind me had said softly, "Cén t-ainm atá ort?" *What's your name?*

Turning to look, I'd been jostled by the crowd. I'd peered into each male face that had come close, but all had seemed confused or irritated by my staring. I'd told myself that it had to have been asked of someone else, not of me, though the gentle, confidential tone was an intimate voice that I trusted and longed to answer.

After these two incidents, I braced myself each time I walked on the streets, anticipating the sound of spoken Irish, longing for it and fearing it at once.

But now, here I stood staring at an inscription in gold on the window. I touched the painted words with my fingertip.

The letters dissolved before me, and I heard Maighread's voice echoing in my mind. "It's you who will be unmoored in the world."

A man's face came suddenly into the light within the shop, peering out at me with a smile and beckoning me in. I stepped back, startled, then continued on.

Approaching the quays, the air grew rife with the river's smoky, well-traveled odor. The gulls, usually wheeling over the water, huddled in subdued clumps on the bridgepier.

By the time I reached Essex Quay, the snow was gathering in drifts. Dublin had become mystically quiet. Every sound cast an echo: my own footsteps in the soft snow, the creak of a shop door, the muffled cough of a pedestrian across the road.

Under the pristine whiteness, the sooty gables and dormers of the taller houses appeared charred. My hems were sodden, and the dampness came through my boots. I turned suddenly south away from the river into a narrow, winding lane that descended in a curve, spectral-looking houses leaning over the cinder paths that ran before them.

There were no other pedestrians in this narrow lane. A bird flew close above me, and I crouched, holding my hand up over my brow. I looked up when it was clear of me, white wings in a flutter rising up and landing at a dovecote near a green eave. The dove stepped back and forth, softly warbling on the ledge of a dormer window with a dim light within. Beside the lit window a sky blue plaque—ANTIQUARIAN BOOKS—was carved in gold lettering.

I felt the cold now and smelled a coal fire. I opened the door at street level and ascended a narrow flight of creaking stairs. When I reached the floor where the bookstore was located, I saw another sign. This one read, THE ALCHEMISTS DEN. My heart sped up as I opened the door to the shop. The rooms within looked more like a library than a bookshop. Tall, heavy oak cases filled with cloth and leather volumes were illuminated by oil lamps. A heavyset man wearing round glasses met my eyes from his chair behind a desk. He nodded at me, his face betraying no feeling.

"It's very wet out," I said by way of apology for my sodden shoes. He waved his hand: my dampening his floor was of no consequence to him. As I moved softly in between a high row of books, I saw a woman sitting at a small table upon which four or five large vellum-bound volumes lay. I gave her a smile. She stood and took my arm. "Stand by the fire," she said, "and get your blood moving again." She fanned the embers until the coals went bright, lighting the grate and the edge of her dark dress.

I stood warming my hands before the flames and noticed on the mantel an etching of an empty room, the bricks of the wall artfully detailed and shadowed. The words, scripted in italics beneath, imbued the image with meaning. *Celluris Memorium.* The room of memory, or perhaps more precisely, the storage room of memory.

The woman returned to her volumes. I saw her dip her fingers into a tin of what looked like lard and begin to massage the leather spine of one of the tomes.

I left the fire and faced a heavy shelf of books, looking directly at titles that rang with foreboding familiarity to me.

Atalanta Fugiens, Aurora Consurgens, the Book of Lambspring. I had looked into each of these volumes in the library in the house in Kenmare early in my marriage. As my fingertips grazed the spine of a volume called *Secretus Secretorum*, I began to sweat with excitement and trepidation.

Only two days married, Manus and I had hidden away together in a remote room of his mother's house, where we'd lain naked on our bellies turning the pages of the *Secretus Secretorum*, which was rife with depictions of sexual intercourse, the metaphor for the alchemical process: the marriage of one metal to another. Manus had explained to me that the alchemists had struggled to produce superior metals by intermixing them.

In this book we'd found *The Courtship of Sol and Luna*, a series of particularly graphic, step-by-step illustrations of the marriage of gold to silver, the sun being the man and representing gold, the moon being the woman and representing silver. In one picture we'd clearly seen the male genital entering the female.

The discovery of this mystifying book had fused itself in our minds with the discovery of each other's bodies. We had read phrases of the text to one another as we'd made love.

"'I will sow my gold,'" Manus had quoted to me once, the volume fading from his breath, "'in your silvery earth.'"

Once, still breathless after a feverish bout of sex, Manus had told me that he believed this book held the secrets of the universe, if only we could interpret them.

But this book had also frightened me. Once, while Manus had been sleeping, I had leafed through the pages, encountering horrific, terrifying things: beheadings, a man swallowing a child, a creature half-cock half-toad exuding poisonous smoke and fire from its mouth. Two-headed dragons being disemboweled by monks. It was as if these were the serpents guarding the gates of Paradise. Out of lust, I'd managed my way through the random labyrinth of ugliness and sadness, arriving eventually, shaken, upon the sexually exquisite ones.

My fingers moved across the titles, and I returned again to the *Secretus Secretorum*. It felt enormous and heavy. The man looked up at me over the round windows of his glasses as I carried it to a small table in the corner, where I sat down to look at it. Out of his view, I took a deep breath and found myself relieved that the image I'd opened randomly upon was not of a particularly horrifying nature. A man lying ill in a bed, a woman standing at his bedside gazing down at him. Out a window behind them, a black night sky filled with stars. Like many of the alchemical pictures, the image itself was framed by an elaborate mandala, at the corners of which were depictions of the four elements: billowing waves, flames, a tree growing from a plot of earth, a cloud. Fierce animal heads blew fire and swirls of wind from their mouths.

I read the text beside the picture.

> The ores that are not gold are ill and require cleansing. Unless gold is acheived in the coupling of the metals, illness remains and the state of the world is such that the whole house and the generations that might follow are in the thrall of a great sickness.

A wave of nausea moved over me. I stared at the text but could not read more. I sat back from the book, and my eyelids grew heavy. I remembered that it had been this way before with these books. I had never been able to take in more than a few phrases of the written text at a time.

I could still hear the woman beyond the bookshelves at work rhythmically massaging the vellum. My eyes wandered around the room and then fell back on the text.

> . . . houses in the thralls of terrible curses. As in the Greek houses, Atreus and Thyestes.

My eyes fell on another phrase:

It is an illness which separates body from soul.

I heard the squeak of the woman's chair and in my peripheral vision saw an approaching shadow.

I heard her voice. "Are you all right?" She touched my shoulder. I started and looked up into her face.

"Yes," I said weakly. I closed the *Secretus Secretorum* and stood.

The man was not at the front desk as I moved past to the door and descended the stairs.

Outside, the wind was up, and the snow, stinging my face, revivified me, bringing me back to the world. The gutters had gone to slush, and I could hear horses clopping on the main road along the quays. I turned away from the traffic and moved deeper into the maze of streets. It stunned me to see that the clock on the wall inside a shop said half three. The afternoon light was failing and some businesses had already lit the gas. The clock over the Ballast Office had said eleven when I'd left Sarah Dooley on Westmoreland Street. Was it while I'd been walking that so much time had passed, or was it in the bookstore? How long had I gazed at the picture of the man lying ill in his bed, his wife standing beside him? I had invited something dangerous close to me.

I could have asked someone for directions, but I felt fragile and shied from people's faces. I kept wandering, remembering some ancient Greek story about a man killing his son and feeding him to his guests, the curse of that sin then to be borne by the generations that followed, and all the children to suffer with the sins of that parent, to be brought down with it into tragedy.

I began to make note of the street names: Ross Road, Bride Road. Bull Alley. I heard the jingle of harnesses, and an ambulance car went rushing past. When I saw the Carmelite Church on Whitefriar Street, I knew again where I was and found my way back to Dame Street, where I saw a stalled tram car filling with snow.

A woman shivered in the doorway of a vacant shop. "Two for a penny!" she cried out to me. I selected two banberry cakes from the wooden tray harnessed around her neck, then went on my way, but found I couldn't stomach them.

It was late, almost six, when I finally reached Merrion Square, the arches flickering on the stately houses. The air smelled of burning coal, and plumes of smoke from the chimneys ascended high into the dark sky.

When I came in, Manus, Maighread, and Caitlin were sitting to supper. Their eyes were large, surprised looking when they saw me. I sensed a din on the quiet, the ring of unfinished conversation. My clothes were deluged, but it was my face they all seemed fixed on. Moving into the hallway I saw in the mirror my florid, fevered color.

Mrs. Daley peered at me from the doorway to the kitchen.

"Would Madam like tea?" she asked dryly.

"Yes, thank you," I said.

I did not go upstairs to change, and was shaking faintly when I sat to join them.

I saw a Kilorglin postmark on a letter beside Manus's plate. When he saw me looking at it, he pocketed it. I looked at Caitlin, but she would not hold my eyes. Mrs. Daley came in with my tea. I drained my cup and set it back on the saucer. I was dizzy and not inclined to speak to them or to ask about the letter. I stared at the silver tureen centerpiece and saw through it, and through the table beyond it. I focused on flecks of wetness on my nose and eyelashes, entranced by the way they glinted in the lamplight.

After the meal I went into my little back room, not caring that the hem of my dress left a damp trail behind me.

I stared at the vase that I'd left on the shelf. It was made of liquid, I thought. It had been poured. Viscous, dark blue liquid. It caught and made distortions of everything in the room. How, I asked myself, had I ever imagined I could draw such a thing?

A gust of wind blew the shutter open suddenly, and a bit of powdery snow flew in through the screen. I went to the window and stood in the blast of it, a south-blowing wind. I could smell ice on it, just as I had been able to smell the glaciers on the Greenland current when I was a child living on the Blasket. That wind caused grain and grass to stream steadily in one direction. In spite of its coldness, it was a fertilizing wind that blew the spores of plants and trees on the island, displacing them, carrying them into unexpected places, so an ear of barley might appear close to the beach, or a lone potato plant on the windy summit, growing impossibly between stones. Thus was the strangeness such winds encouraged. Things growing in isolation, blown away from their like.

I left the window open and sat before my drawing pad. The gust caused a loose strand of my hair to graze against the nape of my neck. I fancied that Caitlin had come into the room and was touching me with the tips of her fingers. I pressed the point of my pencil to the paper, afraid to turn and look. Instead I looked at the angel in the painting, coming suddenly upon the Virgin when she was alone; how the Virgin must have heard the angel first or sensed it there before she'd turned to see it. How she must have been afraid. Did she sense the Holy Ghost above her? Did it change the smell of the air? The temperature of it? Did it send the errant hairs grazing at her temples and neck?

I had a sudden intense desire to have a child inside me; a child not of Manus's body but only of mine. A child between me and this wind; a crumb of fecund fire blown to me on its back.

I thought of my daughters and closed my eyes, picturing the quiet estuaries of selfhood in their eyes, intense privacies that excluded me. And I knew then that I could not have borne to have such intimacy again and to lose it.

From the beginning it had been difficult with Maighread. On the third day when my milk had come in she'd sucked a bellyful, then begun to shriek, turning her head side to side, then spit it all up.

"Some babbees cannot drink mother's milk," Mrs. Grey, the

midwife, had said to me. But I had refused to believe and had tried again to the same result. The third time I'd offered Maighread my breast she'd refused it, red and shaking, understanding my milk to be poisonous to her; the shrillness of her screams, outcries against me.

It would be weeks before we found the right formula for her. She could not take cow's milk, and we came at last upon the milk of a certain kind of goat that she could stomach. It had to be brought in special for her from Drogheda.

Maighread cried when I held her, vexed and impatient, her arms trembling, and one afternoon, beside myself with grief, I called Mrs. Grey close and asked her in a fervent whisper if she would keep Maighread and care for her.

She did not understand, and she admonished me in a harsh whisper. "Some babbees have fierce constitutions, but they are as soft and helpless as any infant."

After Maighread's birth, the pious contemplative face I had shown Mrs. O'Breen was shattered. Maighread had exposed the weakness of my nature. I almost didn't rise to the challenge of her.

I remembered a babbee I'd seen dead on the Blasket, put to rest in a little wooden box after having suffered with a terrible illness. I remembered my grandmother's words, "Ah, sure. Nothing can hurt that child now." I had thought of how safe it was under the ground in quiet, perpetual sleep. I wished Maighread dead sometimes that her suffering might stop.

In her third month she evened out, and I breathed a deep sigh, the difficulty riding away like the tides of a storm. But that beginning and my fear that I was wrong for her would always live between us. And it would always be there in the air between Mrs. Grey and me, that I had offered her my girl. And it would always be in my own thoughts that I'd wished my girl the peace of the grave.

Caitlin came a year later, mewing like a lamb, a soft, temperate cry. She nuzzled up to my breast within an hour of her birth. For weeks I'd lie easy with her, startled from dreams, confused as to whether she was inside or outside me, so woven together were we two. She was a pet, smaller than Maighread had been and marbled red with tufts of fair hair and a tiny pink mouth that puckered to a star shape when she sucked. She could not get enough of the milk from my body. She loved to be in my arms, yet there was a strength to Caitlin. She had more resources in herself. It confused me, and it took me years to understand that Maighread, the one most vexed with me, needed me the most. She had nightmares, and in the throes of half sleep clung to me with desperation that moved me like nothing else ever had, the darkness between us filled with a kind of passion.

But children grow out of love with you. Slowly, their growing is a process of cleaving away. It was meant to be this way, Sarah Dooley once told me. They wanted the far reaches of the day and the night.

Once my children had not seen me as separate from themselves, invoking me constantly. But now, like their grandmother and their father, they saw the truth of me.

The memory of infant Caitlin at my breast seized me with a sudden visceral power, and a flux of dampness soaked through my dress at both breasts. I could feel again the strength of her suck, and I could hear Maighread's little suffering cry and smell her newborn skin, like dark, warm honey.

I hunched forward and wept.

I did not feel the hours pass, though I remember the dark deepening in the room, and for a while my pencil cast an elongated shadow over the paper where it lay. Mrs. Daley found me sitting in the dark, my head at my chest. She called Manus in, and he led me out and up to my bed.

I fell ill that night. For three days I dreamt about empty rooms, my sickbed in the drafts of *Celluris Memorium*, a dove coming in the window circling me, a panic of wings.

THREE

At fourteen years old, my parents' deaths were an explosion to my senses, the singular blast that unsettled the particles of the world.

My grandmother refused to dismantle their great bed with the iron headboard but kept it as a monument to the two of them, the curtain always drawn around it. "So they'll have their privacy," she used to say, as if their return was expected, even after they were under the sod.

The cottage we lived in was a single room and the yellow curtain around the bed they slept in the only partition. I recall hearing one night, the wind charming the latches to sing and the soft shuffle of their steps coming into the room. The embers deepened suddenly, and the smell like the smell after a storm, cold and sweet and gusty, filled the house. "Aaaahhh . . ." the whole room seemed to say, faintly like a chorus of children's voices, pulling me back from the threshold of sleep and the straw shifting behind the curtain. I lay in a paralysis without breathing, every nerve at attention, the curtain moving almost indetectably. And I do not know if I really heard her saying it or if I was just anticipating it so intensely, the thing my mother used to say to my father in a breathless moment of tenderness: "Is braithim as titim an saol." *The world is falling away.*

Why, I had always wondered, and would continue to wonder all my life, had she said such a thing in joy?

There was something stunning and misbegotten about what had happened to my mother and father. And the shame of it had been great. A priest brought in from Ventry refused to bless their bodies and said they must not be transported across the sea for a Christian funeral but buried in the island graveyard, a place for vagabonds, nameless sailors, and unbaptized babies.

I'd been the one who'd found them, and it was whispered among the islanders that no one, child or adult, should have witnessed what I had.

If my grandmother spoke I cringed from her, and it took a few moments before the sense of her words became clear to me, my hearing deranged after the death, all sound coming to me a few beats after the visual in the way thunder always follows after lightning. Somewhere within myself, I had decided I could not live close to that memory. I would always be putting something between myself and it. I watched the moods of my grandmother's grief with terrific caution. A flicker of nerves in her face warned me that she might grow convulsive with tears.

In the place where the memory should have resided, what I saw was whiteness, a kind of celestial blizzard, streaming over landscape and sea. Their passing caused remarkable changes in the laws of the natural world. I took to wandering outside to escape the vagarious moods of my grandmother's sorrow, and sitting on the rocks, marveled that I could not hear the sea, though it exploded before me and I felt the shiver and rush of it in my bones.

People seemed afraid to touch me. They squinted in my direction and turned their faces obliquely as if they, too, saw the blizzard within me, horrible and too bright to look at. From their doorways, they watched me pass. I had become something both less and more than human, a strange, isolated being that had, because of some fateful mistake, remained on the wrong side of death.

A month or two after the tragedy, my grandmother and I left the island for good and went to stay in Ballyferriter, with her sister, my great-aunt.

Now and then at that time, I was overtaken with flashes of one or the other of my parents' faces. I had come to feel their death as a singular one. They had succeeded in becoming one abstract idea; one shadowy, faceless creature. But the startling appearances of their faces reminded me that they were differentiated beings. Whichever one I saw before me in a particular moment shimmered there, piercing me, so I felt the loss to the very quick of myself, and grew breathless with sadness. After it dissolved I could not recall it. Even still, for a day or two after I'd seen the face, I felt the presence of that parent, sharply real to me, more real than the stones and the walls, the spoon and the porcelain bowl, things I could not always feel when I touched them. But mostly my parents remained dark, difficult to concentrate on.

Eventually, I invented faces for them. They were strongly boned, fierce and romantic looking, and edged with light. I saw their figures always leaning into gales of wind. Unbearable feelings gave way to a kind of ecstatic idea of who my mother and father had been.

And that is when I began to listen to my grandmother talking to her sister, telling her the life story of Molleen Mohr, my mother. It felt safe to listen if I kept the face of the romantic figure in my mind.

My grandmother went over certain details, as if she were struggling to put order to things; revising, organizing her memories in such a way that she could live with them.

Molleen Mohr had adored her own father. After he drowned during the run for mackerel when she was six, she stopped speaking and gave herself over to daydreaming, lying on the pallet on the floor all day, staring up at the ceiling, captivated by what she saw moving across her field of vision.

When my mother was fifteen a certain schoolmistress came to the island, a widow, Mrs. O'Hearne, and her son, the splendid young man named Macdarragh, who was a mute. They came in summer to settle themselves in preparation for the school year coming.

Immediately Macdarragh was disliked by the island men, the way he left his mother to do her own fetching and carrying and getting settled into the cottage, not making himself useful in the usual ways of an island man.

He had soulful eyes that looked deep into a person, and a strange self-containment. He seemed never to be thinking beyond the moment he was in and walked slowly, contemplating the flowers and the rocks and the sea. He preferred the soft company of women, who were, in turn, drawn to him.

He was eighteen and fair and lovely of form. The men said he was too soft, that he thought himself a woman. But they were wrong about him. He possessed a manly grace not to be denied, a strong sexual undercurrent. Even one of the older island women, Kate Beg, in her fifties, pragmatic and careworn, took to wandering after him. And so the men hated him more because the women had gone dreamy since he'd come, pining for some unlived desire in themselves.

From the first moment Molleen Mohr met Macdarragh face-to-face near the Way of the Dead, a pure recognition was evident between them. And if the constraints of society and propriety had not held, they might have conveyed themselves into each other's arms like long-lost friends. So strong was the sympathy between the two that some even said that Molleen's voluntary muteness at six anticipated Macdarragh's coming. Other young women who'd had their eye on him may have felt a tremor of jealousy, but the power of the connection between Macdarragh and Molleen Mohr was not to be denied; the disappointed girls became her ladies-in-waiting.

After that day my mother and Macdarragh were always together, and my grandmother did not worry about Molleen being compromised, though the two might wander off, because they were never completely alone, women and girls always following after, standing in the peripheral fields, enchanted.

Macdarragh wore, under his jacket, a piece of armor, a knight's tunic. And on mild summer nights he took off his overshirt, walking along the headlands in the heather, he and my mother holding hands and girls and women following easily after. The lowering sun glowed on the facets of the metal, igniting it, and the strangeness of such a thing was eclipsed by the very romance of it.

Molleen began to speak, her voice at first creaky. She became Macdarragh's mouthpiece. One day she explained, translating Macdarragh's signs to the women, who sat in a circle all around him, why he wore the armor. Because of a certain affliction, he had fallen once and broken a rib.

One day in the company of five women, including my mother, Macdarragh was seized by a fit and fell, beating the ground with his fists, a terrible thing to see him convulsing and drooling, making wild noises like some agonized animal, half-bird half-horse. The women encircled him, fretful, uncertain about what should be done.

"We wait!" Molleen cried, shaking with emotion, having been given instruction by Macdarragh in case this should ever occur. "We watch that he doesn't hurt himself and help him as best as we can. But we wait!"

Eventually the convulsions slowed and his eyes were the only thing fluttering, and all the women around him stroking his wet temples, smoothing his hair, chanting. "Gra mo chroi." *Sweetheart.*

And rising up exhausted, it was as if he were returning from battle, a kind of hero, a resurrected look to him. Molleen, more alive than ever since her da's passing, descended the hills supporting him in her arms.

It was near September when the fit came again upon Macdarragh, and this time he fell and broke a leg. A storm started up suddenly as his mother and two island men were taking him across the bay to a Ventry doctor, and the boat went down.

My mother took again to her pallet on the floor, squeezing in one hand a little brass figurine that Macdarragh had given her at the pier before his boat had departed; a little centaur, half-man half-horse, that she would treasure all her life.

The dead were the longed-for ones. Death rendered Macdarragh more beloved than ever. Women gathered heather from the warrens and left it in clumps at the door, treating Molleen as if she'd been his wife. The island women had a great affection for dead men: husbands, brothers, sons. And the newly dead, especially. In Macdarragh's death, he belonged to each of them.

Three years would pass before Molleen would happen out of the house for a rare walk up the hill and come upon the man who would be my father, Liam O'Coigligh, who had left the island as a boy but was now returned. A man who kept mostly to himself, and who cut turf sometimes alone on the north face of the bog; a splendid, lonely figure of a man. Over six feet tall and as straight as a candle.

He was famous for climbing in the crags and the screes, lifting thrushes from their nests, reaching into the crevices of the cliff rocks and capturing the whippeens and bringing them in by the bunches, twenty or thirty birds tied to the ropes around his body.

That day she'd ventured out, Molleen saw him descending the hill with thirty dead birds tied around his body, a feathered, uncanny figure. She stared at him with her jaw dropped, and in response he raised his arms strangely and squawked. Molleen recoiled, terrified.

"Ah, Love, no! I'm fiddling with ye only!" he said softly to her and then unraveled the rope from around his body to show her he was human. But she was not fully convinced; bloody feathers stuck to his flesh. She undertook to remove each one, carefully between her thumb and forefinger, a bold, intimate gesture for two people who did not know each other. He kissed her out near the screes, and she came home smeared with blood, the color up in her face. Liam O'Coigligh married her within the month, and to my grandmother's joy, there was always a bird or two roasting in the house. Liam's hands were often torn and streaming with blood from their bites and their claws, though he hardly noticed it. My grandmother clucked at him as she washed and tended his cuts.

When they'd married and he'd moved into the cottage, he brought with him an iron washstand and the headboard, something an ancestor of his had dredged up from the shallows of the sea floor west of Woman's Island. There'd been much speculation about the origin of the iron furniture. Maybe an Armada ship, maybe a Danish one. It was impossible to say. Over the centuries so many south-sailing vessels had wrecked in those precarious and unexpected rocks, so far out in the waters from the mainland.

Liam's great-grandmother had used the headboard to dry fish on, and his grandmother had used it as a trellis for viney flowers in her garden. In spite of its roughened black texture, the dovetailing curves of iron had always caught my father's fancy. "The headboard of a bed for a king and his queen," he told my mother, sanded it, and painted it the pale lilac color of her choosing.

"Liam Baun, I called him," my grandmother said. "Fair Liam. For wasn't he the flower of men!"

According to my grandmother, he couldn't take a step to the right or the left unknown to my mother, for the shafts of Cupid had pierced her to the quick, and those days in Ballyferriter, I remember thinking, as my grandmother talked about him, that the same affliction was on herself.

"But even after he'd roused her up from her daydreams, Molleen was never a help at cleaning the hearthstones or cooking the food, for she was off following him, climbing the screes in her purple dress. He made a hunter of her so. I was washing the blood out of her purple dress every night, the two of them on the cliffs of the island in all weather.

"It was another sort of thing he woke in her. A thing of the body," my grandmother whispered to my great-aunt, the two drinking together that night, the porter running as freely as my grandmother's mouth. Lowering her voice, she said, "They had a way together behind the curtain with the breathing and the sighs. And wasn't I after hearing every day from one soul or the other that they'd been seen sporting indecently in the heather, or washing one another in the rock pools in nothing but their skins. And even still I was praying the rosaries to myself one after the other with all the times they woke each other in the hours of one night.

"That first spring they were married all the eggs the hen lay in the straw had chicks in them, and Molleen remarked that the cock had been busy, and I said then that every cock in this house was busy, and Molleen had narrowed her eyes at me but Liam had smiled, not a bit of a blush on him. I thought he'd made things right for her, and it should have been so. But it hurt to look at her, the way she loved him, every sinew of her straining toward him. I tried to tell her he was hers, what more was she wanting when she had him so in her bed as her husband. The love she had with him, rousing a kind of devil in her. She mistrusted happiness. That's what it was," my grandmother said, sucking at her pipe and sending up a cloud of smoke. "Afraid of happiness, she was. Blind as a herring leaping in the bay, inviting sorrow into her life, so. God forgive me for saying it, though I love him with my heart, I wish Liam Baun had not come to us. When we were at peace in our boredom and me railing at Molleen to get up off the pallet and make herself useful.

"If he'd be gone a few hours she'd go demented and be off after him. There was a terrible uneasiness on her over him, like she thought the sea would take him from her like it had taken Macdarragh and her own da."

But when my grandmother started in about the unhappiness that the two had wrought between themselves, how my mother had taunted my father with her love for the dead Macdarragh, and I heard mention of the Skellig isles, the birds screeching and circling, I turned away from her and wound the music box I'd brought with me from the island, my parents' music box, a wedding gift bought in a Dingle shop, from my grandmother to the two of them. The melody added to the romance of who they'd been, so as I listened, I kept them splendid and mythic in my thoughts.

I woke to hear my grandmother weeping one night and saw my great-aunt getting up, starting a rush light from a glowing cinder in the hearth. My grandmother said she had seen the two of them, Liam and Molleen in the darkness, Liam throwing a brace of birds down before her and asking her to cook them and eat them, because the food of the dead had a lovely, unearthly taste.

"'Twas a dream only, Peig!" my great-aunt cried, and she brought the fire up with a bellows and the two huddled in close to it.

I pretended to be asleep still, and I heard that night my grandmother confide to her sister that she could not keep me. I was the relic of Molleen and Liam's sadness, she said. I would always drag them after me. If she kept to me, she said, she'd have no peace the short time she had left before she was herself under the sod.

And it was that same night in Ballyferriter, after making certain to her satisfaction that I was asleep, that my grandmother told my great-aunt about the dreadful thing I'd done myself. The thing that had made it unbearable for us to remain on the island. The thing that made her worry that I was stone mad and that I'd go on to break her heart as they had. The dreadful thing I did, which would draw prayers and astonished noises from my great-aunt.

But that I remembered. That I remembered as clear as I heard the flames lapping in the old woman's hearth.

It was after the explosion, the death. The fracture in the two sides of the world. I'd followed my friend Eileen to visit another friend, Sean, who was working alone in his father's field. I sat on the stone wall listening to the talk between the two of them, watching the cat looks she gave him. He dropped his hoe at something she said and chased her, and they fell and rolled together in the grass, and I saw his hand roaming under her skirt and her laughing and throwing open her legs. And the laughter and rolling came to a halt, things having grown suddenly serious and them holding tight onto each other for a moment or two before she struggled up, jumping to her feet breathless and running off, leaping over the wall like a goat and disappearing down the road.

Eileen and I had been vying for Sean's affection before the blast, and now it was clear enough who he preferred. That agonized me and I felt a kind of fierceness that he not be distant with me. I sat on the wall shaking over it, panting, wild for the touch of him. Pulling my skirt up over my knees, I opened my legs and held his eyes and him now with his eye on me and such a look in it.

A shiver went the length of me. "Come down off the wall, Deirdre," he said. I stared at him with a little surge of fear.

"Come here to me, Deirdre," he said again, and that was the first time I felt the thrill in the soft places of my body, a kind of revelation. He came closer and closer to me, his eyes holding mine and the feel of his rough hand running up the length of my thigh and grazing at its destination. "Jayzus, you're a ready one, aren't you?" He'd brought me down off the wall and was pulling loose the buttons of his pants when the voice of his father pierced the air.

"The Devil take him," Sean muttered. "Come back to me here tomorrow," he said. Before leaving he put his hand between my thighs again and gave me a tickle, sending me into a paroxysm of excited confusion. My curiosity was so tortured that I couldn't wait for the sun to set and rise again. I would have dispensed with my maidenhead with little thought, nothing seeming of much value to me those days.

All night I lay in a state, remembering each detail of his presence, his self-assured roguery; his wide shoulders and strong arms. The magnetic pull between male and female seemed the only mystery worth attending. I breathed softly and sighed, my loneliness transformed into heightened sensation, located now in my body. But the next morning was as dim as late afternoon, the sky like gray green linen, soft and heavy, light permeating from behind its layers so things took on an exalted look, like candles burning behind curtains.

The Winds of Pentecost started blowing ungodly in the screes, bringing torrential waves so the tides ran up the cliffs and near the doors of the houses. The sea battered the rock face on the north and western heads, the spume flying so high into the air that it rained down on me.

Still I ventured out, fighting the gale that screeched across the passes, the waves churning up the stones. My grandmother fetched me, pulling me home, the two of us almost blown to the rocks.

The storm lasted four days.

The crops from the previous year had been poor, and the storm swept away any nets put out for mackerel and bream. Before the storm we'd been subsisting on a seal clubbed to death in the cave; the flesh of those creatures would always turn my stomach and our cottages stank of it, the cresset lamps filled with the oil from their livers.

My grandmother and I got so hungry those four days locked in the cottage that we took to sipping the oil from the lamps.

The morning it cleared, the pebble dash houses were a brilliant, glittering white. There was a commotion on the cliff and I ran toward it; a broken ship was stuck in the rocks, the sea bobbing with all sorts of riches, barrels, and boxes. Swarms of men in curraghs struggled to collect them all and to bring them in at the quay. On the White Strand, men and women unpacked the barrels, marveling over sacks of grain and great wheels of cheese, jars of preserved fruits and bottles of clear alcohol. There was flour and lard, petrol and wax. The ship had been abandoned, not a soul on board, and it was generally agreed upon that when the hull had broken and the ship had threatened to go down, the crew had left on lifeboats.

"God save their souls," someone said.

A man named Fearghall, who had lived seven years in Dublin, recognized the writing on the boxes as Danish and said the ship may have been headed to Iceland and could have been blown south off its course along the Greenland current. Cooking implements were brought out, waterlogged blankets and pillows. Mattresses dried on the rocks in the sun. A great service of delft crockery decorated with windmills was collected and divvied up among the families so every household ended up with a few plates and cups and saucers. For days, men gathered in groups on the rocks around the shipwreck, their heads bent over instruments of nautical brass: compasses and telescopes and mysterious wheels with moving arrows, strange ciphers that pulsed, sensitive to the warmth of a hand or a heated breath. The men sat on the sand, Sean among them, his head bent over a map, struggling to decipher the symbols.

That night when the water was low in the rocks around the wreck, the men broke the boards from its sides and burned them on the shore. People gathered to drink the sweet clear alcohol and eat the fruit and cheeses. Sean sat with his arm around Eileen. Once he met my eyes and quickly looked away. After that there was singing and dancing and I stood in plain sight of him, waiting for him to take me in a reel, but it was as if he didn't see me there at all.

The world of the dead seemed the better place, for it was unbearable to be left such an outcast in the world of the living. I hated Sean in my heart, yet I still would have let him sweep me off into a cave, the anger seeming only to add fodder to the fire burning in me. This struck me as a mysterious thing: I was suspicious even then that I had a strange nature.

On the fourth day after the ship had come, I climbed down to investigate the ruin, which had been slowly dismantled over the days. The hull rested now at a slant in a peak of sand, and just before I reached the door, a slew of kittiwakes rushed out at me in a panic, taking to the air above my head. I stepped inside the frail interior of what remained, the metal-and-board skeleton creaking with my weight. Sand had gathered in storm water pooled on what was now the crooked floor. A point of light came through a crevice in the wall. I had heard that the men had been unable to get into the boiler room. They'd pried and wrenched at the door, but it had not given. I saw a small red button under a handle, walked up and touched it, and the door pushed out as if something were pressuring it from behind, the room exhaling a concentration of steam. I moved back, tripping on the uneven floor. The fog issuing out wet my skin and made it impossible to breathe, a strange smell carried on it like overripe fruit. After a few moments, a gust of wind blowing through the hull diluted the fog, and as it slowly cleared I saw a young man lying inside the boiler room on the floor. His head and neck and shoulders leaned against a pipe, raised higher than the rest of his body, giving the impression that he was struggling to get up from his prone position, the rest of him submerged in a pool of seawater. All around him mechanical structures gleamed a coppery color, some having gone faintly green.

His open eyes shined. It occured to me that he was dead, yet his expression was alive and nothing like the looks on the faces of the dead that I'd seen before. There was nothing resigned about it. Yearning or hope held to his features and his eyes held to mine, at once seeing me and not seeing me. I stepped in, and in the dimmer light his look intensified.

The pool of water that held him sloshed and stirred. His long, reddish hair moved like seaweed around his neck and shoulders. He kept peering at me, the weight of him shifting with the movement of the water as I knelt down beside him. At first I was ashamed to study him so closely, his eyes still gazing hard at mine. But soon, kneeling at his side in supplication, I reached into the water and touched the curved palm of one of his hands, which lay facing his thigh, and I clasped it with both of my hands.

This close, he had about him an intensely sweet smell like the Easter lilies brought from Dingle that had rotted on my grandmother's shrine to the Virgin. His smell, his eyes, full of the qualities of life, confused me, so in conflict were they with the stiffness of his form.

The shock of him settled in me, and I felt a thrill as I peered at him. My grandmother had said once that the dead were very close to us; closer even than the living. How old was he? I wondered. Maybe sixteen or seventeen. He looked the same age as Sean, and there was a roughness of whiskers on his chin and above his lips. I ran my fingers through the hair near his neck and it felt like any living person's hair in water, and I closed my eyes and sang to him.

❧

In the full dark the starlight leaked in. When the tide was high it came up the beach and rocked the hull. He stirred when it thundered, and I hoped the tide might lift the hull and carry us off. I watched the starlight on his eyes. In the middle of the night the sky must have clouded, because the light grew creamy and diffused and it began to rain in the hull outside the boiler room.

I lay beside him in the pool, my arm around him, and I think I slept, because I startled up once shivering with the cold, my teeth chattering.

And as I remember it now, deeper into the night there were candles, myriads of them around us, though I cannot say where they came from. I held my face in his two hands. Now and then a flame would extinguish itself and make a sound, like a human sigh. Its smoke would unravel, and it would fall into the pool we lay in. Another would light mysteriously.

"Is braithim as titim an saol . . . ," I whispered to him. *The world is falling away.*

I have broken memories of the morning; of the men prying me from him. I fought them bitterly and wept, my head on fire, my body racked with cold.

I had been making the death passage but was cruelly interrupted. My grandmother said later that she'd done everything to keep me in this world, rather than let me pass into the other. She did not understand why I'd railed against her after that day and hated her for keeping me back.

'Twas after this incident that an even greater shame came down on my grandmother and me. I took to my parents' bed behind the yellow curtain, and when my grandmother found me there she went mad, accusing me of desecrating a shrine. But every chance I had I returned to that bed, though the covers were rough and cold and the straw it was stuffed with was rife with insects. This was the end for her. She said she was too old and tired now to keep such a creature as me. She was finished too with the harsh weather and the uncertainties of island life. She had her mind set on the mainland and was making ready to leave the Great Blasket for good.

I decorated the iron curves of the headboard with strands of seaweed, and lying there, I knew when the tide was high because I could feel the ring in the hollows of the iron, tuned as it was to the temperamental vibrations of the sea.

In my wakeful hours behind the yellow curtain, I wound the music box and listened to the dinny melody of Donal na Grainne.

FOUR

Throughout March and April, I heard very little talk about Enfant de Marie from the girls, and I imagined, against my better judgment, that it had passed from their minds like a fancy. I went secretly to the prioress at St. Alban's and told her that the girls would be back. She said I needed to sign a promissory note in order to hold their places, so with a shaking hand, I did so.

Near the end of April, a letter came from Mrs. O'Breen addressed to me.

Dear Deirdre,

   I hope you are well.

   I'm so pleased that you have made such a wise decision in relation to your daughters. The environment at Enfant de Marie, as you well know yourself, builds strong character.

   By way of further aiding the girls in the transition, it might be to their benefit to come to me here in Kenmare on their own early in the summer to stay, perhaps for June and July and you could join us in August and spend the rest of the time until we see them settled in rooms at Enfant de Marie. I think it will be good for them to get used to being away from you while they still have all the ease and comforts of home at hand.

   Again, I am extremely proud of you for your thoughtful concern over your daughters' development.

                        With love,
                         Mother

I handed the letter to Manus. He read it, then met my eyes. Neither of us spoke, and he was placing the letter in his own pocket when I reached my hand out for it.

"It's mine," I said.

"Oh," he said, taken aback. He handed it to me, and I walked up the stairs with it. I sat in the girls' room with the door closed.

In the hours that followed, I thought I might fight it somehow, but the more I read and reread, the more overcome I was; the more defenseless I felt at the force of it.

The morning they left for Kenmare, I stood in the vestibule looking out at the waiting carriage. Maighread moved past me, giving me a quick kiss on the cheek. I thought Caitlin might look sad, reluctant to go, but she met my eyes with a kind of ease, brushing her lips across my chin and following Maighread down the steps and through the gate.

When they were gone, I faced Manus, who was standing behind

me in the vestibule. His eyes wandered immediately from mine. He colored faintly, then walked toward his study. Before he closed the door, he turned to me.

"You'll see them in two months, for God's sake," he said with irritation, then closed the door.

So I was left alone in the big Georgian house on Merrion Square. Alone with the ministrations of Mrs. Daley as she cleaned and put things right downstairs. Alone with Manus, who would come in later from work at half five, maybe with McMartin, his business partner, to sit in the study and smoke and go over his papers and his blueprints.

Manus, who had long since become a creature of habit, lived a separate life behind the eyes, kept his own counsel. The rift between us hardened with time. He had grown short and disapproving with me. But I had seen, in unguarded moments, his face so different with the clench gone from his jaw. From under the armature of manly bones, the Beloved peered out from one eye now and again like a boy trapped in a tower. But such appearances were fleeting. Gruffness had become his way of managing.

The perfect scripted habits of Manus's life, unchanged by the girls' going, threw into terrible relief the sudden emptiness of my own.

For years the neutral waters of repetition and routine, the rhythms of everydayness, had kept me afloat: moving from one simple task to the next, I had acheived a hypnotic steadiness, a kind of half sleep to stave off any outbreaks of emotion. Before I'd received the letter from Mrs. O'Breen, I had usually spent the early hours after the girls had gone to school making their beds and straightening their room, attending to their clothes; sewing and darning stockings, presiding jealously over these tasks, having forbidden Mrs. Daley to undertake them herself. To keep some semblance of power over Mrs. Daley, I had made lists for her. Chores less related to the girls.

I had no inclination to make her a list this day, and I realized, when she did not come asking for one, that it had been a dummy show on my part. Perhaps all these years she had merely folded it and put it into her apron, not even giving it a glance. I felt ashamed, adrift as I was now in my own house. I hid from Mrs. Daley.

Moving back and forth in the girls' room between their unmade beds, I realized that it would be the last time for a long time that I would make them. I put it off and looked out the window, the chimes ringing in the wind, the branches of the tree waving in the morning sunlight. Two months would have to pass before I'd see them again. How would I bear it? And then I'd be with them only a brief time before they'd be gone again.

Cold air wafted from the ruffled drapes. I gazed at the small white porcelain figures of nuns their grandmother had given them. "Caitlin's the nun, but Maighread still might surprise us," Mrs. O'Breen had once said offhandedly.

My heart beat hard at a clatter of hooves from the street. For a moment, I entertained the magical thought that they had come back, and when the hooves passed, going south, I sank down onto Maighread's bed, sitting forward with my elbows on my knees, my face in my hands.

Enfant de Marie. Caitlin might manage, I thought, but how would Maighread? Manus had gone on about how girls with money had a completely different experience there than the orphans. The rooms were nice and kept well warmed. It was a sought-after place, he'd insisted. His mother had gone there before me, for God's sake, and would she want her granddaughters there if it were not a quality place?

I remembered how it had been for me, new to the convent Enfant de Marie. In a dark chapel while we'd waited outside the nuns' office, my grandmother had said to me in a low voice, "Never speak of what happened with your mother and father, Deirdre. You've only a hope left in this world if you never breathe a word of it."

She'd looked at me with her old, wet eyes, and though she did not repeat those words, I heard them again and again on the heavy chapel air, building in urgency each time so my heart began to race.

We had already agreed upon a story that she'd tell the nun: After my parents died crossing the bay in a storm, she had raised me herself in Ballyferriter but was now too old to keep me.

She'd squeezed her eyes shut and shaken her head. "I never thought I'd live to the day where I would tell a bold-faced lie to a holy nun!"

We'd had to wait a long time for the nun, so we'd knelt at a shrine to Our Lady where the flames of the candles had pulsed and leaned toward us, giving off a warm, pacifying smell of butterfat.

When we'd been admitted to the Reverend Mother's office, my grandmother had spoken to her in English, and though I had not been able to translate all of what she'd been saying, I'd seen apprehension on her face. She'd colored like a girl in front of the nun and stuttered, so the nun had looked at me sidelong with a suspicious flash in her eye.

After the interview my grandmother and I had said good-bye to each other, and she'd left me alone in providential night.

It was in my early days at Enfant de Marie that I saw it all again: the memory that had been buried under whiteness. It came in flashes at odd moments when I was set on some small chore or another, or struggling to write an English word on my slate. The hot glimmer of sunlight on water, a rare scalding sun that burned my scalp; the little empty boat moored by rocks, its underside a wet sheen of sealskin.

And when I'd be thinking on it, it was like the outside world and the inner world mixed. The streams of girls around me moved and eddied like water. I stayed in the sunlight, thigh high in the tidepools. "Da!" I cried out once, so a girl said, "You're da's not here!" and a group of girls laughed.

It confused me to hear the sweetness of the girls' voices at vespers and morning prayer, in conflict with the laughter and whispers I knew were about me. I would not look at them. I hardly remember seeing them that first year except in peripheral. I looked past them or through them, because I was trudging in the water, a sheet of moss stretched out on the surface of a wave like fine green cloth, or gazing off in the other direction, south toward the skellig, the bay beyond as calm as new milk.

The first thing I learned at Enfant de Marie was that it was safer to disappear into the background. If you were quiet and obedient, the nuns believed you were good. They did not suspect you of harboring a lie at the heart of yourself.

My bed was separated from the other ten in the room, and faced out to the long stone corridor that culminated at the nuns' kitchen, where a cast iron oven squatted on four crooked legs like some headless monstrosity. A pulse of blue light, which dwindled deep in its gut, reflected on the windows behind it.

One evening after the meal, I went to those windows and looked out. On the cloudy glass, I discerned the ghost of a self reflected back, her eyes as intent on me as mine were on her. I was enthralled to see my own face. I had thought my face had changed after my grandmother had told the lie to the nun. There you are, I thought. It became my habit to stand at that window at that hour, but it drew attention to me, and one of the nuns detected what I was doing and ordered me to stop, admonishing me, dubbing it vain.

The nuns did not allow us to keep mirrors. Girls were even discouraged from trying to gaze at themselves in the sides of the teakettle.

It surprises me to recall that another girl who had a hunger to see her reflection, the girl I followed one day out beyond the yards past the nuns' kitchen and behind a carpenter's shed where we were forbidden to go, the girl who took me through boards and ruins of furniture to what once must have been a massive mirror, now scored with thousands of cracks, was a girl with a harelip.

Her name was Bride, and she had hair the color of pewter. She showed me how to bend a small bit of the cracked mirror at a crease so that a piece could be broken off that could fit into the palm of a hand.

We flashed our mirrors on the broken walls and at the stones.

"Mirrors are magical things that reflect what's often unseen," she said to me. A girl who never spoke in class or in the dormitory. A girl who stared at things with an expression of mistrustful astonishment. Except those days when we'd gone trespassing. We sat outside in dead grass and flashed our mirrors at the sky.

"The only way to see Pegasus moving across the sky," she said in a slow, dramatic voice, "is with a mirror held at an angle to the clouds.

"In some ways," she said, leaning in close to me and piercing me with her eyes, "it was terrible for Pegasus. To be of both earth and air. The horse's element is earth, but it had the wings of a bird!"

Her voice grew quieter but increased in intesity so she spoke in a stage whisper, "Worse still is the chimera! An animal and a human confused into one. Mistakes of nature. Two natures in one body. But the Pegasus is a kind of beautiful mistake. There are beautiful mistakes and there are ugly ones."

Once, after examining her face in the mirror, she drew her scarf around her mouth and said, all the drama gone from her voice, "Look how beautiful I would be if I lived in Arabia!"

Mostly we each lived our separate isolations, but now and then we spent a free hour together. One day we took a risk, running like mares into the dead yard, her braids flopping and slapping at her face, my gray skirts tripping me as I went.

My windpipe ached as I ran, laughing and screaming her name. We were giddy that day with disobedience.

But she was not there long, a few months at most before an aunt came and fetched her. I felt a certain jealousy watching from a second-floor window as Bride held her aunt's hand, the two crossing the courtyard together. It did not matter that this aunt was not her mother. She was like a mother. She would keep Bride under her wing. The two, I imagined, would be a kind of team, each doing for the other.

I did not take Bride's departure well. I told the other girls that Bride was very ill and that the aunt had taken her home to die. I told them to make them suffer. I told them for retribution because they had been cruel to her about her lip.

I fed the fire of their terror, telling them that I'd heard a finger scratching at the glass at night so that the others listened and were certain that they heard it too.

They did not sleep well, and I had company in my night wakefulness. I sat up on my bed watching their silhouettes and listening to their uneasy, fervent prayers.

But hatred could never long occupy me. Anger in me has always been a hay fire that burns wild and bright and goes out quickly. It would not be the thing to save me.

I was consumed with the memory of Bride, amazed by her. I came to believe that because she had looked deeply at the flaw in her own face, searching out its mystery, she had changed her dire circumstances. I trespassed alone into the yards, breaking odd pieces of mirror and hiding them in various places so I'd always have one.

One day I sat in Sister Dymphna's class, holding my little edge of mirror in my hand, angling it up from my lap to try to glimpse my face. But the more I searched the mirror, the more featureless I looked, until what I saw reflected back was the white flurry of weather that had blotted out the memory of my parents.

"Deirdre from the Blasket!" Sister Dymphna cried. "What do you have there?"

I did not move or speak, but I would not surrender the mirror. She tried to force it from me, prying my fingers apart, and I don't know if all the blood between us was my own, or if she had cut herself too in the struggle. Eventually, she extracted the jagged glass from my hands.

After that day I hid behind my unkept hair, wincing and weeping if the nuns tried to comb it or tie it back.

ၜၜၜ

This was the place, I thought with agitation, where my girls were going.

Eventually it had been Manus who'd rescued me from Enfant de Marie. Manus who made me forget the hunger for mirrors and in whose eyes I would see myself reflected back. Where was that Manus now, I wondered? The beautiful boy I had married. Where was he? The boy with whom I had discovered the *Secretus Secretorum*.

When Monday morning came I walked as usual to the National Gallery but could not bring myself to go inside. I continued on along the quays and found my way back to Antiquarian Books.

Once inside I walked directly to the shelf where the *Secretus Secretorum* was kept. I took it to the corner table and opened it. Leafing through the decorative pages, I passed extraordinary images of night skies, bright with spheres and planets and stars.

In one, a descending human figure moving through a zone of mist, and the words:

The water that breaks at birth is symbolized by the white or lunar tincture that precedes the solar reddening.

Though I could not grasp their meaning, I felt enamored of their poetry.

I turned onto an etching of Hermes wading waist deep in ocean waves, the sun and moon presiding. I read:

Mercurial water flowing down into the darkness of matter to awaken the dead bodies of the metals from slumber.

Everything struck me as full of portent and resonance, but when I tried to clarify what things meant, I could not. The rational mind was not what the words and images engaged, yet I felt the shadow impression they made upon me. Language and configurations from a dream. I found myself swimming through the mistiness of it all, letting my eye stop where it was drawn, drinking in phrases.

The deeper I went into the book, the stranger the images grew.

An eagle chained to a toad on a hill overlooking a great city, the heavily robed alchemist walking beside them pointing at the clouds, the words "dissolution or bonding" written beneath.

Turning the page I came to a picture that caused my heart to plummet. A naked woman, having torn her heart from her own body, offering it to her male counterpart as if she were offering him no more than a rose, the man himself gazing far past her, oblivious. I caught, floating in the midst of the text, the phrase, "the melancholy of human transactions."

Just as I thought of closing the volume, I turned unexpectedly upon *The Courtship of the Sun and the Moon.*

The first image depicted the bride with the head of the moon, alone in her chamber, sitting at her vanity and gazing at herself in the mirror. The second depicted the bridegroom with the head of the sun, striding with muscular legs across landscapes. In the third image he had arrived at her window and was leaning in. She had seen him in her mirror and was turning to look at him.

In the fourth picture she was standing facing him with an outstretched arm, and he was midclimb into her window, one leg in the room. This was the picture in which the dove appeared on the air between them. The dove that presages union.

The pictures filled me with a keen loneliness. I remembered Manus stroking the curve between my waist and hip as we'd looked at the figures, his breath catching as he'd whispered, "Oh, Luna, about to be folded in my sweet embrace."

My heart drummed hard and I closed my eyes, remembering how being near him then, every cell in my body had shivered with electricity; how I had been unable to resist kissing his naked skin.

When I opened my eyes again the afternoon light had deepened and was traveling slowly across Sol and Luna, their eyes locked one upon the other.

I closed the book and stood. Then I purchased the *Secretus Secre-torum*.

As I walked home along the quays, embracing the book in both arms, the river was dark, reflecting a multitude of lights.

When I arrived at Merrion Square, Mrs. Daley had made boiled beef and cabbage, but she said that Manus had not come. I ate a little and she asked about the girls' unmade beds and I stiffened. "Leave them," I said plainly. She said nothing, and I did not meet her eyes. I went upstairs to the girls' room. Mrs. Daley left, and as night filled the house, my mind gave itself over to dark fancies. Alcoves and shelves in the deepening gloom looked like they tunneled into the walls.

Maighread's snow globe on the dresser cast an enlarged shadow on the wall behind it, and the snow flurried suddenly in the shadow. A doll on the shelf behind me began to breathe.

It was after midnight when the door downstairs opened and closed hard and I heard Manus getting out of his coat, his footsteps sounding as he came up the stairs. He paused before the half-open bedroom door, having brought with him the mundane world, the smells of pipe smoke and alcohol; of rain and soot from the Dublin streets. A bit wobbly on his feet, he gave me a bemused look, then dismissed me and moved off to our bedroom. He coughed and cleared his throat, and I heard him take off his clothes and get into bed. Tightness left my chest. In spite of his drunken condition, tonight I felt grateful to have him home, his presence neutralizing the danger that darkness and an empty house had wrought. The house conformed again to daylight laws; the arcane passages dissolving, giving way to benign decorative architecture and white gloss walls. The doll, which I'd fancied breathing, put on an orderly face. The snow stopped moving in the globe. Manus exerted a force over chaos. Manus ordered things into their places.

When I heard him snoring, I crept into our bedroom and sat down to watch him sleep. He was active in sleep, sweating, the antithesis of the harsh husband he had become. He moved and paused in postures of flight, the supple curve of his upper arm thrown over his head.

In sleep, his true face returned to him, the past alive in the present. The Lost Manus. My Beloved.

I could smell again the sweat of a horse that had just been galloping and the aroma of leather, hot and chafed.

PART TWO

Mysterium Amoris

It is said: Woman dissolves man and he makes her solid. That is, the spirit dissolves the body and makes it soft, and the body fixes the spirit.

—AURORA CONSURGENS

FIVE

1895–1897
West of Ireland

When I first saw Manus in church at Enfant de Marie, we were sixteen. I was faceless then and squeezing a mirror in my palm, hiding behind a head of roughened hair.

When he passed the aisle where I sat, he left behind the vital smell of horse sweat, a rousing aroma deeper than Christmas pine and myrrh smoke from the swinging censor. In empathic reaction, my own body broke into a gossamer sweat under my woolen clothes. I would learn later that he'd come directly from riding, but for a very long time I would not separate the smell of horse sweat from the idea of maleness. He was rather like a horse himself, with an equine face, beautifully boned, and dark-eyed with long eyelashes and a colt's mane of windblown black hair. Besides the frail, bald priest, the sixteen-year-old boy I saw there that day was the only male I had ever seen in this chapel. This was a service attended only by nuns and convent girls.

He was with a woman and a girl whom I assumed to be his mother and sister. He and the girl resembled each other remarkably, black-haired and cream-skinned, though she looked to be the elder of the two. She held herself demurely, keeping her eyes to the altar or cast down, while the boy's eyes roamed the aisles of girls and nuns, or gazed negligently at the eaves of the church, studying its structure, ignoring the Mass. The mother stood between the two, wearing a dark hat with a veil that hid her face. Yet I could see her strong jaw and chin, and when she lifted her face to look at the crucifix, a flash of her plaintive mouth. Though I could not see her eyes, I read devotion in the steady movements of her lips as she prayed silently. The three were exquisitely dressed in dark woolen clothes, their stately bearing I imagined to be the result of some familial wisdom.

I studied each of them fiercely, but my eyes always came back to the boy. His features retained an adolescent softness, but he was already taller than his mother and stood on the precipice of manhood.

After Mass, with all my senses still tolling, I followed them at a distance and saw the woman talking to the Reverend Mother, handing her an envelope, which the nun, nodding her head enthusiastically, hid immediately under a layer of her habit. The three went out and took a turn in the courtyard, a gentle animation between the girl and her mother. The boy was reserved, almost sullen.

Later I would hear about them in the dormitory. The O'Breens were a wealthy family of stonemasons. The father had died, leaving them with a big house on Kenmare Bay, where white horses roamed the acres along the sea. The mother was a great benefactress to the nuns. And the girl, it was said, would be coming to Enfant de Marie as a postulant.

"They are an ecclesiastical family," I heard one girl say. I longed to ask her what that meant. How mysterious, I thought! How could a family be ecclesiastical?

I could not understand why, with such a family, the young woman wanted to be a nun. The orphans in the school, in particular, were urged to sign on as postulants. I had listened often uneasily to these talks, no other future in sight for me. It was terribly difficult, we were told, for orphans to find places in the world.

"As a nun you have a family of sisters. You have safety and shelter, and you are espoused to Christ Himself," Sister Carmel had explained.

The O'Breens peopled my daydreams, and restlessly I imagined them, romantic figures ascending and descending staircases, riding horses over rolling green property.

Three weeks would pass before I saw any of them again, and then it was only the mother and the girl, but the memory of her brother's face was present in the girl's. And there being so much time between, all the feelings the three had once roused in me, and the ones her brother had especially excited, I read now in her. She was taller than I remembered, and without him present I was aware of a note of masculinity to her features. She was for me both the brother and the sister, as if she had absorbed him into her own nature.

Once Bairbre O'Breen had donned the veil of a postulant, I sought her out, though I never spoke directly to her. I breathed her in deeply. She did not smell like her brother but rather like some exotic spice, an eastern wood, which wore away the longer she was there, replaced by the odor of the coarse soap the nuns used, which dried and reddened their skin.

Every Sunday Mrs. O'Breen attended service, her face hidden behind the dark green veil, an edge of animal fur on the collar of her jacket. During the Agnus Dei she always cried, and with ritualistic grace she'd take a linen handkerchief from her bag and part the dark green curtain before her face before applying it to her eyes.

Perhaps, I thought, the term *ecclesiastical family* meant that they were consecrated somehow in the eyes of the church.

I imagined an elevated love and understanding between this mother and daughter, and I felt outside of their secret. Desirous of it, I was also hungry for the intelligence they seemed to represent; the order.

Bairbre gazed to the altar during Mass. When I saw her in the corridors, she wore a mild, pious expression, a circle of inward focus around her, which I struggled to emulate.

She taught lacemaking and her pieces were displayed, pinned to dark velvet and preserved behind glass frames in the corridors outside the nuns' antechambers, so that we saw them each time we passed into and out of the dining hall. She was not so very much older than the rest of us, only two years, but her expression afforded her the authority of an old soul. She taught the girls to make chapel veils, geometrically divided into sections of flower and snowflake.

I was all thumbs at it though, and was allowed to sit at a separate table and draw. Still I watched, struggling to fathom her. She being of her brother's blood and of his coloring, I swooned faintly in her presence, a prickling sensation running up my spine. When I was alone I sketched her face. I drew her with her mother's face and her brother's always there behind her; sometimes as moons, sometimes as planets, inseparable as they were from one another in my thoughts. It was Manus O'Breen at the forefront of my thoughts, and his mother; but poor Bairbre, who seemed the least defined, was my close link to the other two. I thought of them as a Trinity. The Mother, the Son, and Bairbre, the Holy Ghost. She bore the natures of the other two within herself, and in her presence I felt the mystery of all three.

In my less mystical contemplations of her, I was faced with the confusing paradox of a girl who had everything, leaving all of it behind her.

One Saturday afternoon I followed from a distance as she walked into the empty chapel. She knelt, thinking she was alone. Exhaling deeply, she crossed her arms over the railing before laying her head upon them. A quiver ran through the middle of her body, and I found myself shocked by her awkward and vulnerable posture, out of character with the graceful young woman I had been watching so closely. I knew from the undulations through her back and waist that she was weeping, though she restrained all sound of it, except for the occasional winded and uneven draw for air. When at last she lifted her head from her arms and sat back in the pew wiping her eyes, I withdrew from the chapel.

After Mass the following day, Bairbre went off as usual to walk in the courtyard with her mother. I followed them and saw the mother take a package out of her bag and give it to Bairbre, and, after the two exchanged affectionate looks, Bairbre peeled the gold paper away and gasped, a small white book revealed. The two stood together, heads bowed over it, studying it, then embraced. Bairbre's face, pressed between her mother's neck and shoulders, looked ecstatic, her half-open eyes lit with tears.

That evening just before vespers, I managed to sit behind Bairbre at an angle so I could see over her shoulder as she ran a fingertip along the white, finely tooled binding, then moved the book back and forth, letting the gold leaf on the edges of the pages catch the dim light of the candles. She leafed through, stopping at the brilliantly colored illustrations. In one, over which she seemed to linger the longest, a devil with all the characteristics of a human man, except for horns and beautiful green skin, whispered seductively at the ear of a daydreaming Christ in white and scarlet robes.

When the priest arrived at the altar we all rose, and she left the book on the pew. In the hour of chanting that followed, I rarely removed my eyes from it. The book hummed, a pure citadel in itself. Once near the end of the hour, in Bairbre's shifting from kneeling to standing, the folds of her white linen skirt knocked the book sound-lessly to the floor. My heart raced. I wanted to touch her back and tell her, no one else seeming aware of it, but she was so engaged in the service that I did not dare.

When everyone filed out at the end, she had forgotten it. I stayed on, pretending to pray. She stopped, standing for a moment in the aisle at the end of the pew, and looked at me. I met her eyes, and it went through my mind that I should tell her about the book, but something held me back. I put my face into my hands and squeezed my eyes shut. She disappeared with the rest out of the chapel, and I was able to confiscate the little book unnoticed and steal away with it back to my bed.

Inside, below the title, *The Passion of Christ,* was an inscription: "For my beloved Bairbre on her engagement to Our Savior. With love from Mother."

I hid it inside the casing of my pillow, and when I went toward the dining hall for the evening meal I saw her with two postulants looking frantically around.

She met my eyes.

"What's wrong?" I asked, addressing her for the first time.

"We're looking for a book," she said, approaching me. "Have you seen a small white book with gold on the edges of the pages?"

"No," I said.

"It was a present. I need to find it."

"Can I help you look for it?" I asked her.

"Thank you."

I followed them about the convent in a daze, pretending to search until the falseness of my actions wore on me and I slipped away to my bed and lay on the pillow under which the little white book was hidden.

I will never forget the day that followed that one: wild spring winds tormenting the lace curtains in the vestibules and corridors, and sporadic light; broken, westward-moving clouds; my heart beating deceptively as the search continued.

Bairbre seemed set on me. She watched me, but I told myself she could not have known, because there was such regard in her face. I was convinced it was because of my concern the day before.

Once I stood alone in a corridor looking out the window to the back of the nuns' cloisters, where I saw the mysterious pieces of a postulant habit pegged to the line, drying in the wind.

All the girls and nuns were engaged in the search. Girls were looking in the most unlikely places. In rooms that had been uninhabited for years. In the larders and the potato bins. Eventually everyone seemed to forget what it was they were looking for in the first place.

Near the end of the day she approached me in the corridor.

"Did you find your book?" I asked her.

"No," she said, looking into my face with a sad intensity. "I was careless with it. It was so beautiful."

Her eyes grew damp. We stood together in silence. She touched my hand and I felt intoxicated by her presence. But I did not once think of returning the book to her. Her loss bound us exquisitely.

Bairbre's grace was formidable; her presence at once soft and commanding; her height when I stood face-to-face with her, something almost imposing in its strangeness. This close, her white robe smelled like cut pine and unlit candles. It was in that moment that I began to imagine nunhood as a romantic state. It was the only answer. How else could Bairbre have left the white horses of her girlhood? I wondered if silences and demure behavior, like the voluminously layered robes, hid secrets.

I found a place at the dining hall that night where I could watch her from across the room through the din and movement of the girls. In the course of the meal she looked up from her plate and found me set on her. I blinked when she smiled, tore my eyes from hers and looked back at my own plate. But I felt her there, aware of me, curious; watchful.

That night I opened my eyes through half sleep and saw, with a thrill of terror, a glimmering on the corridor wall and heard faint, repressed noise, a shuffling and breathing. My heart went wild, and for a few minutes I sat rigid, hardly breathing, as the procession of soft noise and light advanced, brightening and growing louder. It passed the corridor door, what looked like a single elongated creature composed of shadow and shuddering flames. When it was gone, I slipped from bed to peer out after it. As it ascended the stairs I recognized three white veils and understood that it was a procession of postulants bearing candles. Leading them, a nun in a black veil bearing the heavy cross that ordinarily hung in the entrance hall.

I followed once they'd ascended the stairs. The corridors up there were wider, and my eyes, having grown used to the dark, could discern each different postulant. It seemed to be part of the ritual to follow one another very closely and to remain in step. Bairbre was at the back of the line, her white veil wavering behind her. I restrained an overwhelming impulse to go to her; to stand close behind.

I returned to bed with galloping pulses, amazed by the strange procession.

I was trembling the next day when I stopped Bairbre in the corridor. She looked startled at what she saw in my face.

"I want to be a nun," I said.

"Deirdre," she said softly, "from the Blasket." It stunned me that she called me so. She had clearly spoken to someone about me to learn that I was called this. My first reaction to the name was one of unease, to explain to her that there was a mistake, that I was not that girl.

"I am not from the Blasket," I said. "I am from Ballyferriter."

"Oh," she said, seeming disappointed. "I like the sound of it. *Deirdre from the Blasket.*"

I wished in that moment that I could invent for her an entirely other childhood story, not the one that my grandmother and I had settled on telling, but one of lost privilege and luxury. Wouldn't it have been better to have lost, through difficult circumstances, some fine and dignified place in the world? I wanted her to think I was worthy of her.

"Can I still call you *Deirdre from the Blasket?*" she asked, the name that had once felt demeaning transformed to a term of affection by the softness of her voice.

Emboldened by her sweetness, I touched her shoulder, and that gesture roused from her a response, so subtle, like a warm gust of weather. A little issue of vulnerability. She shifted slightly on her feet.

"You're my friend," she said, then averted her eyes from mine and walked away.

I went to Sister Hildegard, the prioress, and told her that I was ready to attempt the early trial period of Holy Instruction.

A few days later I was transported, with the rest of the postulants, to the cloister in the old battlement behind the convent, where we were kept isolated from the others.

Six

In chapel, wearing the white robes and veil of a postulant, I sat in the pew behind Bairbre and off to her right so she remained always in my peripheral vision. At night in my cell, or when I walked alone through the corridor, I still saw her before me as if she were burned there, and I felt her presence everywhere, in the way, I imagine, I must have been expected to feel the presence of God.

Sometimes in chapel I sensed her quieting her own voice that she might listen to mine, a delicate communication between us. Only once or twice a day the first week did we manage to find an unfettered moment to exchange a look, and always it was she who withdrew her eyes. That intensified my longing.

Every day each postulant was allowed, if she wished, to choose a psalm to recite during the Divine Office. I saw the psalms as my opportunity to speak aloud to Bairbre and made my selections carefully.

"I will worship toward and at your holy temple in reverant awe of you."

As I spoke these words, she listened with a heightened attention, unmoving. When I finished, she kept staring straight ahead, but I heard her exhale very faintly.

And it felt to me that I had lived for that tiny exhalation, which, because it could barely be discerned, made it even more exquisite and true, and filled me with wondrous thoughts; that she understood my affection. In some mysterious way, she reciprocated it.

During the hour of deep meditation the silence was so generous and immense that I could track a change in her breathing, and when she leaned forward over the rail, I could hear her heart beating like a very distant drum, and I followed the changes in its rhythm, wondering what her thoughts were when it quickened. When I was supposed to be pleading with Christ to clean iniquity from my soul, it was Bairbre's presence that I pleaded with. And how could she have helped but feel my intensity? I longed for the boundaries to be lost between us; that we might become infused one with the other. Particles of her brother and her mother, particles of her dignified place in the world might enter into my being. Might closeness to her not elevate me?

In the long hours I chanted inwardly to her, *I worship you,* repeating it so often that it seemed to become audible of its own accord, and I heard my thoughts as if spoken aloud. I worried and had to look at the nuns and other girls to be sure they had not heard.

Each day came the chance to recite, my voice breaking onto air, bald with emotion, *"You cause my lamp to be lighted and shine. You illuminate my darkness."*

It was that pleading that wore her down, that drew at her so she'd turn her face that I could gaze at her profile, as if she could not, at times, resist my adulation.

But it was that same pleading and repetition that began to intrude on her. My thoughts and intentions to become one with her so filled the air between us that I saw it physically weary her, so she had to hold on to the back of the bench in front of her and hang her head, unable to add her voice to the refrains.

One day, a month or so into our postulancy, Bairbre seemed particularly vulnerable to Sister Vivian's instruction; Sister Vivian, who was more soft-spoken and intense than Sister Carmel. Old Sister Vivian with her benevolent face and peculiar way of opening her arms to us when she spoke, as if she were calling lambs in from a dark field.

"Christ sees into our hearts. He knows our worldly passions. We must lay them at His feet. Unharness your hearts, my daughters, so they are clear and cool as glass."

Bairbre slumped as she listened, and later, when I passed her as I was returning from Communion, I saw a look of painful self-searching on her face.

One day she devastated me by moving from her place before me to a distant corner. An hour or so into prayer she turned and found me facing her. I saw her read everything in my face at that moment. She knew I had no vocation, that I was there for her. She stiffened and gave me a harsh look in which I sensed a warning.

She stood for Psalms and recited, *"As for God, His way is perfect. The word of the Lord is tested and tried."*

I felt myself falling from a great height. After she knelt, I stood and recited, *"In dumb silence I hold my peace, so my agony is quickened and my heart burns within me."*

She met my eyes and I grew hopeful that the words had served as an appeal to her.

The next day I recited, *"All night I soak my pillow with tears, I drench my couch with my weeping. My eye grows dim because of grief."*

But she would not return to her place in the pew before me, and she did not meet my eyes without a harsh expression on her face.

One day in mid February, I approached Bairbre in the corridor. I touched her arm, and she withdrew as if I'd hurt her.

"You're making this very difficult for me. I'm trying to go into my vocation with my heart open to God. You're making it impossible for me!"

I stumbled off, went outside into a wet frost, and contracted a fever. I lay on my pallet, Sister Vivian tending to me with hot drinks and extra blankets. Eventually she brought me into the little infirmary, where I could barely be induced to sit up long enough to take a cupful of broth.

I felt heavy. Giving up on Bairbre, a terrible lethargy overtook me. I lay unmoving in the infirmary at night, the wind beating and whistling in the fractures of the wall.

Lying long hours in my sickbed, the prayers we'd been for so long repeating played and replayed themselves within my mind; refrains and ejaculations speaking themselves automatically and against my own will. If I could not address the words to Bairbre and the O'Breens, they were rendered meaningless.

Bairbre had seen through me. I had no vocation. But did she know that not once in all those months had I sensed God there? I struggled to articulate to myself exactly what it was I believed in. I had never been able to resolve myself with God as I was taught to think of him: the bearded presence in the granite chair. What I believed in instead was sky filled with luminaries; air flooding with wind and light. A tremendous energetic vibration infrahuman and indifferent; neither punishing nor compassionate. It was not a thinking entity that I sensed but something more diffuse. Not one face but millions of them as numerous as stars and planets.

I suddenly pitied the nuns, bent and vehement with prayer. It did no good to plead with the indifferent sky.

◈

Two weeks passed before I got up one morning, dressed, and walked shakily into the chapel, where the sisters were engaged in Lauds. Bairbre had returned to her old place in the pew in front of the one I used to sit in. But afraid to intrude upon her, I sat far to the back. She turned, feeling the sense of me on the air. She stood and recited slowly, distinctly, *"My voice shalt thou hear in the morning. I prepare a prayer for you and watch and wait for you to speak to my heart."*

I lifted my head slowly, understanding that her words were for me. Each morning that week she recited the same words, and each time she did I felt my heart begin to fill again with hope.

One day I answered her softly, *"You cause my lamp to be lighted and shine."*

Winter drabness began to trail away, and I could feel the coming spring.

It was March. A lightness filled me, and knowing the prayers inside out so I did not have to concentrate, the incantation of familiar phrases produced a kind of liquiddy emotion in me. Looking up at Bairbre in her place, her face at its usual oblique angle to me, I saw a misty replica of her between us, facing me, holding her hand out to me. And I thought, *I can do this. I can be a nun if that extension of her will remain reaching toward me.* The air was our conspirator, carrying our messages between us.

That Saturday we had free hours in the afternoon. I went out in the sunlight and saw Bairbre facing me as if she were waiting for me. I followed at a distance as she turned and walked slowly ahead, the bracken beginning to green with buds.

Soon she stopped and went very still, facing away from me. I approached and stood nervously before her, but she kept her eyes averted from mine.

"When you were ill . . . I realized how terrible it would be if you were not here," she said.

It was her face but with other shadows playing on it. Her eyes but not the holy eyes I was used to seeing. It struck me like a blow that the pious face she usually wore was studied. She had, as I'd witnessed the day I'd seen her weeping in the chapel, cast off the graceful, controlled demeanor as if she were tired of upholding it. Her true face, the one I was seeing now, was more fragile, strange and exposed.

She struggled with her words, trying to explain. "When you were gone . . . the air was different in the chapel. It was dead air. You are what made those long hours alive. This is so hard," she said. "This life. I don't know that I could bear it without you here."

We walked together, and I asked her if she had really had white horses and lived in a great house and did she miss those things.

"I don't miss those things."

"Why not?"

She shook her head, looking thoughtful, but would not answer the question.

She kept looking at me, so I felt her agitation over something. We stopped near the wall at the very edge of the garden and stood in the shelter of a pear tree, still naked from winter. And I sensed, as I had months back when we'd spoken about her missing book, the palpable gust of vulnerability; something warm rushing forth from her.

She touched the side of my face and I moved back from her slightly, surprised. With a gust of audible breath, she took my chin between her thumb and forefinger and peered at me. It happened quickly, a moment of aggression, soft and convulsive. She brought my mouth to hers. A powerful curiosity made me open to the sensation of her kiss, amazed by the warm pressure of her mouth and the heat of breath through her nostrils. My heart jumped when her tongue moved into my mouth, yet I was half receptive to it, my entire body tolling with astonishment and arousal. She broke from me and, looking into my eyes, struggled to quiet her breathing. Then all at once, the confidence that had so animated her drained away.

"What have you opened in me?" she asked, then turned and walked swiftly back up the path, her white veil rippling behind as she disappeared into the cloister.

Even more shocking to me than what I had just experienced was the idea that I could affect anyone with such power. I had not meant to break her down so. I had only meant to rise up to her.

Bairbre avoided my eyes for a few days, and when she began again to seek me out, it was always in the company of others. We ate our meals together and walked in the free hours when other girls peopled the courtyard. She indulged my curiosity about her house and horses. She told me that the house had so many rooms in it she had not been in all of them. I pressed her to describe them, the setting, to tell me the names of the horses, what they looked like, what they ate. I held back from asking about her brother and her mother, careful lest she learn that my fascination with her extended to them.

"I heard once," I said, "that you come from an ecclesiastical family."

"Yes," she said quietly.

"What does that mean?"

She thought for a moment, but before she could answer, I asked, "Is that a kind of tradition?"

"More than that," she said. "A kind of necessity."

"What do you mean?"

She did not answer and I withdrew from the topic, a stiffness come into her demeanor.

But the next day, strolling in the courtyard, she said to me suddenly, "I have a brother who died."

"You do?"

"Yes, his name was Tiernan."

"How old was he?"

"Eighteen." She stared off beyond the walls.

"I'm sorry," I said.

I wondered if it had been this brother she had been crying for that day in the chapel. "How long ago did it happen?" I asked.

"Ten years ago. I was eight."

A few moments passed before she said, "I saw him once. After."

"After?" I asked.

"After he died. I saw him in one of the corridors of our house, staring out the window." She did not look at me, but we continued to walk for a while before she stopped and faced me. "He studied almost his entire life to be a priest."

"How did he die?" I asked.

"He'd had typhus the year before, and after that his health was fragile." She stared off past the wall for a few moments and seemed to be undergoing a physical change, as if all her energy were abandoning her. When she spoke again there was a flatness to her voice. "He was prone to fevers."

A chill passed through me as I watched her walk slowly away.

Because of Mrs. O'Breen's patronage, the nuns tolerated Bairbre's choice of poetry, which she read aloud to the girls during the lacemaking. I sat drawing alone at the table in the corner, and a few times as she read I looked at her, and, when she sensed my eyes, her voice grew less steady and lost volume.

Once she came and stood behind me and read over the noise of my pencil: " '*What times of sweetness this faire day fore-showes, / When as the Lily married the Rose.*' "

At night in the privacy of my cot, I opened the little stolen book and, pressing my face into it, relived the moment she had kissed me.

One day, while sitting in the dining hall, having just finished a meal, she pressed me to tell her about the Great Blasket Island.

"I told you, I don't come from there," I said.

She held my eyes and I could see that she knew I was lying, though she could not have known why I did not want to claim the place. She knew there was something I was hiding.

"I know you come from the Great Blasket, Deirdre," she said.

I felt myself crimson.

"Why don't you want people to know?" she asked.

I moved as if to leave, but hidden by the table, she grabbed my forearm, squeezing it, holding me there. I met her eyes.

"You are from there, aren't you?" she asked in a low voice filled with certainty. I did not reject her question. I waited a moment, two moments, three, the seduction deepening.

"I am," I said softly, and she loosened her grip.

That night I wished that she would find that strength that was so attractive in her and trespass into my little cell. I touched myself restlessly but stopped short of rapture, afraid to reach the little death alone.

SEVEN

From high in the choir loft in Mass on a March morning, where I sat with some of the novices, I watched the celebrants filling the pews. Mrs. O'Breen came in with Manus. In the initial seconds that I fixed my eyes to him, my heart leaped. He was more formidable than when I'd last seen him, tall and wide in the shoulders, a mustache over his upper lip.

Two years before, he'd been boyish, yet on the verge of transformation, and that more youthful other had imprinted itself on my memory. He seemed now almost a new self; enhanced, come into profound focus.

He sensed my attention on him and looked directly up at me, his eyes the very salt of Bairbre's, but without their concentrated stillness; a more tumultuous sea. A thrill shot through me, blushes rising under my clothes. I tried not to look at him for the rest of the Mass but could not stop myself, and each time my eyes settled on him he sensed it and looked back. Mrs. O'Breen glanced at Manus and then at me, and I registered a trace of a smile on her face.

Bairbre shifted her attention from the crucifix to her mother, then to her brother, whose eyes in that moment were on me. When Bairbre's eyes met mine, I averted my own. After an interval, I stole a look at her. She had stiffened, and her focus was again given to the crucifix. The priest read from Teresa of Avila, about the soul in its terrible isolation.

As the Mass progressed, Manus fumbled with his watch, tapped on the back of the pew before him, then caught himself, struggling at formality. A man with the suppressed irreverence and impatience of a lad. All the original curiosity and fascination coursed through me, a physicality that could not be diverted. I closed my eyes and heard the wild beating of gulls over Beginish. I tried to banish the sounds, the burden of their cries threatening diminishment.

When the Mass was over I watched him leave, the tallest figure there. I remained alone in the choir loft until the rioting of my blood quieted, then went out to the vestibule, where Mrs. O'Breen stood with Bairbre, speaking in hushed tones. I passed through, pretending not to notice them.

"Who is this girl?" Mrs. O'Breen asked.

"Deirdre," Bairbre said.

I stopped, bowing my head. My eyes went directly to her face before lowering again.

"This is my mother, Mrs. O'Breen," Bairbre said.

I held my breath, then lifted my eyes to meet hers.

"Hello, Deirdre," Mrs. O'Breen said.

"Hello," I answered and nodded. This was the first time I had the

chance to gaze into Mrs. O'Breen's eyes, which were clear and beautifully gray. She smelled of rare flowers. A finely wrought beadwork
enhanced the lapels of her jacket, and when she breathed, the beads
shimmered.

At that moment, Manus appeared under the arch. The burn of a
flush moved like a force upward from my heart, and I felt myself
shrink. His footsteps as he crossed into the room were loud and
unapologetic, echoing, as if he were leaving broken masonry in his
wake.

It was like being approached by a creature of another species; a tall,
bold animal, who'd brought in with him the air of another, richer,
more foliated wood. With him present, even the walls of Enfant de
Marie felt female, marled with pink.

"Deirdre, this is my son, Manus."

He held his coat toreador fashion over his shoulder, his chest high,
and I would have thought him unapproachable but for something soft
and half disclosed in his features; a flush of sensibility on his cheek, a
tiny spasm of uncertainty that crossed his upper lip. "Hello, Deirdre,"
he said, the depths of his voice strummed with softness.

I nodded, unable to find my own voice.

When I bid them good day and moved off into the corridor, I
stopped and listened.

"What a remarkable girl," Mrs. O'Breen said.

Bairbre hesitated, then said, "She is my favorite."

"She's the one who likes to draw your laces?" Mrs. O'Breen asked.

"Yes. Deirdre from the Blasket."

"An orphan?"

"Yes."

"The pet."

"Yes."

"And pretty as well," Mrs. O'Breen said. "Do you think so, Manus?"

"I do," he said.

I was transported by their approval of me, and about to rush off
lest I become detected listening, when I heard Mrs. O'Breen ask, "So
she has no one to visit of a weekend now and again?"

There was silence before Bairbre said, "No, I suppose not."

"You'll both come to Kenmare together Saturday next, Bairbre," Mrs. O'Breen said.

Again there was hesitation from Bairbre before she said, "Yes, I'll invite her."

That evening at the meal, Bairbre was silent and far away while I waited for her to ask me to come to Kenmare. When she finished eating, still not having spoken, she got up abruptly, and I followed her.

"What's wrong, Bairbre?" I asked.

"I'm not feeling well," she answered.

She sat on a bench in the corridor and I sat beside her. The bell for Vespers rang, but neither of us obeyed its call.

A long silence passed and I began to despair that she would do her mother's bidding and invite me.

Unable to hold back, I asked, "Will you ever go to visit your family in Kenmare?"

She stiffened slightly. "I don't know."

I waited. "I wish I could go with you some time. I don't think I could bear it if I never left Enfant de Marie again!"

"I don't like going there," Bairbre said.

"Why?"

I thought of her dead brother's ghost but suspected that her anxiety was related more to the living than to the dead. I was afraid to say more, for fear of upsetting her. After a few moments' silence she sighed and said in a soft, patient voice, "You asked me once about my ecclesiastical family." She faced me. "It goes back two centuries. I had an ancestor who was a bishop in Donegal, an important political voice among the clergy. Apparently he was very handsome and worldly. Bishop Hugh O'Gara. He created a scandal when he left his vocation to marry a wealthy woman of royal blood. She was a Portuguese duchess, a descendant of Philip II of Spain. And she was a Protestant. Bishop O'Gara was threatened with excommunication, but before his wedding he made a pact with the cardinal. He was so charismatic that he convinced the other clergy that God had spoken to him and that he must father sons who would be priests and that all his children who married would produce children to carry on the tradition of a great ecclesiastical family. The papers they drew up were complicated documents. His wife would be converted to Catholicism. Fortunately he fathered ten children, two of the sons became priests, and three of the daughters, nuns. And he was allowed to keep a place among the clergy. It was consecrated in Ireland, though kept secret from Rome.

"But over time the tradition has died out. Branches of the family have dissolved, plagued with daughters, many of whom did not marry, or those who did did not produce children who would take up the religious life. Many emigrated to America. But my mother's branch of the family has remained loyal to this heritage." She went quiet, her hands fidgeting softly on her lap. I wondered why she was telling me this now, and how it related to her not wanting to go home.

"My mother was devastated when Tiernan died," she said suddenly. "So much rode on his becoming a priest."

I was curious why Manus had not been sent into the priesthood after Tiernan's death but trusted an intuition that I should not press her, especially after she witnessed his attentions to me earlier in the day.

When we parted that night, nothing still had been said of my visiting Kenmare. I did not sleep, agitated that my chance might not materialize.

The days passed and still Bairbre said nothing. But as if Mrs. O'Breen knew that this might happen, she issued a letter to Sister Carmel saying that plans had been made for the two of us to come to Kenmare the following Saturday.

EIGHT

The morning Bairbre and I walked outside the convent gates, birds twittered and a dampness held to the bright air. Manus, who stood near the waiting carriage talking to the groom, turned and smiled when we approached, sweeping aside a strand of loose hair from in front of one eye. He opened the carriage door, giving us each an arm in. Bairbre and I sat side by side and Manus across from us. As we moved into the wide vista of the landscape, it impressed me what a great chasm separated the medieval city of Enfant de Marie from the open world.

Bairbre pressed her shoulder and upper arm against mine and stirred unhappily. The carriage rocked and bounced on the hilly road. I felt Manus's eyes on me, but a long interval passed before I returned his gaze. He looked at me with a bold curiosity, the corners of his mouth poised before a smile.

Bairbre startled me by taking my hand and securing it possessively in her lap, then casting a dark look at Manus, who blinked and looked away, growing thoughtful. For a while the tension between brother and sister made my chest ache.

Bairbre kneaded my fingers in her two hands as if she would milk them. I wished she would stop, the way she was knitting uneasiness into my very skin. I stole a look at Manus in the long, jostling silence of the ride. The strand of hair he had earlier swept aside he now left to hang negligently before one eye.

As the carriage brought us closer to Kenmare Bay, I was surprised at how deeply the humid, saline vapors of the ocean unsettled me, bringing back a younger, lonelier time. The house that came into view as we turned a mountainy road was like nothing I'd ever seen, palatial and rising up before the sea, the gray-white stones of it polished by the rain. When we descended from the carriage, throngs of gulls rose from the many blue gabled beams, pleading in the sky, swinging back and forth in intricate arcs.

The central area of the house had a monastic look to it, pinnacled as it was with a church tower, complete with a bell. The wings to either side were more modern looking, as if they had been grafted on at a later date.

"The original house was an Augustinian abbey," Manus explained to me.

"Really?" I said.

He walked a few strides ahead then turned and, pointing, directed my attention northerly on the grounds to the ruins of a single stand-ing wall, weed choked and overgrown in ivy. "Hundreds of years after the rectory had fallen around it, that particular wall still stands."

I was still looking at it, marveling, when Manus disappeared with the groom, walking the horses to the stables.

Bairbre and I proceeded to the main door of the west wing, climbing the stairs between two massive stone urns in which camellias flourished. Bairbre did not respond to the salutations of the servant who ushered us in. Behind the dull thrum of silence that filled the vestibule, the sea's low roaring continued to echo.

We moved directly into a grand room. Through the window the backs of the waves glimmered in a mild sun that appeared sporadically through the gray. The sea moved slowly, not as I remembered it, the waves now powerful in their lift and swell, yet somehow constrained.

"Are you glad again to be near the sea?" Bairbre asked softly, coming behind me.

"Yes," I said, though I struggled against a feeling of vertigo. I turned to face her but found myself distracted by the play of waves on a copper vase just past her shoulder.

As we'd stood together in the main room I'd heard the entrance door open and close and footsteps on the stairs. I'd believed it had been Manus going upstairs, so as the serving woman led Bairbre and me up to our rooms, I expected to come face-to-face with him, but was startled at every turn in the passage to meet with a different statue. Most were religious in nature: saints or marbles of women at prayer. Occasionally something more mythical appeared: a lion with wings, a unicorn with a silver horn. The deeper into the maze of hallways, the darker the passages grew. Figures gazed somberly from every alcove as if each had once trespassed into this place as I was doing now and had been paralyzed with fear. I was entering into the dark mystery of a family, queasy as if we were coming closer to a central room that enshrined a Eucharist. I could not separate the sinister from the sacred, as I could not separate my foreboding of the place from my fascinated attraction to it.

The bedroom where I was to stay was drained of light, the bedsilks crimson and deep green. The servant went to the window and parted the curtains, but the daylight did little to cut the dimness.

Bairbre told me she was going to rest in her room a few doors down the hall, and that she would come back for me when the servant called us down to tea.

She left, closing my door behind her. I strolled, awestruck, around the room, touching things, looking into drawers and cabinets and little wooden recesses, carefully oiled, where I found prayer books and icons; a white folded cardigan, handkerchiefs and pillowcases. A statue of the Virgin stood on her own pedestal, her cape spread, her eyelids heavy, as if she were struggling to stay awake.

At an angle and facing me from one corner stood a grand dresser with a large oval mirror. Approaching my reflection, I took off my postulant's veil.

The clarity of my own figure filled me with wonder. It was not as I'd imagined it, having for so long only seen my incomplete face in the small edges of mirror. There was a fluidness of line to my tall self. I moved my arms in graceful motions and turned my face this way and that. Laughter of pleased surprise surfaced from within me.

I looked outside over the cobbled drive and beyond the property walls at flatlands and ditches running beyond to the unreachable horizon. Dead blackberry creeper ran along the wall directly below my window toward the back of the house, where I could see a neglected garden, all out of character with the rest of the transplendant facade.

I had lain down and closed my eyes when I heard horse's hooves and a creaking and turning of stiff wheels. Peering out I saw a carriage stopping, swaying slightly as Mrs. O'Breen descended from it. My heart clamored wildly as if she were the one I was in love with. She stood a moment, brushing her skirts, adjusting the fitted ice blue jacket she wore, then turned with authority toward the house, a stately yet feminine figure. I heard the doors open below, and she disappeared from my view.

An embankment of clouds moved to cover the sun and the day deepened. I lay down again, struggling to relax, waiting for Bairbre to summon me downstairs.

Startled by a soft knock, I sat up. The door opened soundlessly, and as Mrs. O'Breen peered in, I stood.

"Deirdre, I'm sorry I wasn't here to meet you when you came."

"Oh no," I said breathily. "It's fine."

We both hesitated a moment, regarding one another.

"Let's sit," she said, gesturing to two richly upholstered chairs. She turned the flame up in a small lamp, glancing as she did at my postulant veil, which I had draped over the footboard of the bed.

In her presence I earnestly assumed the demure and pious demeanor learned from Bairbre.

She gave me such a look of approval that I tingled within.

"Did you know, Deirdre, that I was once going to be a nun?"

"No," I cried softly.

"And at Enfant de Marie!"

"Really?"

"Yes, I was always meant to be a nun. As a tiny girl I received instruction. I even wore a veil and learned very young to accept solitude. While my sisters played, I stayed in my room and prayed. And I was the youngest, so it was very hard." She paused. "But life presents us with surprises, doesn't it?"

"Yes," I answered quietly. Her words felt rich with portent. I looked beyond her at the glimmer and order of the room.

When I met her eyes again, they were so set upon me that a little thrill rushed me. "I was her beauty, my mother had said. Her flower petal. She said it was right to offer her most beautiful one to Christ. All the paintings of the female martyrs depicted them as romantic beauties.

"We were always told, Deirdre, that we must uphold those who came before us. That we were responsible for our ancestors. Being from an ecclesiastical family was like having royal blood. She had no sons, but she had a beautiful daughter. She gave me the looking glass, and while my sisters wore their hair in braids, mine was left loose and long."

I was exhilarated by her presence, drawn into her story, but confused by her desire to lay herself so plainly before me. She'd seen me only from a distance in the choir at Enfant de Marie, and had spoken to me very briefly, yet she was confessing to me as if we were close.

She paused and was gazing beyond me at the window, a thoughtful intensity about her. When her eyes met mine again, they looked wistful. In a softer, even more confidential voice, she went on. "A fortnight before I was to become a postulant, my mother read an advertisement in the *Evening Chronicle*. A man was looking to publish a book of photographs depicting saints, and he needed models for them. We traveled across Ireland to Dublin by train. My mother put rouge on my cheeks and mouth. She thought I might be selected to represent Saint Thérèse of Lisieux, the little consumptive nun, but I was chosen to be photographed as Saint Lucy and as Saint Cecelia. The man, his name was Mr. Holohan, said I had a natural flair for the dramatic.

"In Dublin I inwardly reveled in the romance and theatricality of my own nature. I swelled with an awareness of my own beauty and worldly potential, and then my mother took me directly from that experience back across Ireland and to Enfant de Marie. It seemed like a form of cruelty at the time, but I have come to understand why she did this. In order to make the sacrifice greater to God. She had produced no sons, but a beautiful girl with gifts was as close as she'd come in this life to offering God a priest.

"Francis O'Breen saw the photographs in a gallery in Dublin. He wanted to meet me. Mr. Holohan gave him my name and told him I was a novice at Enfant de Marie. He wrote to me."

I was hoping she'd go on and tell the story of how she'd come to leave the convent, but all she said was, "Ah, well then. In the end I did not become a nun." She sighed. "Sometimes, Deirdre, I imagine what it must be like to give oneself fully to God. Fully. Body and soul. What my mother wanted for me. And I think, Deirdre, there could be nothing finer. No finer, truer life. And seeing that you are embarking on such a life, you must be in agreement with me."

I ached to reveal myself truly to her, to tell her I was not meant to be a nun, but I was flooded with an urgency to say whatever it was she wanted me to. "I am in agreement with you," I said.

She studied me with thoughtful curiosity, then said, "You have magnificent hair."

My hands flew to smooth it. "It's always been difficult to control," I said, and smiled awkwardly.

"There's so much of it and such waves!" She smiled at me. Leaning slightly toward me she asked in a quiet voice, "May I touch it?"

I tried to hide the little pulse of shock I felt. "Yes," I uttered.

She stood and walked around to the back of my chair. I felt the faint pressure of her hands on the outer nimbus of waves. Very gently and with one finger she tucked a strand of fine hair behind my right ear, and a pleasurable shiver took me, gooseflesh rising on the back of my neck. I closed my eyes, reduced to most primitive longing, resisting the memory of my own mother's touch and soft ululating voice at my ear.

Mrs. O'Breen's hand brushed past my face, soft and smelling like cake flour.

"In the Middle Ages, voluminous hair in women was a sign of fertility," she said, then came around in front of me.

"Was it?" I asked.

She nodded, her eyes picking up the lamplight.

"Don't wear your veil down to tea," she said. She took a jeweled comb out of her own hair and arranged it into mine.

"Look," she said, taking my hand, leading me to the mirror. Amazed, I moved in close to the glass, tilting my head in different directions to watch the jewels glint and sparkle. In the dimness of the room I looked at her image beside mine in the glass, a swift answering flash of admiration in her eyes. Through her I sensed my own potential.

She led me out to a wide marble staircase, and we began our descent into the dining hall. I had never imagined that a ceiling could be so high. The walls were a deep cornflower blue, and the ceiling was painted an even deeper shade of blue and damascened with gold and silver stars.

Escorting me down, she held the tips of my fingers and smiled at me. I told myself that she was not one to be deceived; that she recognized something in me. I took a deep breath. I would not disappoint her. My poise intensified, my movements were slow, weighted in time. It was Bairbre I had studied this grace from, but now it went beyond Bairbre. I could be a daughter to Mrs. O'Breen as well; a different daughter. I would dizzy myself with pleasing her. I would take the poise further.

After we sat down together at the table, Bairbre appeared on the staircase, and I saw a spasm of confused emotion on her face as her mother leaned close to me, adjusting a strand of my hair around the jeweled comb. But like a momentary ripple that had passed over a still surface of water, Bairbre's pain was suddenly undetectable. She nodded to her mother as she took her place, then seemed to enclose herself in a circle of silence, her eyes cast beyond us as if she were in a religious revery.

The table was set with a multitude of cutlery and crystal, dozens of candles lit at its center in elaborate candelabras. Beneath the branch of each candle hung a clear jewel pendant.

Manus appeared, storming through the front door, which he left open behind him. He threw his riding gloves down on a side table and walked with a jaunt into the room. Mrs. O'Breen suppressed a smile, her eyes widening and lighting up at his irreverence.

"Mother," he said, and she extended her face to him obliquely, and he kissed her cheekbone. "Bairbre," he said as he crossed to his own chair, and when he kissed the top of her head, she squeezed her lips together almost indetectably.

Under his close attention I kept my eyes cast down.

Mrs. O'Breen reached for her snow white linen napkin, and as I followed suit, I was mortified to see that my fingernails were dirty. I withdrew my hand suddenly and felt everyone's eyes on me.

The fire of a flush burned my skin. I winced, looking down at my rough postulant skirt. Silence filled the room.

"What is it, Deirdre?" Mrs. O'Breen asked.

I did not know what to say. "I've never sat at such an elegant table before."

A look of empathy moved over Mrs. O'Breen's face. "Do you think knowledge of such things has anything to do with a person's character? It means very little in the grand scheme of things, Deirdre, and I will guide you along."

She made the sign of the cross: "Pray for us honorable vessel, vessel of singular devotion. Mystical rose."

A man in a black coat served dishes of cold segmented orange and chopped apple, and Mrs. O'Breen pointed to the fork I must use.

Mrs. O'Breen and Manus spoke as the meal was served, about profits on various properties. In a silver pitcher on the table I caught my reflection, the jewels a riot of twinkles in my hair.

I glanced at Bairbre, prim in her postulant veil, and with downcast head, looking as if she had collapsed into herself. She seemed on the verge of disappearing. At last Mrs. O'Breen addressed her with questions about this nun or that, and about the timetable on our novitiates. I gazed at Bairbre as she responded. She had her mother's eyebrows and long fingers.

Unused to wine, three or four sips relaxed and warmed me. I stole covert glances at each of them.

They were of peerless lineage, their skin like cream, black hair heavy and straight as fine silk, while mine was coarse in its abundance and like brambles, dark but wrought with browns of various sorts, some strands coppery, some light pewter.

My eyes were drawn up to the heights of the room. As afternoon deepened outside the window, shadows consumed the upper stratosphere near the ceiling so I could barely discern the gold and silver stars I had seen there only half an hour before.

Looking down once from the ceiling, I found Manus searching me with his eyes. He looked shyly away, that softness out of character with the swaggering, more self-assured persona. The flush on his cheek made my heart swell.

Emboldened by the wine, I kept looking at him. His hair was the blackest of the three, and burnished with the most intense cobalt blue; a blue that could hurt the eyes with its brilliance. Like an Immortal! I exulted within myself.

That evening I walked with Bairbre along the darkening beach. I was wearing my postulant's veil again, having taken Mrs. O'Breen's jeweled comb from my hair. Not wanting to part with it, I had placed it in a dresser drawer in the room I would sleep in, thinking I might put it on again at night before the mirror.

Along the sea the sky was immense and streaked with darkening clouds, the last light of day filtering away. We held hard to each other, bowing into the force of a cold, cleansing wind. I had been hesitant to walk along the beach, afraid of the old sadness the waves might rouse in me, but here they came in in steady, rolling sheets. They were nothing like the chaotic crash against Blasket rock or the weedy, straining water running up the White Strand. Here the shore was majestic, and the sea struggled for poise and conformity as it drove inland, foaming at its edges and discreetly withdrawing.

"I don't like the way the two of them are together," Bairbre yelled over the noise of wind and waves. "You know how he came in tonight all jaunt and canter, acting the very lad. He does that for her. Manus isn't really like that. And all that talk about the properties. I know he doesn't care about profits or properties. He puts it on for her, and they're very cozy together. His little dance for her. I don't like to be near it."

The sea's roar diminished and returned. I looked at her, struggling to understand her words. It would not occur to me until later, when I was alone in bed, that she had seen my euphoria and had not liked it.

But she had not dampened my excitement or my intrigue. Alone in my room, I opened the drawer, looking for the jeweled comb, but it was gone. My heart fell at the thought that someone had been in here, but I told myself this was not my house, and Mrs. O'Breen had not given me the jeweled comb, only loaned it to me.

That night, unable to sleep, I got up and opened the curtains, looking out until the dusk came gradually in over the trees and flowers, causing the cobbles to glisten below.

The next morning was brilliant. I dressed and wandered through the hallways in search of the staircase that led down to the drawing rooms and the dining hall. But I got lost along the way and passed through a long gallery of marble busts on pedestals, ghostly white and with vacant eyes, and I knew I was in a very old part of the house, the

walls leaning slightly, the window frames deeply recessed, the mold-
ings primitively carved, and the ceilings low.

I came to a door festooned with decorative carvings, which I
opened and went through, stunned to find myself on a balcony in near
darkness, looking down into a chapel.

As my eyes adjusted to the dimmer light, I could discern the
ribbed vaulting of the ancient walls. On the altar, two candles were lit,
signifying the presence of the Eucharist, one to either side of the velvet
curtained chalice. A faint smell of frankincense held to the heavy air,
along with smells of old stone and dampness. It struck me that the
balcony I stood on had once been a choir.

I was about to slip out and try to find my way downstairs again
when I saw another door farther down along the balcony and slightly
ajar. As I moved closer to it, I saw the quiver of candlelight on the wall
within. I knocked softly, and the door creaked open wider. I waited a
few moments longer before fully opening it. On a large black wood
dresser with iron handles sat the curtained hat that Mrs. O'Breen had
always worn to Mass at Enfant de Marie. A pair of her soft leather
shoes with the buttons on the sides were set on the floor a few feet
away from me. I stepped in further and saw an elegant bed under a
wood canopy, the coverlet glinting with gold embroidery.

The room was night dark except for dozens of candles flickering
before three pictures that hung on one wall across from the bed. The
central canvas, an oil painting, was the largest. I moved in close to
study it. Set before a lugubrious backdrop of storm-distressed clouds
was a young man whom I recognized immediately as Manus. His features were composed into a velvety calm, a gently penetrating expression shone in his eyes.

The picture to the left of it was not a painting but a photograph.
The young Mrs. O'Breen, I thought, her face coming delicately forward into light, a luminous oval and one white arm rising from
shadow. Saint Lucy holding the saucer with two disembodied eyes on
it, and seeming to offer them like delicacies to an abstract presence
above.

The photograph to the right of Manus's portrait was of young Mrs. O'Breen as Saint Cecelia. In this one her statuesque body was apparent, the voluptuousness of it out of character with any other depiction of a saint I had ever seen. An underexposed angelic figure loomed behind her as she sat before a harpsichord, her fingers grazing the keys, her intent expression in the act of listening, not to the music under her fingers but as if she were sensing out the barely imposed angelic figure behind her. I was amazed by the artistry of the image and by the soft young girl with the receptive eyes, mouth slightly open, an expression somewhere between rapture and astonishment.

I looked again at the portrait of Manus, confused and uneasy at the romantic expression on his face. I was embarrassed by the size of the portrait and its place of prominence here in his mother's bed-chamber. A sudden prickly sensation moved over my scalp.

I went back onto the balcony and exited through the door I had come through. I walked a while longer through the corridors when I found myself at a window that faced out over the sea. I watched the water for a few moments and was about to go when I saw a figure on horseback moving at a leisurely pace along the foreshore. I went close to the window glass, peering out.

The moment I realized it was Manus, he looked directly up to the window where I was. He pulled the reins so the horse twisted its head and shifted direction, coming back to the house. My heart began going so hard it hurt. I remained where I stood, waiting, not knowing what to expect, and afraid that if I left this place, he might not find me. I heard his footsteps, saw his approaching shadow darken the doorway. When he was there at last beside me, tall, breathing heavily from his ride and from scaling the stairs, an earnest expression on his face, there was not a trace about him of the irreverence his mother seemed to enjoy.

"How did you find your way to this part of the house?" he asked, and broke into a little winded smile.

"I went through the wrong corridors. I was trying to find the stair-case down."

He nodded.

At a loss for words and looking for something to rescue us both from awkwardness, my eyes fixed themselves on a pin set into his lapel. A golden sun with a serious face, engraved inside a triangle.

"What does that pin represent?" I asked.

"It's a Masonic symbol. My father was a Freemason," he said.

"Freemason?" I asked.

"A secret society of craftsmen."

"How old were you when your father died?" I asked.

His face darkened. "We don't know for certain that my father died."

"You don't?"

"He went off on an expedition, a ship into the High Hebrides of Scotland, and never returned. The ship and no one on it was heard from again."

"How long ago was that?"

"Fifteen years ago."

"So you were very small."

"I was two. He'd gone in search of something called fire marble. On one of the obscure islands in the North Sea there is supposed to be a big wall of this marble hidden in the rock cliffs."

"It must be extraordinary marble to have drawn him so far away after it."

I felt him quicken at my show of interest. He pointed down the hall. "Would you like to see what it looks like?" he asked.

I nodded, and he pointed to a small, insignificant-looking door a few feet to my left. He drew a key from his pocket and slid it into the lock.

Going through that door we left a corridor of well-lit, cream-colored walls and persian rugs, paintings of trees and lakes framed in gold ovals, for a corridor all rough stone and exposed brick, rampant with echoes. The windows, low to the ground and deeply recessed, had no glass in them, and the wind blew in. As we passed through, I saw three large, thatched nests occupying an alcove high up in one of the lintels.

"Ravens," Manus said, pointing at them. "You see, this house was very much a work in progress for my father.

"There are one hundred and twenty-one rooms, many of them altogether forgotten," he said thoughtfully. After a pause, he said, "In fact when I was little and my father had been lost in the High Hebrides, I thought this part of the house was called The High Hebrides; that my father was lost in this part of the house and that one day he would find his way back." He paused a moment, perusing the walls. "My mother won't come to this part of the house."

"Why not?"

"She hates the way he took things apart back here."

"Why doesn't she have this area renovated?"

"This house is too big. These rooms are not necessary to her. I'm glad she doesn't touch them. This is where my father's things are."

Dead leaves and flowers littered a wide staircase, which we descended onto a vast panoramic room below, what once must have been a great hall of some sort, roofless in one area now and covered in ivy. Broken, carved faces in niches high on the wall were discolored, exposed to the elements. Through a break in the stones I could see a wild orchard. A sudden wind sent pink branches straining, and a slew of blossoms came through the glassless windows.

I followed Manus through corridors, passing rooms that contained great stores of rough-hewn stone, quarried slate, and marble.

"My father believed that the old must always be resuscitated, grafted with the new. This abbey was sacked in Cromwellian times. A century later, a family of Irish Papists, the Fitzpatricks, moved in and built on the newer wings, but that family was dispossessed by English Protestant landlords. The house has been tenanted on and off over the centuries. It's had a shaky history at best." Now and again he'd stop to point out a faded inscription carved into a window recess, or the relief of a sculpted angel or a heraldic bird.

We came at last to his father's study, a room fully fortified and protected from the elements by reinforced doors and windows. The chimney breast was crumbled, and shelves were piled with books and papers. Against one wall a group of mysterious contraptions were displayed.

"This is an alchemist's laboratory," he said.

"Alchemists? . . . Didn't they try to make gold?"

"Yes, centuries ago."

My attention was drawn to an elaborate oven of some sort with knobs and various dials attached to it. "This," he said, "is an athanor, a kind of furnace where metals were melted down."

He pointed out different objects set on a shelf behind the athanor: tongs and a bellows; various crucibles of earthenware and glass; a mortar and pestle.

"You see, Freemasons used to study alchemy, searching for secret and sublime knowledge." I felt him watchful of me now, trying to suss out my reaction to his words. "They study the elements; they believe that that's how we'll discover the true nature of the universe and thus of ourselves."

When he looked expectantly at me, I nodded.

"I'm sure the nuns wouldn't approve of you looking at these things." He waited for a response, and when I didn't know what to say, he went on.

"Perhaps such things seem"—he hesitated, searching for a word—"*godless* to you."

"No!" I cried. "I'm intrigued."

He looked at me in earnest.

"You don't think it's godless?" he asked again softly, looking sidelong at me.

I took a breath, moved by his need for my reassurance. Emotion caught in my chest, a deep desire to reassure him, which became a desire to validate him. "The Church can be intolerant . . . and cruel. I don't place much store in the beliefs of the Church," I confessed. My face suddenly on fire, I lowered my head. I had never said such things aloud. A brightness issued suddenly from my nun's clothes, but I did not sense his judgment on the air between us.

He remained silent for a few moments, then said softly, "I try to explain to my mother that many Catholics are Freemasons. And that alchemy once flourished in the Franciscan and Dominican convents of Europe." I looked up at him, and he smiled and said, "Of course I don't tell her that the most passionate alchemists were condemned as heretics."

I smiled back, then averting my eyes from his, studied the alchemical laboratory.

"How did the alchemists produce gold?" I asked.

"Through great heat they transmuted one metal into another. And they used mercury, which they believed had magical properties and could inspire gold or silver out of a coarser metal."

"Inspire it?" I asked, amazed.

"Yes, persuade it."

"As if," I began, "coarser metals contain the potential for gold, or that the seeds of gold are present naturally within them."

He focused on me, his face lit at my excitement.

"Yes," he smiled. "To awaken the spirit in matter. My father was passionate about this idea. When he was younger he actually did experiments with these things. But as he got older he kept them really as museum pieces, collectables. He tried to take it literally when he was younger, but with maturity he became interested in alchemy for its metaphors. He wanted to understand nature, and he felt that modern science was cold; that there were secrets in the medieval science. He saw it as an esoteric science. And I can attest to the fact that the old books are confusing. I struggle to understand them. There were warnings in some of the texts that the uninitiated should not read them."

"Why not?"

"It's all so difficult to decipher. Alchemical texts are filled with strange imagery."

Manus opened a drawer and took out a little velvet bag. "Let me show you the fire marble," he said, drawing out a streaked milky green stone and handing it to me.

"Come to the window and you can see it better," he said. We stood together side by side and I held the stone in the light, my blood rising at his proximity, my nerves taut as harp strings. The stone was scored with deeper greens, the smoothness broken by three veins of a clear reddish gold, a kind of hardened ambery syrup. "You'd think by its name it would be red," he said. "But it's not."

"Why was he after this?" I asked, keeping my focus on the stone to steady myself.

"He must have wanted to build something with it," he said softly.

As he returned the stone to the drawer he said, "As a builder, he was a great idealist. He loved his work and spent much of his time in this part of the house and even kept a bedroom back here so when he worked deep into the night, he could sleep."

I let out a surprised laugh when we heard the beating of ravens' wings in the hallway outside the room and their echoing, melancholy cries.

Manus smiled, and an awkward silence ensued.

I broke it by saying, "Your father sounds like a remarkable man."

"Come and look at this picture." I followed him to one of the shelves, where he showed me a portrait of a man and a small child. "That's me with my father," he said. "I was twenty months old. He used to dandle me. Bairbre remembers it. She says I tried to eat the carnation in his lapel."

The man's eyes were pale and blurred, as if they had shifted away from the lens in the precise moment the picture had been taken. The impression was of a man capable of great intensity, his big hand around his tiny boy's arm and chest, a study in gentleness.

"I know so little about him. His family in the north had made a fortune in flax but at the time he met my mother he was estranged from them. My father had been living in France for five years before he came back to Ireland. The story goes that he was studying dolmen stones in the field in Kilorglin when he saw my mother in her white novice robes." He paused, his eyes quickly traversing my white habit from hem to neckline before returning with a faint smile to my face.

"My mother says she was praying, that she'd wandered off the convent grounds in a holy revery." He smiled ironically. "But that's not the story my father told my brother. He says that they arranged a rendezvous.

"Anyhow, my father bought this house for my mother. He was renovating it as they lived in it."

"Your father must have been very much in love with her."

Manus went thoughtful at this. "Yes, but my parents were different from one another. And because of that, this is a house with two faces. My mother loves the decorative, but my father had very different tastes. I don't think he liked modernizing the house to the degree that pleased my mother. He had his own separate life back here, raven haunted and full of echoes. I think he liked that this was a lifetime project."

He drew in a deep breath and looked around the room. He seemed so animated talking about his father.

"I want to show you a picture," he said, but did not move. He extended his hand toward me, and after a moment, I gave him mine.

He led me to a corner of the room, where, affixed to the wall with small nails, hung an etching on old parchment. Most of the picture depicted an earthly landscape intricately detailed with rocks and hills and overseen by a large, thoughtful-looking sun. The image was contained within a wash of blue, but to the left of it, in the corner of the picture, a gold and cloudy firmament filled with planets, mechanisms like wheels and sundials. A man in robes who was in the act of crawling on the land in the foreground on the earthly side of the image had just broken through with his head and one hand into the bright yellow world, peering up at the planets and the universal workings of the firmament. Engraved at the bottom of the etching were the words: *One is the whole, and from this comes all, and in this is all, and if it does not contain the whole, the whole is nothing.*

"Do you really understand what these words mean?" I asked.

"No," he laughed. "I struggle with it. But I think it's trying to say that heaven and earth are closer to one another than we think."

He gave me a warm smile, and I felt, as I had the first time I had seen him, a premonition of intimacy. He took a step closer to me, and as if he were bestowing a great confidence upon me, softly said, "The alchemists concerned themselves with the sky and the wind; the territory between the earth and the spheres. What I want to do as a builder is colonize the sky. Build in that in-between place."

It struck me as a magical thing to say and I smiled, feeling myself color. I broke the look between us, turning away, feigning interest in the books on the shelves.

"I've applied for an apprenticeship in Dublin. Most likely the work I'll be doing for a few years will be basic, restructuring, renovating. Maybe government buildings. Nothing as interesting as my father's work, but I'll be learning. And there's a Freemason lodge I hope to become a member of." He paused, then said, "You'll have taken your vows by then." My heart fell. I had felt up to that moment that his confidences were admitting me somehow into his life. But he had the wide world before him. I had Enfant de Marie.

"My father was more prone to go to the lodge of a Sunday than to Mass. I've promised her . . . my mother . . . I'll always go to Mass. I will always," he said as if it were important that I know this. "And that she can depend upon me. She's lost my father. I'm the man of the family."

I wondered why he was telling me this. I continued to gaze at the books, at a loss for what I might say.

"And what about your own family, Deirdre? We've talked so long of mine."

"I feel I've always been at Enfant de Marie. I hardly remember myself before that."

"Bairbre says you were born on the Great Blasket Island."

I did not respond.

"You've a wild look to you."

I turned away from him, pained.

"I like the wildness about you."

"I don't want to be a wild girl. I want to be like you."

"Maybe you and I are a little alike."

"You're free and unfettered. You don't have to be quiet and contain things in yourself."

"I have things to contain . . . ," he said wistfully. I held his eyes. "Just as my sister has things to contain. Did you know that Bairbre wanted to be a stuccodore?"

"No . . . I didn't."

"She didn't tell you? There's rooms throughout this house where she did stuccowork."

"She never told me," I said, amazed.

"After all," he said, "she has the Masonic blood in her as well."

"Bairbre's very sad," I said.

He froze, taken off guard by my words, and for a few moments, neither of us spoke.

"I don't blame her for being sad," he said. "Now she makes lace. Can you imagine how hard that must be for her?" He looked abstracted, as he had in the carriage. "Reduced to fidgety repetitive movements of the hand, when once she stood on ladders and scaffolds to spread and sculpt plaster on high walls."

We left his father's study and he led me back up the corridor and up the stone staircase until we reached yet another area of the house. He opened the door of a vast and empty dining hall. Drawing aside a heavy curtain, the room filled suddenly with light and an effusion of swirling white dust. The wall opposite the windows was covered with numerous sculpted rams' heads, childlike in disproportion; the room was a kind of workshop, the walls having been used as canvas, the floors still speckled with dried spills of plaster. On another wall were studies of urns looped with laurel leaves; on another, a tableau of dogs overcame a stag.

"Bairbre did this?" I asked, studying the snarling lips and sharp teeth of the dog.

"Yes, and there are more rooms like this."

"Manus," I said. "Bairbre has explained to me that yours is an ecclesiastical family—"

"Yes."

"And that your older brother was going to take up the cloth. . . ."

He nodded.

"Why was it, well, why was it that you weren't sent into the seminary yourself, after your brother died?"

"It was my superstitious aunts who decided it. My mother's sisters. They were afraid that God had not yet forgiven my mother for abandoning her vocation. They'd read of a similar case in the family history. Generations ago, another young nun had left her vocation and was replaced by her sister. There were no repercussions. It seemed God had accepted the replacement. So they decided that rather than try to groom me as a priest, Bairbre should replace our mother as a nun and the family sin would be forgiven. And I would be left to bring in a new generation."

I felt stunned, filled with pity for Bairbre.

"Out of the deep Dark Ages, isn't it?" he asked.

Peering at one of the stucco rams, I said, "Bairbre must be wondering where I am."

Manus led me back through the house and directed me to the staircase I had been searching for earlier.

I found Bairbre in the dining room drinking a cup of tea.

"Where were you?" she asked.

"I was talking to your brother."

"What were you talking to him about?" she asked.

"He showed me the back part of the house." I paused. "And he told me that you wanted to be a stuccodore."

She lifted her cup to her lips.

"You never really wanted to become a nun, did you?" I asked in a soft voice.

"The ties of blood rule," she said, looking at me.

"What do you mean?"

"I told you, it's an ecclesiastical family."

"Your mother told me she was going to become a nun once."

"Yes. And she left her vocation, like my ancestor Hugh O'Gara, the one I told you about. She feels it even more incumbent upon herself that she pay God back for having left."

"Manus told me that your aunts said you must replace your mother as a nun."

She stared ahead of her silently for a moment, and then said, "It wasn't my aunts that decided it. My mother says it was my aunts, and Manus believes her. My aunts wanted Manus to be a priest. It was my mother who found the story in the family history of one nun replacing another. She fought my aunts and convinced them that this was what was necessary." She paused for another few moments. "It isn't a sacrifice my mother would ever ask of Manus."

"She wouldn't?" I asked.

Bairbre was silent. I thought better than to press her on this painful matter.

How could it be normal, I asked myself, to lay down one's life for one's mother? Perhaps this too was the way of the world, for what did I know of such things? Still, I could not help but ask, "Why, Bairbre? Why would you give up your own life . . . ?"

She set her lips and would not look at me. I moved closer to her, waiting for her answer. She pushed her cup and saucer away and stood, then walked woodenly from the room.

The next morning after a congenial breakfast with Mrs. O'Breen and Manus, Bairbre and I boarded a coach and were on our way back to Enfant de Marie.

When we were on the road and the house was no longer visible, Bairbre leaned back in her seat and sighed, then turned to face me, taking my hand, lacing her fingers through mine.

"Thank God," she said. "Thank God we're going back."

A few moments of silence passed, and she said, "Deirdre, I see that you're counting on Manus, but you shouldn't."

My heart stopped, but I did not speak.

"There's a girl in Dublin I've heard him speaking of. He wanted my mother to meet her." In a soft voice she added, "A girl from a good family."

The coach rocked gently from side to side. I could still hear the vague murmur of the ocean. Slowly I freed my hand from Bairbre's and gazed silently out the window at the passing fields.

Nine

That September, cloistered in the ruined battlement, breathing

again the chill of ancient air, we began our novitiate: a fragile

community of seven girls and three officiating nuns who led us in

shifts. Our days were given to the fevered enterprise of prayer:

nightly matins, morning lauds, Vespers at twilight, and finally

compline.

We got up in predawn darkness and moved single file into our

places in the ancient Ursuline chapel to plead with the Lord to show

us His face. And though we still chanted the ecstatic language of the

Psalms, and sang *The Psalter of the Virgin*, and the *Magnificat*, most of our time was given now to silent meditation.

The nuns lit fewer candles in the chapel to encourage deeper thought. In such reclusive darkness, the damp arches and winding galleries around us were barely visible, and after a certain hour, no candles were lit at all. Often we crept through blackness. I smelled my way from one passage to another, sensing the closeness of a wall, or, from a shift on the air, the openness of a room before me.

A somberness pervaded this time. Often in the blackness I heard weeping or whimpering. One evening, Sister Vivian addressed us, her voice quavering with compassion. She told us that she remembered this period of her own preparation as a nun as a difficult time because it required a new level of surrender and maturity.

I could not completely extinguish the cinders of hope that still kindled in me for Manus. But as the weeks passed, and the months, they dimmed.

I found myself prone to trances, often shaken out of them by Sister Vivian. "You mustn't sleep when you pray," the old nun whispered.

I did not tell her that I wasn't sleeping. It was in such a trance one day that I had first found myself in brilliant sunlight in a little boat crossing the bay from the Blasket to the Skellig. I was looking for the place where my father had moored his own boat in the rocks. This place which I had avoided, which I had tried to blot from memory because I knew it to be the place where I would find them, the place that held them. The unapproachable place. I stood thigh deep in water before the cave but would not enter it.

I learned to remain a long time in a trance without being discovered. And attention was diverted from me by another novice, Ann Carey, who was given to weeping fits during meditation. I heard, through my trances, her sad voice, as if from very far away.

I began to live an entire life around what was enshrined in the skellig cave, the little bay and the rock pools. Things began to happen there when I visited each day that had not actually happened. The little boat that had brought me there sailed away from me as if someone were rowing it. I found objects in the water: Manus's Masonic pin with the sun's face, glinting up from between dulse and sea lettuce; fish sliding sideways above Mrs. O'Breen's jeweled comb.

Manus and his horse waded with me in the bay.

"You know what's in there," he said, pointing to the cave.

"Yes, I know what's there."

"You know what you'll see, so why don't you go in?"

"Yes, I know what I'll see. But I won't look."

"You think you cannot bear to look at it, but you are always seeing it," he said. "You have never forgotten it. Even when you look into my face, you are seeing it.

"I'm sending the horse in," he said, "and if he returns, we'll know it's safe for you to go in and look." The horse went in on his instruction, but it did not return.

Sister Vivian shook me and my eyes opened, and I felt them roll. She shook me again. Mass was about to begin. Candles were lit on the altar.

"The horse didn't come back," I thought.

The priest pointed at the crucifix. "It is the divine who undergo the divine punishment."

From the dim corners to either side of the choir, female martyrs stood in calm, exalted postures. Cool stone, white and resurrected.

"Corpus Domini nostri," the priest said from the altar, and we rose single file.

I lifted my face, and the priest put the Host on my tongue. "In vitam eternam."

Bairbre was always present, watchful of me, smiling mildly when I met her eyes, taking my arm now and again, walking with me. Leaving little things on my cot. A holy medal. A bit of crochet work.

She had grown even stealthier in the dark than I had, and once, making my way through a corridor, I walked directly into her arms. She held onto me and said my name barely audibly. I stayed in her embrace, allowing myself to take comfort for a while before blundering away from her.

One night, several months into our novitiate, I couldn't sleep and crept from my cot through the blackness until I found the door that opened into a roofless, eroding tower, the walls covered with creeper that had been green in the spring and clotted with blood-colored berries, withered now from the sharp autumn winds.

I sat here on the broken stairs, shivering, looking up at the stars, leaning my face against the cold, ancient wall.

I thought about how I'd come to be there: my grandmother speaking to the Reverend Mother, nervous to be lying to a nun, dabbing her forehead, which had glimmered with sweat. The nun's eye suspicious on me. My grandmother blushing torridly, like a shamed child. My grandmother on her old legs running. Had she run? I don't think she had, but it seemed real to me in my memory. Why did I remember her running? And then the boom of massive doors as she'd closed them.

The door in the wall opened suddenly.

"Deirdre," Bairbre said. I knew she must have heard me leave my cell. She sat beside me on the broken step.

"You've gone so quiet with me," she said, hurt. Looking at her face illuminated by starlight, I saw how sincere her desire was to forge an intimacy with me.

We sat a while in silence and she asked, "What is the thing at the heart of your life?"

She'd always known I had a secret. I wondered if I could tell her about the memories that moved constantly through my mind, the bright interior sunlight that contrasted so sharply with the darkness of my exterior world. I wondered if I might try to articulate to her what I had never spoken aloud.

But something in the beseeching expression on her face caught my attention. I smelled guilt on the cold, starlit air, and it occured to me suddenly that she may have lied about the girl she'd said Manus wanted to introduce to his mother? Before this instant I had not even considered that it might be a lie; but now it was as if I were breathing the truth of it into my body.

I looked away from her, my pulses galloping at the idea of such a betrayal. Struggling to understand, I told myself that a heart that had been as blighted as hers was a desperate heart. Though Bairbre was capable of great compassion and I knew that she genuinely cared for me, I could never trust her fully. Desperation might drive her to tell my shameful secret if she needed to, in order to ensure that I never leave her.

I looked up at the stars on the night sky and recalled the carriage ride back to the convent from Kenmare. My excitement over the interest from her brother and mother had been too painful for her. She had told me about the girl, then had added the words, "a girl from good family," to deepen the blow.

Feeling my retreat, she leaned toward me, trying to read my face. "What is it, Deirdre?"

I shook my head. "I'm cold," I said and stood. As I made my way back to my cell through the dark battlement, I sensed her behind me. When I was under my blanket again, I knew she was standing in the doorway of my room. Very softly, I heard her sigh before she left.

As the winter months went on, Bairbre's melancholy desire to be close to me grew. At all hours, her focus was upon me, and that intensity exhausted me, as my own toward her must have once exhausted her.

It was weeks before, out of loneliness, I crept out onto the ruined stairs in the cold, where I knew she would follow me.

She did not ask me again to tell her my secret, but instead, as if in a show of devotion, she laid herself open before me, telling me stories of her own childhood, which she knew would interest me.

The first night we met, she told me about Tiernan.

"It was my mother's checks to the seminary that kept the priests tolerating him at all. From the time he was fourteen, he was in revolt, drinking and failing his studies. He was ten years older than me, twelve years older than Manus, so neither of us knew him well. When he was home, there was such a strain on the air. My mother was doing everything she could to persuade him of the importance of his role in the family. He never openly defied her, but reports of his behavior at school were always coming in. He acted as if he were listening to what she said, and that gave her hope. Hope that was always being dashed.

"When he was sixteen, he was almost expelled. He'd gotten drunk and thrown a rock through the stained glass window in the chapel. My mother persuaded the priests not to expel him, and disciplinary measures were being considered. At that time, Tiernan contracted typhus. He was in a sanitarium for a month, and sent home afterward to fully recover. His health remained fragile. Every time he got better and was preparing to return to the seminary, he would get ill. Because of the inherent weakness left from the typhus, simple influenza could make him bedridden. And he was prone to fevers. It was in the throes of one of those fevers that he died."

She spoke again of Tiernan the next night, rambling on about him, often repeating details she'd already revealed, and I sensed how unresolved his death was for her, how it gnawed at her.

"Mostly I was furious with him. I don't feel I ever knew him, and he had no time for me.

"When I was little I used to hide because I felt as if the entire house were suffering around us. I felt like the world was going to end. My mother was so unhappy because of him."

I ached to talk about Manus, and one night I said to her, "I had the feeling, when I spoke to him, that Manus loves you very much."

She stiffened slightly, then turned and faced me. "What makes you say that?" she asked.

"The way he talked about you."

"What did he say?"

"He was filled with admiration for your gifts as a stuccodore. He feels badly that you don't get to practice your craft."

She remained quiet for a few moments, then blurted out, "Manus is an innocent! He's never grown up because he's never been required to."

With these words she seemed to be dismissing him. I was afraid she would try to speak of something else, so I made something up. "He said that you were close when you were little."

She considered this. "We were. He followed me around. He wanted to play with me all the time. We had our games, as siblings do. Our secret hiding places." She paused for a few moments recalling that past time. "I didn't blame him then that my mother loved him so much. He was the baby of the family. Yes, mostly we were harmonious playmates. If anything, I dominated the games. He wanted to please me. It always mattered to him so much that I approved."

She stumbled upon a memory. "There was a maid, a parlor maid, who used to tell me how much Manus adored me. 'Don't ever ask Manus to jump out a window, Bairbre,' that maid said to me once, 'because for you he'd do it! For you and no one else!' " She shook her head and laughed, amazed to recall it. "I think that woman felt sorry for me, because she was always saying such things to me."

There was one particular day Bairbre would tell me about many times. She was eight years old and it had been decided that she would be a nun. I came to know many of the details of this particular day: that her mother had worn a green dress and a scarf, and Bairbre had worn a black-and-white dress; that the brisk, windy weather in the morning had changed by afternoon to mild and sunny.

"That day that she took my hand and we walked far into the field, I was so fully in her graces." Mrs. O'Breen had taken the scarf off from around her own neck and placed it over Bairbre's head like a veil. She'd looked into Bairbre's eyes and cried and touched her cheek. She'd kissed her temples and called her her "Soul's Saviour." They had wandered together, fasting all day, kneeling and praying in the field. They had lain that night on the chapel floor together and slept.

"It was this day that my mother explained to me the necessity of the ecclesiastical family. She told me how she had been filled with terrible weaknesses as a young woman. How when she'd received letters from my father who she'd never met, but who had seen her photographs in Dublin, she agreed to meet him secretly one day in the dolman field outside the grounds. She said she met him twice, then told him they should never meet again. She tried to resist him but he was persistent. Though he was older than her, he was handsome and worldly. He wasn't a religious man, and she admitted to me that there was a perverse relief she felt over this fact at the time. She pleaded the folly of youth . . . and, as I said, weaknesses of character.

"She continued to meet with him in the field. When he asked her to marry him she told him she would if they could think of some way to appease her mother. My grandmother had always been impressed by wealth, so my mother thought that my father's money might help, but she knew it wasn't enough. My father bought her the house in Kenmare, which to him was an architectural curiosity. The altar and nave within the abbey were still intact. A house with a church right at the heart of it! My mother thought maybe my grandmother would love this house, and come and live there with them.

"But she refused. It was a terrible falling out my mother had with her mother and sisters. My aunt Ethna was pregnant at the time and lost the child, and this was blamed on my mother's terrible rebellion. And then everything fell apart. Ethna's husband left her. Moyna never found a husband. My grandmother accused my mother of having thrown off the balance of nature."

"Those things weren't her fault!" I cried.

"My mother says they were," Bairbre said. "She explained to me that things had to be set right again. She'd devastated her mother and ruined her sisters' lives. Within a year of her marriage, my grandmother was on her deathbed and wouldn't see her, but my mother begged so vehemently that she at last agreed. My mother begged her forgiveness before she died. You see, she'd been her mother's favorite, the one she had placed her heart upon. My mother could not bear to have fallen so far. To have lost her mother's love. My grandmother told her then that the only possibility for redemption was if she had a son or a grandson who she groomed into a priest. She had to carry on the ecclesiastical family. My mother promised her on her deathbed that she would. And only then did my grandmother allow my mother to kiss her.

"That day when I was eight, Deirdre, my mother told me that my becoming a nun bonded the two of us. That it was a kind of marriage, a union of the spirit between us. She spoke of the silent dialogues among angels.

"I felt a kind of joy I can hardly describe. A kind of joy, Deirdre, that I would almost die to experience again."

⁓⊙⊚⊙⁓

How many nights was it that Bairbre and I met like that? Maybe ten or twelve, and Bairbre underwent a change those nights. I could see it in her, during the hours of prayer in the chapel; her pull upon me had lessened and I began to understand that at the back of her longing for me was the memory of that day of closeness to her mother.

"I learned that day that I was capable of making my mother happy," she had said to me more than once. And she'd asked the air one night, "Will it come again like that? Yes, it has to! I can smell the promise of it when I'm near her. It's there. If only I could find my way back to it."

The last night that we met on the ruined stairs, it was raining and we huddled together under the bit of roof that remained on the tower, our faces pressed to the dead creeper on the wall. The story of that day she was eight had become now the only story she wanted to tell.

The battlement door opened, and the light from a cagework lamp blinded us. I made out Sister Carmel's figure and soon could identify her disapproving face afloat over the brightness.

We were lectured the next morning about the danger of particular friendships, and our nightly meetings came to an end.

So a year passed.

A few days after my eighteenth birthday, I was filing out of the chapel among the other novices after Vespers, when I saw Mrs. O'Breen standing in the courtyard in the evening light. Bairbre, having seen her as well, rushed to her. Mrs. O'Breen embraced her.

I continued on my way with the others when Mrs. O'Breen called out to me, and I went to them. "I've come to congratulate Bairbre, of course. I just wanted to congratulate you as well, Deirdre."

"Thank you," I said.

"I've spoken to Sister Carmel and I know that most of the novices are going home for last visit. I've received her permission to bring you both to Kenmare for a few days before you take your vows."

Bairbre said nothing, her eyes lowered, all expression erased.

"Unfortunately," Mrs. O'Breen said, "Manus cannot be here this week. He has to remain in Dublin. So it would be just the three of us."

Bairbre looked up, her face altered at this news. "This is a very important time for Bairbre and me. I want to have a celebration before the ceremony." And though I knew her mother's interest in me made Bairbre uncomfortable, she was shivering with excitement and seemed moved by her mother's words and said that she would very much like to go.

They both turned their eyes on me.

Without speaking, I nodded my head. Mrs. O'Breen told us that a coach would be dispatched to pick us up the next day.

It wasn't until I was in my cot that night that dread began to course through me. Dread at the heights my hope might dare again to take me.

The next day after Bairbre and I arrived, we ate a meal with Mrs. O'Breen, then enjoyed a solitary walk on the property. Bairbre's spirits were up, her face flushed and mobile. She chattered on about this novice or that, about the ceremony itself and the crimson cowl we each would wear as new brides of Christ. Cells were being prepared for us in the Mother House, and Bairbre said she hoped ours would be next to each other's.

But being there with no hope of seeing Manus was an agony to me.

In the evening Mrs. O'Breen led us to a little altar she had created in the woods, frail cables of lanterns looped and moored to branches, tinkling and swaying in the balmy breeze. We stood in a clearing under the luster of the moon. A silent serving woman who had accompanied us lit a fire until it was banked high and red, then disappeared through a dark opening in the trees.

"The Soul," said Mrs. O'Breen, looking at Bairbre, "unhindered by the body tends naturally toward God. He who is the center of all existence." She gestured weakly at the sky. "God's yoke is sweet and light."

As Bairbre lifted her hands and looked to the sky, I saw Mrs. O'Breen look at her from the corner of her eye, and for that flash of a moment the world slowed down and I saw that her heart was not in this. She was doing this for effect and more for Bairbre's benefit than mine.

But Bairbre's elation was real. I guessed that this ritual was an old one between them. A smoky hiss rose into the air when Bairbre turned, as if on cue, and tossed frankincense into the flames.

In the bedimmed radiance, Bairbre's eyes fixed themselves dreamily on her mother's face.

Mrs. O'Breen gave us each a rosary, then went to her knees. When Bairbre followed suit I did as well, and we spent the next hour in prayer, a faint sickness sighing in my heart.

In the middle of the night, unable to sleep, I got up and, carrying a lamp, moved through the dark halls until I found the staircase and descended. Down one long corridor I came into a kind of library, where family photographs were displayed on a shelf. I held the lamp to them, searching for an image of Manus, but I soon realized that these were pictures of the dead, some very old, archaic photos on metal and glass; daguerreotypes, even. The most modern one was of a teenage boy in a priest's collar. Though his face was less equine, Tiernan bore a striking resemblance to Manus. As I gazed into his eyes, which were piercing and prominent and more closely set than Manus's, the air grew suddenly frigidly cold, and an intense sadness infused me. I backed quietly away, then turned with a start, afraid of what might be behind me. On my way back to my room every shadow terrified me.

I hid under the covers in the bed, my mind working wildly around the idea of Tiernan's ghost.

Deeper into the night, still huddling stiffly in the bed with my eyes squeezed shut, I heard galloping footfalls, which came to a stop outside, and the unrest of a winded horse below. In a little while there was noise on the stairs and I heard a man cough, his footsteps pass my door.

I knew that Manus had arrived unexpectedly. Relief overcame me and exhilaration, which rendered the previous hours remote and as unreal as something dreamed.

TEN

❧

Early the next morning I wandered into the gardens and along the grounds, looking up at the house, raking the windows for a sign of Manus, but I saw no one looking out.

Hearing the nervous neigh of a horse I turned and saw Manus coming toward me, drawing after him a black stallion, very tall with a white star between its eyes. Its coat glistened as if it had just been brushed.

"He stands sixteen hands. His name's Ivanhoe," Manus said. He jumped onto the horse's back, and it danced sideways, fighting the bit and stretching the rein. I moved away.

"Come up," Manus said to me.

I was surprised at the request.

"You're not afraid," he said. "You're not."

He reached out to me and, sweeping me high, pressed me between himself and the horse's neck. Before I had a chance to breathe, we were galloping, wet sod flying from the horse's feet, the three of us one creature. I sustained the impact in my teeth and bones, bent forward, squinting against the wind. We were on the beach, along the white stretch and into the tide, the horse losing traction, struggling to regain it. The sting of the sand on our faces. Manus cried out like an unfettered child, letting loose raucous screeches on the wind.

At last he pulled the reins, and, slowing Ivanhoe to a winded canter, we returned to the grounds of the great house.

As he lifted me down, still breathless with exertion, he said, "I'm going to be a wayward man! I'm going to run off to the Continent!"

I laughed, quivering with excitement.

"Will you come with me?"

"What about your future in Dublin?" I said.

"I'll chuck it!" he cried out, happy with himself. I smiled and he held my eyes.

"You've nothing on earth to lose at all, have you?" he asked.

I cringed, thinking they were cruel words, but there was a zest to the way he looked questioningly at me, as if it were a state he envied.

"Not a thing to lose but this absurd rag on your head. This veil," he said and pulled it off.

I was quaking, a gust of cool air rushing me so I felt the wet state of my own skin. I backed inadvertently against the horse, which stood solidly with its face down in the grass grazing, hot from running. One of its muscles twitched against my side.

Manus reached out and touched my hair, a look of wonder on his face. "You've wild hair," he said. "I could no more get a comb through it than I could get one through Ivanhoe's mane." He gestured with his chin toward the horse.

We had caught our breath, but I could still hear his, though it was slower now. Ivanhoe's massive body stood between us and the house, obscuring us from view. Manus looked into my face. I had a sudden feeling of transparency, and the profound sensation that he could see the truth of me, no matter the contradiction I presented. I felt a shock of love as his face moved close to mine. A shared euphoria encased the two of us together. Our two mouths touched softly again and again, and I felt as if my body were comprised of hundreds of subtler bodies thin as veils, but concentrated, all ignited and brushing at each other.

He took my hand by the wrist and pressed my palm to his pants. I started at the warm, taut thing I felt there. But he seemed to know by the willing tension in my hand, or maybe by what he saw in my eyes, that I was not going to shrink from it. His own hand detached from mine and hovered near.

We heard the noise of skirts on the damp grass and flew apart. Manus began unharnessing the horse as I walked off in the opposite direction, struggling for composure.

"Deirdre," Bairbre said.

I turned to her. "I've never gone so fast on a horse. I thought I'd fly off!"

With a distressed expression she searched my face. "Your veil!" she cried.

"It flew off. I just barely clutched it in my hand."

Manus bent down and grasped it from the ground, then threw it at her. She watched his face. I saw his upper lip shimmer and tense, but he kept his eyes off me, then tugged on the horse's reins and drew it roughly from its grazing.

"What are you doing here?" Bairbre cried.

"I'm home for a few days," he said and then led the horse away.

Bairbre looked at me strangely. "You're sweating."

"It was a rough ride, didn't you see?"

"I saw from the window, but then I lost sight of you."

"We went to the beach. I thought I'd fly off and break every bone in my body!"

"He's wreckless!" she said angrily.

I wanted to defend him but held back.

I went with her a long way through mud and brambles and ditches, following her on black earth still wet from the morning rain, and squelching underfoot. The farther we got from the house, the more I struggled not to turn and look back at it.

From the clearing where we finally stopped, the house appeared to rise out of the sea. I could hear, faintly, the screeching of cormorants and shearwaters circling it like they might a ship far from land.

I sat down on some stones, folding my veil in my lap. She grabbed it suddenly. "Put this back on," she demanded.

I held her eyes, vacillating between anger and guilt. I took the veil from her and began arranging it on my head.

"Our hair will be cut at the altar, swept away, and kept in a gauze bag, saved to be buried with us when we die."

"I know," I said.

After a silence she blurted, "Why did you ride the horse?"

"I don't know. It just happened."

"I wish we had not come," she said.

I struggled to respond appropriately, but I could not climb free of my voluptuous confusion. I squeezed and pressed at the drapery of my skirt.

When lightning flashed in a bank of gray clouds, we set off again for the house.

"I miss the convent," she said as we walked. When I made no response she looked at me expectantly, but I remained silent.

Bairbre and I ate a small meal together alone at the grand table.

"Will you draw my portrait, Deirdre?" she asked as the servant cleared the dishes.

"Yes," I said.

She instructed the serving woman to bring drawing paper and a charcoal pencil. Bairbre surprised me by taking off her veil and loosening her hair with shaking hands, spreading it over her shoulders.

She sat very still and I drew, anxious from wondering every moment when Manus would appear.

She watched me uneasily. I carefully smudged the charcoal to make the denseness of her eyebrows, the beginning of her hairline, the shadow at her temples.

"This is a sin for a nun," she said.

"What is?"

"Dwelling on the faces we keep in this world."

I stopped drawing, thinking she had changed her mind about the portrait, but she held her posture, staring past me, given to contemplation. I drew slowly, trying to capture Bairbre, but I was too weak to stop myself from searching out all features similar to her brother's. Now and then her lips moved and I heard words, though barely audible; a prayer to the Blessed Mother. And I saw how she struggled to make the prayers shield her, as she had once shielded herself from me with the psalms.

The closer I looked, the more I could find Manus's face in hers. I stared at her mouth, laboring over the upper lip in the drawing. She emitted a sadness, as if she sensed that the closer I looked at her, the less of her I saw. She seemed to me now, forgetting herself, lost.

I paused with my pencil and said, "When I first saw you and your family in church I thought of you as a Trinity. God the Mother, God the Son, and You are the Holy Ghost." A darkness washed over her face.

It grew very dim in the room, but neither of us made a move to turn on a lamp. I continued to draw and she to sit, as if it were the portrait keeping us there.

"I'll never have a child at my breast," she said to me suddenly.

"Neither shall I," I said.

But in that moment I somehow knew, as she did, that this would not be true.

She stood and looked ambivalently at the drawing, which revealed a sad, almost desperate, look to the eyes. She reached for it and rolled it up.

"Where's my brother?" she asked the serving woman, who said that Manus had left the grounds and would likely not be back until evening. Bairbre sighed and seemed relieved at the news, while I tried to hide my disappointment.

She invited me to go with her to the chapel, but I said I was tired. She watched me ascend the stairs. I remained on the landing, hidden from her view until her footsteps sounded far away and I heard a door open and close again. Then I moved along the corridor as quietly as I could, looking for Manus's room, but none of the rooms I peered into offered any sign of him.

In a separate wing, I saw Manus's riding boots set out before a door left ajar, which opened onto a room with a massive bed, the headboard carved like a great cathedral door, the top of it pinnacled like the facade of a city.

The shirt Manus had worn during the ride lay negligently tossed at the foot of the bed, one sleeve hanging over the side. I approached the bed slowly and touched the shirt, bringing it to my face, smelling it, kissing it.

There, too, also lay a thick draftsman's notebook, which I opened, leafing through page after page of blueprints; complex and with tiny voluminous notes in the margins; calculations for houses and buildings drawn in very fine blue pencil. Some drawings belabored the interiors of rooms, details of walls converging with a ceiling or with a floor. I opened upon a fanciful-looking drawing of a castle, white birds flying out of its open windows. A tiny human figure stood beside it, revealing the structure's enormity. In each subsequent drawing that followed this one, the scale of the castle increased, the human figure beside it tinier and tinier; the birds from the windows were reduced to specks.

Manus dreamt dreams of immensity, I thought, and for a moment I experienced the exhilaration of such an idea: to create at the scale of nature.

I heard footsteps from a distant corridor and my heart beat with anticipation, knowing somehow it was Manus who was coming. I closed the notebook, and while the footsteps got closer, my attention was drawn by two illustrations that hung framed on the wall to the left of his bed. The first depicted two crowned figures, regally dressed, one male and one female, the man standing on the sun, the woman on the moon, each reaching to the other, fingers about to touch, a carnal tension between them.

I continued to study the image as the door creaked open. Without turning I felt him come into the room. In a moment he was standing close behind me.

"I found these etchings at an open-air market in Dublin. They reminded me of things my father had."

I read the words below the image: *"The first meeting of Sol and Luna."*

"Who are they?" I asked.

"The moon and the sun; female and male. Two opposing principles that are attracted to each other." A warmth issued forth from his presence.

I moved to the other picture and studied it: a woman in a long gown standing on her toes on the earth and reaching her arms up, caught in an embrace with a winged god who was leaning down to her mid-flight. The caption read: *"Mercury links the infernal world of Hades with the upper Olympian world."*

"Is the woman supposed to be the infernal world?" I asked.

"Yes. Woman is the earth."

"I thought she was the moon."

"She is both, just as a man is the sun and is also air." Manus stood so close that I could feel his breath through my veil. "He is creative and she is receptive."

He touched my back near my waist, a tremendous energetic heat moving from his fingers into my skin, infusing me so I shivered.

"Mercury is the god of the alchemists," he said. "The bearer of great transformative power."

He drew my veil aside. I closed my eyes and took in my breath at the pressure of his lips on my neck.

When we heard the clatter of horses outside, he broke from me and went to the window.

"Damn it!" he said.

"What is it?"

"My aunts. My mother's sisters."

"You don't want to see them?"

"I never want to see them," he said.

"Why not?"

"Damn them," he muttered without answering me, then led me back to the door of my room. Unnerved and distracted, he went from me down to greet them.

An hour later, in a green drawing room hung with tapestries, Mrs. O'Breen introduced her sisters to me. Both looked older than she did, the taller one wrinkling her chin into a smile and nodding at me. The iris of one of her eyes was a duller blue than the other, clouded and gazing off to the right and above my shoulder.

"This is Moyna Furey, my oldest sister. And this," Mrs. O'Breen said, extending her hand toward a plumper, shorter woman with a scrutinizing gaze, "is Ethna Furey O'Dowd."

"Good to meet you, Deirdre," they both said, almost in unison.

A door was open onto a veranda and the sea air wafted into the room, causing the unlit crystal chandelier to sway and chime above us. Both aunts wore dark clothes roughly cut and no jewelry. Moyna Furey had a long, gray braid, which she kept draped over one shoulder and constantly toyed with. Ethna Furey O'Dowd kept hers bound in a knot at the back of her neck.

I nodded to each and smiled, settling myself into the chair Ethna directed me to take. There was a radiance about Mrs. O'Breen, her eyes brilliant with some excitement she seemed hardly able to contain. She wore a blue satin dress, low cut, and an opulent necklace with icy diamonds and loops of delicate silver chain, which set off the whiteness of her flesh.

"Manus, why don't you tell everyone," she said breathily.

Manus looked hesitantly at his two aunts, then at his sister.

"Go on!" she cried, rising slightly in her chair.

Manus colored faintly and shook his head.

"He was chosen the most promising young architect of his class and has been offered an apprenticeship with Duncan Brady, the most influential master builder in Dublin."

Both aunts uttered congratulations, Moyna, the tall nervous one, nodding and smiling as she looked at him.

Manus did not respond to them. His eyes flashed to mine and then away. Bairbre gazed with diminished energy toward the open door.

"And," Mrs. O'Breen went on, "I've just received word from my solicitor that he's been able to acquire a house for Manus on Merrion Square, on one of the loveliest blocks in Dublin. It's very close to the National Gallery. Manus will receive a key to Merrion park, a beautiful little green oasis in the heart of the city."

The more she went on, the stiller Manus grew until there seemed to be no animation in him at all. It was as if he had evacuated the room, and I entertained a strange thought that there might be two of him; that he had a twin. How could the lithe, energetic boy who had kissed my neck upstairs have transformed into this cool, maudlin-looking man? I took the strange notion further, imagining that my Beloved was somewhere else, in some dark room locked away. I grieved his absence with a palpitating intensity and a helplessness.

Mrs. O'Breen chattered about Dublin, the shops on Grafton Street and an oriental cafe on Westmoreland Street, Trinity College and the Book of Kells. I was struck that Ethna and Moyna were addressed by their first names, though they called Mrs. O'Breen "Madam." However, they behaved with no deference to her. In fact, she exhibited a slight subservience to them, overanimated in a way I had never seen her. Both sisters watched her, and she kept shooting glances at them as if to read her effect upon them.

Bairbre nodded as if listening attentively every time her mother looked at her.

Mrs. O'Breen stopped to catch her breath, her chest rising and falling, and a few moments of silence held the room. She leaned suddenly forward, her necklace set ashiver by her exuberance. "My son is a man with a brilliant future ahead of him!" she said. I saw gooseflesh on her cleavage, minuscule blonde hairs standing on end. In her heightened state, she exuded heat, and I became uncomfortably aware of the sharp odor of her sweat.

I fixed my eyes on the grand tapestry hanging on the wall behind her: a forest with faces peeking through the branches, and just to the right of her shoulder, a fountain and words embroidered in Baroque-looking script above the circulating water. The threads were askew around one of the words so it appeared to read: *I am the water of life, "poisonous" and blue.*

It could not really say *poisonous,* I told myself. I could not have been reading it correctly.

A serving woman came in and poured tea, then circulated through the room with a dish of sweets. Moyna Furey laughed and said, "Take some, Deirdre. We call these penny dreadfuls. When he was small, this was Manus's favorite sweet."

Manus stared vacantly at the plate he held as he chewed the small cake.

I kept looking distractedly at the tapestry. The word must be *precious* I told myself, but the broken threads perfectly formed the word *poisonous.*

That night I crept down the stairs and, following the sound of voices, saw Manus and his mother sitting in a rose-colored light in a corner of the front parlor. From the perspective I had where I hid behind the partitioning wall, I could see only the two aunts' shadows which, because of the position of the lamps, were elongated, moving and shifting upon the wall.

Manus looked more present, though pensive, hanging his head.

Mrs. O'Breen took a drink from her glass, relishing its effect as she swallowed and said, "She's got children in her."

"I can see them," one of the shadows said in agreement.

"Lots of male children, like little lights orbiting her," the higher-pitched, more excitable voice joined in.

Manus remained quiet.

"What is your hesitation?" Mrs. O'Breen asked. "Is it because she's poor? That doesn't matter."

When he did not answer, one of the shadow voices asked, "Don't you like her?"

"It's the opposite," Manus said.

"What do you mean?"

"I would rather marry a woman I have no feelings for."

"Manus!" Mrs. O'Breen said with a soft laugh of surprise.

"Why?" one of the aunts asked, while the other clucked her tongue.

Manus shook his head and looked genuinely heavy with some concern.

"Answer me, Manus!" the aunt's voice piped again. When he didn't, she said, "That was an absurd thing to say, Manus! Wouldn't you rather make a family with a woman you care for?"

He put his elbows on his knees.

There was a general silence as they seemed to wait for an answer or an explanation. When none was forthcoming, the voice of the same argumentative aunt—which I decided now, because of its tone of authority, belonged to Ethna, the shorter, sterner one—said, "Aren't you a lucky young man, Manus? You see how well your mother knows you. The woman she chooses for you is the woman you might have chosen yourself."

He leaned further forward, his shoulders seeming to tighten.

"Take it," Mrs. O'Breen said, extending to him a glass of liquor.

He hesitated, staring at it, the amber liquid sloshing with a little movement of her hand.

"I'm glad you like her. It's better that you have some regard for her."

At last he took the drink and put it to his lips, holding it in his mouth, allowing the fumes to fill his senses. He swallowed, then sighed and, holding the glass in both hands, hung his head.

"She's mild of manner," Mrs. O'Breen said. "She reminds me of the painting of Saint Agnes with her eyes to heaven."

I went back up to bed and fell into an uneasy dream in which I was watching them again from the same hidden perspective. They were drunk, slurring their words. Mrs. O'Breen's sisters were visible, and they were identical to her, triplets, so I could not distinguish one from the other. Manus picked up a handful of penny dreadfuls from a table beside his chair and threw them at the three women, who looked at each other and burst into laughter, doubling over.

I startled awake.

⟨oᴑ○⟩

The next morning Manus did not appear at the breakfast table.

Bairbre waited for me outside in the carriage, anxious to go back to Enfant de Marie.

I moved slowly down the stairs, my eyes raking the landings and the rooms below for Manus, when he surprised me from the stairwell. He looked as if he had not slept, his eyes bleary and red, his hair in disarray.

He gave a nervous look around and, seeing no one else present, handed me a folded piece of paper, hot and damp I assumed from handling. He moved off unsteadily and watched me from a doorway as I read: *"The sun needs the moon like the cock needs the hen,"* written in wavering script.

At the convent, seven little cells had been prepared for each of us who were to take our final vows. I went into one of the rooms and leaned on the narrow casement, staring out at a small view of the courtyard, thinking about Manus's conversation with his mother; thinking about the words on the paper.

For a long time, it seemed, I listened to an approaching echo of footsteps through the endless corridors, knowing them to be Bairbre's, knowing that she would be looking for me, yet I made no move to let her know where I was.

I did not turn when she came into the room and stood a few feet behind me. I could hear her breathing. From some distant corridor the echo of another set of footsteps sounded but soon began to fade.

"You will stay with me, won't you, Deirdre?" she asked. I turned and looked at her, distressed, but could not answer.

"I wish I hadn't brought you there." She started to cry. "I knew we shouldn't go there again! I knew." She was quiet for a few moments before she said in a soft, hurt voice, "I love you."

I could not bear causing her such pain. I stood and went to her, touching her shoulder. "I love you, too, Bairbre," I said.

"Let me kiss you," she said. I held still, but as soon as her mouth touched mine I turned my face from hers, eluding her. She squeezed my arms painfully, and when I pulled forcefully away, she slapped me.

Reeling, I ran from her up the dim, deserted corridor, crying quietly.

The next morning, Sister Vivian interrupted me as I washed the oatmeal pot in the nuns' kitchen. "Manus O'Breen wants to speak to you," she said slowly. I could hear the weight of surprise in her voice. "He's outside in front of the convent gate."

I steadied myself as I dried my hands and unrolled my sleeves. Walking through the passage on my way to meet him, I saw myself now drawn irretrievably along on the currents of what I had wished for.

He was sitting on the bench in the front garden and stood when he saw me coming. I sat down and he joined me, leaning forward, elbows on his knees, and looked at the flagstones. I knew he had been dispatched to ask me to marry him.

When his silence went on, I worried that he had lost heart. I passed my hand softly through his hair. He jumped slightly at the touch and looked at me.

"I've come," he said, "to ask you if you will marry me."

"I will," I uttered immediately without thought or reservation.

The look he gave me then was confused and tender. But some thought plagued him. He blinked and looked again at the flagstones. I ached to press my ear to the muscle of his heart, to hear it bump and plunge.

I touched his arm.

"I'm sorry to be so grave about this," he said and affected a smile.

"It's all right!" I said, struggling to defend the seriousness of his mood. "I cannot imagine that marriage is a ceremony without some sadness in it."

He looked curiously at me.

"It's a point of departure!" I ventured with lighthearted energy. "Maybe the beginning of a new journey, so you leave one life behind to come into another one."

He nodded slowly, taking me in.

"A journey is filled with the unknown!"

The heaviness of his mood seemed to be dissolving. Encouraged by the smile coming into his eyes, I continued.

"You leave something behind, and even if you want to leave it behind, it still makes you sad."

He smiled, then looked down again at the stones. "My mother wants grandchildren. Many of them," he said.

"I'm not averse," I said, "to the labors that might lead to that end."

A gentle light came into his face. He leaned in close and kissed me. His hand brushed against my thigh, and I felt the promise of what would be between us: the Sun about to know the Moon. The baroqueness of the act. The attendant fires.

At dusk I found Bairbre alone in the nuns' antechamber, streams of red light from the descending sun coming in the window, spilling over her.

I wanted to open myself to her, to confess the truth. I reached into my pocket and took out the catechism I'd stolen from her two years before.

"I want to give this to you, Bairbre," I said.

She looked up and gazed unmoved at the little book but would not take it.

"I want you to know that I stole this from you."

She looked away from me.

"I know that, Deirdre. I've always known that."

"Have you?"

"What do you think made me fall in love with you?"

I stared at her uncertainly, and she held my eyes. "Some of us can only get what we need by stealing it."

The words stung me in some odd, unexpected way, and tears burned in my eyes. I felt a surge of guilty love for her.

"He's asked you to marry him, hasn't he?"

I nodded.

"It means that *she's* chosen you. You told me that you saw my family as a Trinity," she said. "You were right when you said that she is God the Mother and that I am the Holy Ghost. But Manus is not God the Son. You are the Virgin, so he is only Joseph, an incidental. The divine component is missing from him. It's really her you are marrying. He's a proper servant to her. You see, Manus would be more suited to the religious life. He's compliant and obedient by nature. But my life has been a reforging of my own will."

She looked at me again, and the face she could not compose appeared, her eyes watery.

"You don't know yet, Deirdre, that you and I are joined in isolation. Do you think that having left me alone here in the convent . . . do you think that you in your marriage to Manus will be any less isolated than I am here?" She turned away suddenly, overcome by grief. "I should never have introduced you to them. I should have told them terrible things about you. But I suppose that wouldn't have mattered. She is God the Mother, and she saw into my heart about you. How could she not take you from me?"

I stood helplessly, not knowing what else to say or do.

When at last I began to walk away, she said my name. "Deirdre," and the sound of it cast a shadow like a bird that followed me along the corridor, then flew suddenly past.

An hour later, as I moved through the darkened hallway returning from the evening meal, I looked out the window into the garden and saw Mrs. O'Breen sitting on the bench. Bairbre in her nun's robes knelt on the ground before her, her face on her mother's lap. The light was such through the downstairs window that it lit up her face, the only bright spot in the tableau. There was devotion in her expression.

And this voluntary submission was part of the larger mystery.

On the morning of her Coronation Mass, two nuns led Bairbre and the other novices to the altar, removing their veils, then ceremoniously unwinding the long coils of their hair so it hung at their shoulders and down their backs. Each stepped up to the altar one by one. When Bairbre's turn came, she trembled as Sister Vivian clipped her hair off, so it fell to the floor in dark drifts. I felt dizzy, my hands frozen as Bairbre stepped toward Sister Hildegard, who carefully dressed her head in the layered veil of a Poor Marie.

The nuns moved off to either side of her, and she stood alone at the altar, the priest approaching and placing upon her head an ill-fitting garland of blue and purple wildflowers.

When the great doors were opened, one of the nuns swept the pile of dark hair out into the vestibule with a wide broom, where another nun waited to gather it.

The priest placed into Bairbre's arms a large wooden crucifix, which she held like an infant. Her eyes were dark, unseeing, the skin around them puffy as she walked slowly down the aisle and was led away by the nuns. For seven days she would meditate in a darkened room in intense isolation with Christ.

After the service I walked with Mrs. O'Breen out onto the grounds, Manus wandering off ahead of us.

"When I was a girl, this willow was only as tall as Manus is now," she said, pointing to the summit of a massive tree. "I only narrowly escaped the ceremony Bairbre has just come through."

I struggled to hide the shock I felt at Mrs. O'Breen's alacrity, yet I urgently maintained the pious, gentle face that I knew she wanted to see, my wish to please her as strong, it seemed, as Bairbre's.

ELEVEN

After renouncing my vocation, I had nothing else to wear at Enfant de Marie but my nun's robes, the old clothes I'd come there with four years before having long since turned to ash in the metal drum where the nuns burned garbage.

Mrs. O'Breen greeted me at the carriage, then led me into the house and up the stairs, where the two aunts in their dark clothes attended my bridal dress, a white, less-substantial figure hanging on the wardrobe door, and shivering each time they touched it.

Ethna fetched a dressing gown from the wardrobe. "Take off your things," she said to me. I froze as the three stood expectantly waiting. Slowly I took off layer after layer. Moyna retrieved everything from the floor, where I'd nervously discarded it. I stood before them in nothing but my undershift, but they demanded that too. Ethna scrutinized my naked flesh so I wanted to hide, then offered me a robe, helping me into the sleeves.

It was Moyna Furey, the maiden aunt, who told me to sit before the dresser mirror. She labored at my hair, seeming aghast at the state of it, clucking her tongue and finally resorting to a nail scissors to cut off hopeless mats and tangles. She rubbed into it an oil that smelled of almonds so the wisps and kinks flowed together in conforming waves. The three talked around me as if I had no will or no voice, asking one another and never me if the set of a certain pin needed adjustment. And I kept my timorous silence, partly grateful that nothing was expected of me, and partly unnerved at being rendered so insignificant.

It was Mrs. O'Breen who dressed me at last in the chaste-looking wedding dress, the high-necked and generously sleeved white linen. The only feature that distinguised it from nun's garb was the organza veil, and even that was discreetly embroidered with tiny asters, which are said to be a nun's flower.

When at last I was fully dressed, I was led through the hallways and down a staircase into the chapel.

I remember little about the ceremony itself, which was attended only by Mrs. O'Breen, her two sisters, a servant, and the officiating priest.

Staring at a figure of Mary Magdalene grieving at the foot of the cross, I focused on the way the candles lit the drapes of her gown, and on the graceful bend of her hand, which covered her face in grief.

Manus appeared suddenly beside me, a stiff, sepulchral figure. With a flash of the eyes, he acknowledged me.

My voice creaked, breaking from a daydream as I said, "I do." I felt the painful brush of Manus's whiskers on my chin and his lips rub against my mouth, leaving a trace of dampness there. And the continuous ringing in my ears, and my heart, which jumped and paused. Jumped and paused, tired now over its exertions.

After the ceremony, Manus disappeared again. There was no feast, no celebration. Mrs. O'Breen and her sisters transported me up the stairs, and through the trail of corridors that opened finally upon Manus's room with the massive bed.

The three women looked at me expectantly, thinking I had never been in this room before. "This matrimonial bed goes back two centuries," Mrs. O'Breen said.

I wondered if it was the bed in which Bishop Hugh O'Gara had consummated his union with the Portuguese duchess.

"Such wealth!" said Moyna Furey, wrinkling her chin into a smile, the vacant eye looking meditatively over my head.

I gazed at the carved faces on the headboard, staring, discontented-looking children.

Ethna and Moyna moved about the room, closing curtains, lighting a lamp, while Mrs. O'Breen approached me, setting her eyes strangely on mine.

As she removed the veil from my head, she said in a quiet, excited voice, slightly higher in pitch than usual, "It will be up to Manus if you remove your shift or not. You will leave everything up to him, and you must lie very quietly and with closed or averted eyes."

Sensing my unease, her voice softened and seemed to strain at gentleness, but she did not waver from her instructions. "You must wear a nun's expression as if you are praying. And you must be compliant."

She leaned very close and whispered covertly, "Manus is a young-blood!" The color came up on her face. "He's a bit of a swain." She walked behind me, and as she undid the buttons of the dress she said, "God invests a man with a certain knowledge as to how he must act upon a woman's body. Do what he needs you to do to enable him. If you remember always that the children you have out of these acts will be servants of God, then you do not have to compromise your purity by enduring this."

She helped me out of the dress, then, pressing it in against her chest, looked intently into my eyes. "Do you understand, Deirdre?"

"Yes," I said.

Ethna and Moyna had finished their tasks and now stood a few feet away, listening.

"You are very dear to me," Mrs. O'Breen said to me. "Your story is so much like my own. You with your great passion for God. God has chosen you to have sons who will become priests. I wish that I'd had more children, but you, I am sure, will have sons. So through Manus, a priest will come."

She looked at her sisters. Moyna nodded and Ethna stared thoughtfully at the wall.

I began to shiver with anticipation for Manus. I longed for the three of them to leave.

"It's up to Manus to bring in a new generation," Moyna piped suddenly. "There are none left. And it's through you that he will do that. Always remember, Deirdre, that a pious mother can influence a vocation in a child."

At Mrs. O'Breen's ushering, I climbed up onto the huge bed. She covered me, then kissed my forehead.

"Remember, Deirdre," she whispered urgently, her face looming above mine, "cover your face with your hands if you must. Close your eyes or avert them. Your face is the last repository of your modesty." She drew the curtains shut against the daylight, lit a lamp, keeping the flame down low, and the three left the room.

My heart was racing when the door creaked open and Manus came in. From under the blanket where I hid, I heard him undressing, the layers of his clothes coming off, then his weight causing the bed to shift. In the low light his expression looked distressed, and I sensed his nervousness, smelled it even in the humidity issuing from his skin.

I had imagined that when we were at last alone, he would be

himself again, but he was detached of manner, gruff and smelling of liquor. He brushed his whiskers harshly to my face and neck, and then his weight on top of me, the old bed sinking beneath us, creaking, and his hands impatient with my shift, and I heard a sigh of irritation and knew it was meant for his mother, perhaps that she'd let me get into bed without being as naked as he was now.

The entire thing was something to be endured, me wincing against the violence of his struggle while I let out little reluctant screams. After he'd torn into me, the pain was miraculously gone, but I could not breathe, the old bed giving little support to my back so Manus's weight half smothered me. He paused from his thrusting a few times as if to collect himself, and I was aware of how silent the house was in those moments and I sensed his mother very close, the faces on the headboard her avatars, listening, watching to see that I was obedient to her instruction.

As he recovered himself, he put his head gravely down against my shoulder, his eyes open, the tenderest moment between us since I'd come to marry him. There was only pain and wetness between my legs. My heart beat hard with disappointment and confusion.

Manus let out a flutter of breath and a heavy sigh. In the dimness I saw his face contort as he turned on his side, facing away from me.

"Manus," I said.

He remained stiff and did not reply.

"Manus," I said again, touching his shoulder.

"I'm tired," he said.

I sat up in bed and wept angry tears, waiting for some response from him, but none was forthcoming. When at length I stopped crying, I found myself listening to his distressed breathing.

Through a small area of the curtain I could see that it was now dark outside. The silence of the house oppressed me.

It occurred to me that Mrs. O'Breen was now a mother to me. That thought filled me with wonder. I had a vision of going to her, of weeping as she took me in her arms, of asking her why Manus had been so harsh with me in bed, so unmovable.

I got up quietly and moved through the maze of halls, following a trail of dim lights left on, drawn irresistibly down, holding my breath at the strangeness of it all, at the eyes of the statues that watched me pass, until I found the staircase down into the main rooms.

I startled when I saw Mrs. O'Breen and her sisters sitting in an embankment of shadows in the parlor, a thin, lugubrious light partially illuminating them. They could have been a trinity of statues; figures consigned to stillness. Mrs. O'Breen's hand quivered, and light flashed on her crystal glass.

I stepped in closer, and all three seemed to see me at once, like they were one entity, but they remained dull, unmoving in their chairs. It was only their eyes that had shifted to take me in. They seemed slowed down, given over to some collective weight.

"Why have you left your husband's side?" Ethna Furey O'Dowd asked.

I did not know how to answer.

Mrs. O'Breen lifted her glass and took a drink, and the taste of the alcohol influenced a kind of deepening of feeling in her eye, and for a moment I was hopeful. I stepped in closer, my eyes locking with hers.

"What should I call you now?" I asked, my voice coming back to me with a high-pitched, childlike quality.

There was no kindness in the look she gave me then, the reflected light made cold on her eyes. "You'll call me Madam," she said evenly.

I nodded, and all three watched me retreat from the room.

I dreamt Manus and I were standing together about to be married. An unnerving sputtering came from the chalice that sat on the altar behind the priest, the silver cup shivering and quaking, then going still again. My perspective shifted so I could see inside the chalice, as if I were floating over it. Submerged in the ambery water that filled it was an elaborate piece of jewelry shaped like a dragonfly. My perspective shifted again, so I could see it closely. It buzzed, attempting to climb up out of the cup. It was alive, a real insect but studded with jewels that weighted it too heavily so it could not affect flight. The jewels were embedded into its body under its very membranes, glistening protuberances. As it buzzed again I had a visceral sense of its agony and its helplessness.

I awakened with a gasp and heard the sound of horses and voices below. Manus was not in bed. I stood and looked out the window and saw the two aunts departing in a carriage.

The only clothes in the room were my nun's garb, which lay folded on the dresser, so I slipped into them. If I could have found a comb I would not have put on my veil, but my hair, which had left an oily, almondy smelling halo on the pillow, was tangled and wild looking.

Manus, who was sitting at the breakfast table, nodded and looked slightly ashamed when he saw me. His mother appeared and he stood up, gravely, imperiously, his shirt open, his chest hair showing. Embarrassment washed over Mrs. O'Breen's face when he approached her, offering his wrists one at a time and she, like a lover, inset the cuff links. Her hand shook with a suppressed excitement. She seemed moved by him, nervous. A nausea filled me at my reluctant intimacy with her; at her strong participation in the mystery that had occurred the night before in the ancestral bed.

As we sat to breakfast, servants came in and out with silver dishes.

Manus ate distractedly, then threw his napkin down, pushing his chair out from the table.

As he ascended the stairs, Mrs. O'Breen stared into her cup, restraining her upset. I imagined that she was enduring his gruff manners because in the end she would win and have the things that she wanted in place. When we could no longer hear his footsteps, she continued her meal, staring beyond me as if I weren't there. We finished our breakfast in silence.

She stood to leave and I asked, "Is there a comb I could have? And something else to wear?"

She touched her chest with her hand. "I'm sorry, Deirdre!" she cried. "Forgive me. I forgot to tell you. I put some things out for you in the little room that adjoins yours."

⌘

At the top of the stairs, I heard movement in one of the rooms and, glancing in, saw Manus looking at some of his papers, a blueprint spread out on the couch beside him. He glanced at me as I stopped at the door, then, with a formality that hurt me, nodded and turned away. My heart began to bang, and I could not swallow with the anger that filled me suddenly.

"I want to go back to the convent," I said, then stormed from the doorway to the bedroom, went in, and tried the adjoining door but found it locked. My heart beat hard with frustration. He had followed me and was standing in the doorway.

"Where is the key?" I cried.

He tried the door, then took a key out of a small drawer in one of the dressers, but it would not open the door.

"She probably has the key," he muttered.

"Get it from her," I cried. He gave me a dismissing look, then turned from me and began to leave the room.

I was shaking now with anger.

I picked up the bottle of attar of roses and smashed it to the floor. He turned, his eyes wide open and lit, a certain animation flooding his demeanor, as if the shattering glass had broken some monotonous strain that had held the air.

I breathed hard, struggling to collect myself. The perfume rose in cloying vapors.

"Why did you marry me?" I pleaded angrily. "Why did you bring me here?"

A flush infused his face.

"Why are you so different to me now?" I asked.

He stood absolutely still a moment, looking into my face, and he seemed to be searching himself, as if he did not readily know the answer himself. He walked toward the bed and sat heavily on its edge, looking at the floor.

"I heard you and your mother that night I came here with Bairbre.

I heard you say you would rather marry a woman you had no feeling for. I want to know why you said that!"

"The marriage was engineered. Very little was left up to me."

I struggled to quiet my breathing, my face and ears hot, as if the sun had burned them. "You didn't want to marry me," I said.

He looked searchingly at me, the smell of the roses sweet and palpitating on the air around us.

"I care about you," he said.

"Then why?"

"I can hardly explain any of it," he said and paused, looking down at the broken glass, the pool of aromatic liquid. "It's my aunts. I told you before I can't stand them being here, nosing into everything."

"I thought they'd left."

"They'll likely be back."

"If it's them you're angry with, why are you mistreating me?"

He sighed, his eyes meeting mine. "I'm sorry, Deirdre," he said.

For a few moments we sat in silence before he repeated his apology. I felt myself softening to him.

Manus, sensing that the storm had abated, got up and approached me, standing a foot behind me.

"You and I have just been married. We should be alone with each other. We should be completely alone without any interference on the air. Come with me into my father's side of the house," he said, his voice lower and more resonant now; a voice I felt like velvet on the back of my neck.

He led me up a hallway I had not gone through before, and it seemed we walked a long time before reaching a doorway guarded by a marble griffin with a baneful, miscreant stare.

Passing through that door, we left his mother's territory for the rougher passages and rooms of his father's. Again we walked a while before descending a narrow, crumbling staircase, the air growing progressively cooler and greener as we did, an arborial smell to it, and found ourselves in a bedroom with worn, dark green rugs and curtains. I had the feeling of being in a forest and thought there might be dew on the wooden doors; their past lives as trees not completed, twigs and buds in the knotholes. He opened two wide doors and pointed outside at an overgrown garden. I had the sense that we were far away from the world of his mother.

He smiled at me and the fury and despair of the past hours fell away.

He drew open a wide wardrobe door in which hung numerous dresses and shirts and jackets.

"My father found all of these old clothes in a trunk. He believed that they belonged to the Fitzpatricks who lived here in the last century. Bairbre and I used to play with these sometimes. Most of the things don't fit me now. The Fitzpatrick men must have been of a shorter stature." He unbuttoned his shirt. "Still . . . there's one jacket."

As he stood exposed before me, a faint blush passed across his face. He picked out a cornflower blue jacket, gently crushed silk, and got into it without a shirt on. It shimmered, the light revealing its patina as it strained at his shoulders and back.

"And here," he said. He ran his finger along the shoulders of the garments, then drew out a creamy white silk with a wide, billowing skirt. I hid behind the dresser door, disrobed, and then slipped on the silk dress. I paraded around the room, long trains of the hems weighted in little ice-colored jewels, catching at the carpet.

The rich air from the garden flooded the room. Birds twittered and flicked through the festoons of weeds and wildflowers.

Manus ransacked a drawer and threw various articles of clothing onto the bed.

"Look at these," he said. "False sleeves." The same excited energy that had filled him the day of the horseback ride filled him now. He caught his breath boyishly, guilelessly, so I could not help but feel moved and confused.

He sat on the edge of the bed, his jacket sleeves pushed up to the elbow, struggling to button the false sleeves along his forearms.

"Will you help me?" he asked.

He offered his forearm submissively, and I moved to him and stood buttoning each tiny shell button, then pulled the jacket sleeve down around it so only the soft, ruffled cuffs showed at the wrists. His hair was unkempt over his forehead. He looked up and met my eyes, a thrill passing between us. He pressed his face between my breasts and I put my palms lightly on his shoulders, and through the silk of the dress I could feel the heat of his breathing and the grazing of his lips and the sudden wetness of his tongue as he licked the silk. He began to suck one of my nipples through the silk with a slow patience. One of his palms pressed itself to my stomach and slowly down my navel and one finger found the cleft of my sex, and grazed the silk of the gown against it again and again. As he withdrew his mouth from my breast, a thread of saliva connected him to the wet silk, and when it broke he looked up into my face, his dark blue eyes catching the facets of the windows, and he wavered, and caught his breath, and that sweetness in his look and that tension at the corners of his mouth made a jet of desire fountain up in me.

Thunder sounded outside and the sky went dark, but no rain fell. He withdrew from me suddenly and went out into the garden. I waited, sitting on the edge of the bed, and called out his name when he was a few minutes gone. The light deepened another shade and I went out to find him. The darkened air turned the white dress I wore a silvery blue. The cool, caressing breeze contrasted sharply with the hot, agitated pulsing between my legs. I saw him hiding from me behind a tree, and as I crossed the weeds and flowers, the dress huskily breathed, as if it were toiling as much as I to get to him.

He peered out and smiled at me, then moved toward me in his blue jacket and his ruffled cuffs. We kissed and pulled at each other and wrestled our way to the ground, until he was on his back and I climbed over him, the skirt of the dress settling slowly, exhaling as it went down.

His hand traveled up under the tent of the dress and nudged my thighs open, his fingers gently drawing me apart like the petals of a flower.

"What did she say to you last night?" he asked.

"She told me not to look at you."

He lay back, pulling me firm in place. "Look at me the entire time," he said, a half smile on his mouth.

He drew in his breath as he guided himself into me. For a few moments neither of us moved. I watched his eyes roll faintly at the almost indetectable tension and shiver of my muscles around him.

I made slippery, uncharted movements, testing the feel of him inside me, testing the borders of our flesh together, feeling the tickle of the ruffled cuffs on my hips. The ice-cold timepiece attached to his pants pocket pressed at my inner thigh. He held my hips and we began lapping at each other; lapping as steadily as water, the weeds brushing and scratching at the heavy drapery of the dress. And when my muscles quavered, I leaned over him, my hands smashing tiny bluebells in the grass.

"*Is braithim as titim an saol,*" I uttered, the unanticipated cry infusing euphoria with sadness.

"*Is braithim . . . ,*" he repeated and let out a rapturous, surprised laugh. "*. . . as titim an saol,*" his voice soft, fogged by ether. A seraphic look passed over his face before he squeezed his eyes closed, half in agony. Lying breathless on top of him in the aftermath, dampness rose up from the overgrowth beneath us.

For three days we would not leave those garden rooms.

It rained intermittently that first afternoon, and when it wasn't raining, pink petals wandered slowly down from the trees as if through heavy liquid. Our stomachs ached for food.

"Couldn't we go back and get food and bring it here?" I asked.

But Manus looked upset at the idea. "No," he said. "We might not be able to come back if we leave now."

"Why?" I asked, but he wouldn't answer. He climbed the wall into a separate garden, where he shook early pears from a tree. We ate as much as we could stomach of the hard, sour fruit. Then he brought in baskets of the pink petals that had fallen, and though they had a bitter, vernal taste, they were far more palatable than the pears, and they quelled our hunger and induced a dreamy, aphrodisiac effect.

We reveled and rested all afternoon into night, moving between rapt stillness and dreamless sleep, to slowly intensifying vigor. A mist came into the room from the garden so the walls, the drapery, the bed-clothes held infinitesimal beads of moisture.

The next morning I opened a dresser drawer and found inside a massive tome; the leather binding, which was cracked at the corners, appeared to be crocodile, or the skin of some other amphibious dragon. Engraved upon it were the words *Secretus Secretorum*.

"Look at this!" I cried.

"Christ!" he said and unearthed the heavy volume from the drawer, then dropped it onto the bed.

It proved to be an arcane alchemical text, thrilling to Manus, and filled with elaborate engravings, similar to the one he had found in the Dublin antique market. We lay on our bellies on the bed, turning the pages, the images within marvelous and strange: a green lion swallowing the sun; a mermaid harnessing a dolphin; a tree whose trunk was the body of a naked woman, her upheld arms laden with fruit and leaves.

The most marvelous and intricately detailed of all was of a handsome god wading thigh deep against the tide, holding aloft in one hand a globe with a caduceus impaled upon it. Beneath, the words *Mercury, Mystery Bearer and Transformative Force of Alchemy*.

Manus read a passage aloud: " 'Inside each of us there is a heaven and a hell. There is a universe, just as there is heaven and hell and a universe outside of us. The human imagination mirrors the vastness of the starry cosmos. We are made of the four elements. The sun and the moon and the planets and the stars. And all the order and all the chaos of the universe exist inside the human heart. Through studying the metals and the moods and humours of the elements, we might come to understand the nature of ourselves.' "

I opened upon an image of a fountain with two plumes of smoke rising off from it in separate directions. I read to him: " 'The created world began with a separation of opposites, the tearing apart of the united opposites. Injustice is incurred by the existence of separate things.' "

Turning another page, we were amazed to discover the words *The Courtship of Sol and Luna*, followed by an etching similar to the one that Manus had found in Dublin. In a banner above Sol and Luna were the words *Materia Prima . . . Lapidis Philosophorum, The Courtship of the Red King and his White Queen*.

One of the engravings depicted Luna taking off her dress, looking at her naked body in the glass, while Sol peered at her through the window.

Manus read from the text: " 'I am hot and dry Sol and you Luna are cold and moist.' "

In the next image Sol climbed in the window while Luna stood naked, reaching her arm out to him.

I read Luna's words: " 'When we couple and come together I will with flattery take your soul from you.' "

In the third image a dove came in through the window while Sol revealed his erection to Luna.

" 'I am possessed by an ever-agitated god,' " Manus read, and we laughed.

In the fourth image Luna lay back on the bed with open thighs while Sol, with his swollen organ, penetrated the pink waves of her flesh.

" 'With the powerful rod of Mercury I will transform you and be myself transformed.' "

In the fifth image, the bed had become a bath, and Sol was completely submerged under the water while Luna, who straddled him, was sitting. From the waist up she was in the air, the expression on her face rhapsodic.

I read Luna's words: " 'Sol, you are now enclosed, poured over with *mercurio philosophrum*.' "

Turning the page, I was stunned to see the words "The death of Sol and Luna," the two lying on a slab inside a fiery oven, naked and embracing. "We don't want to look at that!" Manus said, disconcerted, and turned back to the first image of intercourse. He took my index finger and rubbed it over the illustration where the two sexes met.

Then he climbed up over me and, reading phrases from the margins, began to recite: " 'The red king shines like the sun . . .' " He lifted my gown and entered me, " '. . . clear as the car-bunc-le . . .' " he thrust three times, once for each syllable of the word, and we both laughed. But now, as he went on, thrusting in time to some of the words, his excitement burned into me with a kind of gravity, so I held onto his hair to keep him close to me. " 'Impetuously fluid . . . like-a-wax, re-sis-tant to fire, penetrating and con-tain-ing living quicksilver.' "

Once, opening my eyes, it must have been in one of the mirrors that I saw the brokenhearted image of his mother. But it was gone in a moment, like a reflection in water. He teased me, feeling my urgency, and each time he'd stop I'd weep and wait . . . wait . . . until the next time he pushed.

When I was on the verge of rapture he pulled loose of me and said, "Injustice is incurred . . . ," his words broken by short sighs, "by the existence of separate things . . ."

"No injustice," I murmured, struggling to join his body again with mine, and when I finally succeeded we held hard to each other, eyes tightly closed, moving faster and faster, as if we were riding away on Ivanhoe, riding far away, galloping, conjuring the smell of sea wrack, a wet, amniotic dialogue, currents swaying and turning. I held back a laugh, which finally escaped me and ended in a sob.

I awakened near evening with a gasp. I sat up in bed to discover that the blanket that covered us had grown a velvety green mold.

A dream residue had followed me out of sleep, a feeling of my father's presence, a faint echo of his weeping, so it amazed me when Manus said, "Tell me about your own mother and father."

I watched the shadow of leaves moving on the wall.

"My mother used to taunt my father by talking about a boy named Macdarragh who she'd once been in love with," I whispered slowly. "A boy who died."

"Why did she do that?" he asked me.

I sighed. "I think she wanted something from my father."

"What?"

"She was restless. Dailiness wore on her." It surprised me how clearly the answers came from my mouth; how transparent my mother's motivations seemed to me at that moment. "They loved each other, but they wanted so much from each other. Neither believed enough in the other's love. They flailed and fought. . . . It could be terrible between them, the way they hurt one another."

Manus went up on his elbow and looked into my face. "Let's never hurt one another," he said.

He kissed my temple, and as he looked at me I remembered my father saying to my mother, "You're leading me the life of the damned." And she answering, "It's you, Liam. You'd wear the heart out of a stone."

In that moment I wished that Manus would ask me how my parents had died. I wanted to find words for it, to try to say it, so safe as I felt here in these hidden garden rooms; so removed from the unsympathetic laws of the external world. Manus would not have seen me or my parents as less than human; he would not have started from me in fear. He would have felt compassion. I believe he saw the expectation in my eyes, yet he did not ask, only drew me in against him, and I watched the shadows of gulls on the wall as they passed outside the room.

Over Manus's shoulder I could see the book on the floor where it lay open, and I read the words:

We all come from one beginning, the Prima Materia. The elements were born by separation. The work is to erase the boudaries between spirit and matter.

My thoughts were full now with my mother and father, and the words resonated keenly and tears wet my face. Everything shimmered with meaning. Alchemy, I told myself, was the struggle to soothe the loneliness between men and women.

I breathed the dampness on the air and pressed my face to my new husband's neck, kissed his skin and felt tender with love, a pervasive ache for him in all the tissues of my body and mind.

"Solutio Perfecta," I whispered.

"Solutio Perfecta," he answered back and his mouth touched mine, the language of alchemy having become the language of Eros.

Manus awakened me that night, kneeling at my bedside, showing me blueprints and plans his father had drawn for something he called a "Celestial Mansion," drawings depicting, from different perspectives, a grouping of towers and rooms set upon a disk suspended in air, clouds floating beneath it; geometrically intricate renderings.

"I found these drawings and journal entries inserted between the back pages of the *Secretus Secretorum*," he whispered excitedly, almost breathless with his find.

"Listen to this, Deirdre! He writes that, 'The walls would all be transparent or semitransparent, but not made of glass.' Deirdre, he has this idea that water can be solidified without being frozen or even cold. Air and fire support the mansion," he said, indicating a cloud and a burst of flame beneath the floating mansion, "and there are traces of earth in the hard structuring that scaffolds the walls and in the mortar."

"How could air and fire support the mansion so it would float?" I asked gently, careful of his sensitive state.

"Such a thing might be possible, if only we understand the four elements. My father must have understood this. You see, he searched into secret and sublime things. He calls it Divine Geometry, architecture taking its secrets from nature. To understand Divine Geometry one studies the four compass points and the four elements. And the nature of the winds, because the winds pressure the walls of structures and fortresses.

" 'Everything physical has a spiritual counterpart, a more subtle, less visible replica of itself inhabiting the air,' " he read slowly, thoughtfully.

༄ঌঃঌ

Manus wiped dust from candles and tapers he found in a drawer and lit them in a circle around him on the floor.

I sat with him as he studied the book quietly. He had ventured to the disturbing image we had turned back from earlier, after the intercourse of Sol and Luna. The picture of the two in the fiery oven jolted me. I got up and went to bed but kept casting curious, uneasy glances at the book, which I could see from my pillow. Manus turned the pages slowly. After the slab that bore Sol and Luna emerged from the oven, they were blackened, still embracing. Ravens had descended all around them, picking at their burned flesh. In the last image I dared to look at, they were skeletons and lying separated from one another in a field.

I was afraid of the book now, and of Manus looking at the imponderable horrors it depicted, afraid of the yearning he searched it with.

I felt for him, trying to bridge the gap between himself and the father he idealized, trying with his rational mind to decipher the images as if they were riddles to be solved. I knew then, though I don't think I could have articulated it to him, that the rational mind was helpless against such images, for they were primordial and of the nature of dreams.

The third day Manus climbed the walls into the next garden, where he caught a rabbit. It screamed as he killed it, an agonized, human-sounding scream that echoed between the walls.

I cried as he skinned it, its blood staining his cuffs, but he disregarded me, set on cooking and eating it. The smell of the meat roasting over a twig fire made my mouth water and my stomach throb, and when it was ready, I ate greedily.

With my stomach full, I imagined that we could remain living wildly in this abandoned part of the house and grounds; that I would grow accustomed to the screams of rabbits and the death spasms of robins and jays pierced by little spears Manus might fashion.

I lay down, content with food, and began to close my eyes. "Don't sleep," he said. "Make this a century-long night."

Something was drawing him back to the mundane world.

I went with him outside and we climbed the walls, and he showed me how the house was built over the ruins of an ancient aqueduct. We sat a while looking at the stars, the sky that night full of celestial light. It was the Western Wind—who, he'd learned from his father's papers, was called Zephyrus—with us in that hour, the gentle one who blows away the cold of winter.

By dawn we'd left the gardens and had come around to a crossroads where we could see the front of the house. We built a bonfire, waiting out the last of the dark, Manus's ruffled cuffs torn, the blood of the hare dried, his cornflower blue jacket ripped and flailing in tatters in the wind.

When we appeared again, Mrs. O'Breen did not ask where we'd been. She joined us at the table and I struggled to recapture my pious, demure persona even as I ate voraciously, both Manus and I still wearing our touseled costumes.

"I've got some nice things for you to wear now, Deirdre," she said. "I've laid them out for you upstairs."

I nodded. "Thank you," I said.

Manus leaned in close to me, his mouth full of food, and gave me a kiss on the jaw. A vexed expression passed over Mrs. O'Breen's face.

Halfway into our second helpings of lamb stew, I brushed inadvertently against him as I reached for the sugar, and he grabbed me by the wrist. Mrs. O'Breen looked up from her teacup. Manus pulled me toward him and kissed me. It was his sudden, playful irreverence that caused her mouth to contract, as if there were something in the nature of his intimacy with me that she had not anticipated. Sensing this, Manus made a show of things, pulling me almost roughly to my feet so an inadvertent laugh escaped me.

As we passed her on the way to go upstairs, Mrs. O'Breen seemed to hardly contain a tide of rising hysteria.

But when we got to the ancestral bedroom, he did not make love to me. A heavy exhaustion overcame Manus, and he plummeted into a depression for days and did not want to get out of bed. I kissed and fondled him and begged him to tell me what was wrong, but he was unresponsive.

On the fourth day he got up and resumed work on the commission that was already in place for him in Dublin: an extension of offices for the Land League in one of the very old government buildings on Parliament Street. He worked with a ruler and protractor, a dry kind of work devoid of magic.

For a while the echo of those perfect days and nights in the garden room resounded each time we were close to one another, so it seemed all right that his wonderment did not match that time and that his attention to me was not finely tuned, because I believed it would come again. How could it not?

"Let's go back," I said to him once, but the spirited boy was not there in him. Mrs. O'Breen talked about the job he would be taking in Dublin. The demeanor he must put forth. Never did it occur to him that he might refuse her. He grew heavy when she spoke and he'd stare, his eyes fixed to a chair or a table as if there were some prophecy in it. And when she looked at me she said things like, "If Nature takes her proper course, Deirdre will soon be having a seamstress let out her dresses."

And though his spirits rose enough sometimes that he made a show of irreverence to her, taking little opportunities to hurt her, he could not quite navigate the heavy flood of her words, and sex felt obligatory most of the time, workmanlike as it had the first night in the ancestral bed. I felt sometimes like a small plot of earth he had purchased and was obliged to seed. And that was when I first knew there was a dungeon in Manus's heart.

cococo

Late in the afternoon on the last day we spent in Kenmare, I walked unnoticed into the front drawing room, where Manus and his mother sat together in silence. They were a few feet apart on the red brocade sofa, his right hand and her left clasped and resting on the cushion between them, Mrs. O'Breen's eyes fixed to his face. Manus's head was slightly bowed, and though he was not looking at her, the silence between them was rich and textured. He seemed to be breathing her adulation into his body.

I did not move, as if I were witnessing something of a disturbing yet mystical nature, a membrane of light delicately encasing the two of them.

Mrs. O'Breen became suddenly aware of me and I saw what I thought was a flash of gloating in her eyes, but that passed quickly. She held her head high and looked at me as if I were an outsider.

I shrank from her look, wavering on my feet, and departed in silence.

A month after our wedding, we traveled across Ireland to our new home, far away from his mother. I had thought our lives would be different. On the rainy Dublin evenings early in our marriage, I sensed him moving further away from me.

Gazing at the shadows on the wall, I tried to ease myself to the noise of the Dublin streets, looking to find consolation in the distant voices and the clopping hooves, not yet suspecting that the days Manus and I had spent in the hidden garden room had been the last valiant days of a youthful rebellion.

But there were still the moments during lovemaking when Manus was brought beyond thinking and his soul overtook him, and the sweet face flashed like lightning, glowing and dimming. And in the years to come it would be the occasional flash of that sweet face appearing in an unguarded moment that sustained me. I'd often remember that odd, early impression I'd had that there were two

Manuses. How had I not realized the pure truth of that? Because I would live mostly without my Beloved, though I sensed him there like a revenant watching me, as if he bided in the walls or on the landing, or in some unseen, secret room of the house.

We weren't married two months when the doctor confirmed that I was pregnant. It could have been the very night of my deflowering that the Sun had succeeded in germinating the Moon.

PART THREE

The Torment of Metals

*Fire is the preponderant human element. It reduces
and transforms.
Despise not the ash, for it is the diadem of thy heart.*

—MEDIEVAL ALCHEMICAL TEXT

Twelve

1910

The third day my girls were gone, I sat in my little back room with pencil poised over paper, staring out at the rain. It was a position I took so I might appear not to be lost, although Manus was at work and Mrs. Daley would never come in here if the door was closed.

It was only me and the sound of the rain, and the dimness it had brought with it.

I had lived here now for fifteen years.

The first time I had descended the coach in Dublin in front of this house on Merrion Square, clouds had raced across the late day sky, the dark just beginning to come from the east.

Inside, the lit rooms had smelled of lavender and oiled furniture. Before Manus and I had been married, Mrs. O'Breen had come and furnished this house; a set upon which our lives were to be acted. The windows had been curtained in a russet silk that had matched the color in the upholstered chairs. Paintings had been hung in every room, some walls overcrowded with them: oils of men on horseback, platoons of soldiers. In the dining area, still lifes of fruit and flowers, the breakfront filled with blue willow pattern china. The rooms had given a surface impression of being lived in, of things aquired over time, yet upon close contemplation the objects had all issued a coldness and a lack of sentiment. I had walked into this unknown history and taken it on as my own. I had made myself instrumental in this family's story.

Particularly in the early years of my residence here, I had been reluctant to add anything of my own or make changes, for fear of disturbing some barely maintained balance; or of arousing some resentment in the very atmosphere.

I fell back on what I had learned from the nuns: that there was safety in subservience to the larger will.

In a corridor that led back to the main entranceway of the house, I had been startled that first night by an ungainly piece of furniture; a vast armoire, a dresser with cabinetry and drawers. It had been similar to many I had seen in Kenmare, which had usually had mirrors on one or both doors. This one had had no mirrors, and though it had been heavily and recently polished, the surfaces had been marred in places. It had been the extreme oddness of the carved decorations that had made me recognize the piece as one I had seen at Kenmare when I'd trespassed, looking for Manus the second time I'd gone there: dragonflies with minutely detailed wings and the faces of children peering through vines. A certain abrasion on one of the doors had made me certain that it was the same piece. It had given me an uneasy shiver. Why had Mrs. O'Breen taken such pains to transport this monstrosity?

I had moved farther through the house, on guard now, afraid I might run into one of Mrs. O'Breen's more confrontational figurines, installed there like a sentry. I had ascended the stairs and perused the rooms, but there had appeared to be nothing else.

That first night, Manus had remained in his study with the door closed. I knew now, fifteen years having passed, that he'd been in shock here that night as I had been. I had sat upstairs at the foot of our bed, expectant, waiting for him to come in; watching the faint green haze of the night sky, waiting for it to go full pitch, as if it might put some closure on my agitation. But two A.M. had come. And three. I had not known that nights in Dublin never go to full black. Now and then a lit coach had passed below. I could see over the trees of the park across the way, and through them distant, twinkling lights.

When the clock had said half three I'd descended the stairs, the wicks in all the lamps gone low but still faintly illuminated.

I'd approached the massive armoire. In the dark the carved faces had looked grotesque. I'd blamed the strangeness of the shadows on my exhaustion and the earliness of the hour. On an impulse, I'd pulled open a drawer and found it lined in delicate paper, a silvery fleur de lys design. I'd opened another and found it without paper, inhabited by the dry husks of a few insects. A prickly sensation had moved over my scalp.

In that hour, the surrounding Georgian elegance had struck me as deceptive. Dark, unlit corners had issued smells of damp earth. The air beneath the stairwell had had an untouchable stillness to it like the air within a cave, unaffected by an onrush of wind through a closely situated window.

I'd heard Manus clear his throat and known he was wide awake behind the study door. Yes, we had both been immediately changed by this house and who we were each expected to be in it.

❦

Manus had thrown himself headlong into his work. He'd taken up each new challenge in his apprenticeship with excitement and agitation. He'd slept sporadically and I'd often awakened to find he was not beside me in bed but downstairs in his study, fretting over a blueprint or an idea.

In the beginning there were still intimate moments between me and Manus. I recalled awakening from an afternoon nap, three or four months pregnant with Maighread and only a few weeks installed in the house and coming upon Manus on the landing: the flash of his handsome grin, his arms suddenly around me. The two of us giggling over something and him driving me back into our bedroom for an interlude of feverish sex. There were other tender moments I could conjure taking place in this house. A few times in the first month or two, he slept with his face pressed to my neck. We laughed when I told him I'd had dreams of loud gales of wind blowing near my ear, sending shivers down my spine.

Once we'd been sitting to tea, and while Mrs. Daley had been serving us, Manus had slipped his shoe off under the table and lifted my dress with his bare foot, rubbing my calf, the two of us exchanging conspiratorial looks. Recalling this, my heart enlarged in my chest.

When Mrs. Daley had left the room, Manus had leaned across the table. He'd wound around his finger a certain strand of my hair that always worked itself loose of the pins.

"This one again," he'd smiled.

But such moments between us had grown progressively rare. Most of the time he'd been preoccupied with his work.

It was not long before I discovered that Manus was frustrated by his apprenticeship; that he had strong differences with his mentor, the master builder Duncan Brady.

Brady was a polite and pleasant-looking man with an ostentatious silver mustache. When he did visit the house I had little interaction with him. He usually sat with Manus in his study, drinking brandy and smoking cigars, discussing whatever project they were engaged in.

One evening when my pregnancy was quite advanced, Duncan Brady and one of his other young apprentices, John McMartin, came to the house for dinner. I instantly disliked the handsome, red-haired McMartin, who blatantly ignored me.

Duncan Brady had just taken a commission from the Dublin Building Association, whose mission was to provide improved structural arrangements for laborers. Brady, Manus, and McMartin were working together on the design of a block of working-class flats.

They were discussing the fate of a huge old Georgian house on a street in North Dublin. McMartin favored knocking it down to erect a new building for housing. One hundred and ten rooms with plumbing and minor fittings, while Manus argued against knocking it down.

I sat uncomfortably among them at the table as their discussion grew passionate.

"Either we restore it and build around it, or we just find another site for the flats. You can't destroy an old beauty of a house like that!" Manus insisted.

"Christ!" McMartin said. "Ireland is leagues behind the rest of the civilized world! We're still reeling from the famine and you're worried about some old Georgian house?"

"I just think we ought to be cautious of knocking away at the old. We should preserve beauty. We can find another site for the housing," Manus said.

"That house is a derelict, O'Breen!" McMartin cried.

"It should be restored and not replaced," Manus said.

"Restored for who?" McMartin asked.

Manus remained silent.

"Why are you so set on clinging to Georgian ideals, which are nothing more than symbols of English Protestant exploitation!" McMartin said.

"I'm not devoted to Georgian ideals!" Manus cried out. "But the house itself has great integrity and shouldn't be destroyed!"

"I never expected you to be so conventional at heart," McMartin said.

"For Christ's sake, McMartin! You know that what's conventional makes me bristle!"

"O'Breen," McMartin said, lighting a cigar and exhaling a cloud of smoke, his eyes perusing the room. "Your house is a perfect example of all that is conventionally Georgian."

Manus stiffened and went crimson.

"A mollusk exudes its own shell," McMartin said quietly, lifting his snifter.

"I'm not a mollusk," Manus said.

"We're getting away from the point of things here," Duncan Brady intervened. "The financing from the Iveagh Trust provides for blocks of working-class flats, not for restoring a stately old house."

"Then let's build the flats on Meath Street and leave the house alone."

"The site of that old house is the best for what we need," Brady said.

"And the front windows face east," interjected McMartin. "The first rays of sunlight will remind the laboring man of his duties of the day." He sat back, drawing arrogantly at his cigar.

After a tense silence, Manus said, "I resent the things you've said to me tonight, McMartin. And let me tell you something you should already know. Irish Georgian is not English Georgian. The Irish do Georgian better than the English. It's less pretentious, better built, with more fidelity to the classical Greek."

McMartin snorted. "Georgian is too associated with Irish degradation."

"All history is full of slaughter and degradation, McMartin. You're forgetting that that house is also a symbol of Irish enterprise and innovation."

"I understand what you're saying, Manus," Duncan Brady interjected, "but I'm afraid I'm in agreement with McMartin on this."

Manus sighed and was silent for a few moments before saying, "Why, Duncan, if you have so many bones to pick with my ideas, did you invite me to work with you?"

The older man paused. "I'm glad you're working with me, Manus," he said in a kind voice. "You're a very imaginative man, but for now you've elected to do some work of a less imaginative nature. Compromises have to be made."

When they left, Manus sat again at the table, and covering his face with one hand, said, "For God's sake, when I think about that beautiful staircase gallery and the columned arcade . . ."

A few days later Manus and I were crossing the bridge along Wellington Quay when we saw a gypsy woman in a tattered purple dress with two small children huddled near the river wall. She held her hand out to us.

"Give her something," I said to Manus.

He reached into his pocket and drew out a few coins, which she took gratefully. We started on our way and she said, "Wait!" her eyes on my pregnant belly. She took off a necklace from around her neck, a worn, filthy piece of string with a medal attached, then held it a few inches from my stomach.

"Ah," she said. "You see how it moves from left to right . . . left to right? You've a girl in there."

Manus stiffened. "That's the way the wind is blowing, missus," he said with a bark.

She focused on him, creases deepening on her forehead. She shook her head with certainty. "No wind today."

Manus took my arm and steered me forward.

That evening I found him standing at the bedroom window, staring out in a kind of a daydream. At that moment the baby began to move. "Manus," I said and he jumped, having been unaware of my presence.

I approached and took his hand, pressing it to my belly. He went stiff and my heart quickened. I sensed he wanted to move away, but I kept a defiant hold of his hand and he gave in slightly and let himself feel the ripple of the moving infant.

"Your child," I said.

He pulled away and my heart dropped. I stood back from him.

A change came slowly into his face. He sat on the foot of the bed and sighed, as if he were exhausted.

"What's wrong?" I asked.

"I've been working too hard," he said.

I knew this wasn't it. I shook my head. "We haven't been happy here," I said.

He looked at me, considering my words, though they surprised him.

"I don't like this house," I said.

Without moving his head, his eyes raked the room.

"You will come to like it," he said, but there was no conviction in his voice.

At this late stage of pregnancy, I often had difficulty getting comfortable in bed. Manus usually slept through all my shifting of positions and adjusting of pillows.

But this night he lay sleepless beside me.

I had finally settled myself on my side with my back to him and had begun to drift toward sleep, when he asked, "What was it like to live on the Great Blasket Island?"

The question sent a soft shock through me. For a few moments I said nothing, my nerves on edge. I felt him waiting for a response.

I'd heard an openness in his voice as he'd asked, and sensed his desire to be closer to me.

Yet what I had once yearned for him to know in the hidden garden room, I felt relieved now that I had never tried to utter. It was the story that I had concocted with my grandmother, that I found myself taking refuge behind now.

"I don't much remember the Great Blasket Island, Manus," I said. "I was small when I left there."

"But you started to tell me about it once . . . and about your parents."

"Those were things my grandmother told me," I said.

I could sense his doubt in the darkness.

"My parents were drowned when I was two. My grandmother raised me."

Why, I asked myself, wouldn't I try to tell him.

The truth did not feel compatible with the life we were attempting to lead in this house.

I felt a sting of sadness over the loss of that deep connection we had shared, and the safety we had felt together in the hidden garden room.

There had been times in those first three difficult months of Maighread's infancy when I had gone to Manus, at the end of myself with exhaustion, and he had held me. But I'd felt my neediness wearing on him.

During my pregnancy with Caitlin, Mrs. O'Breen was often around, and there was great pressure and expectation on the air that this baby would be a boy. In the throes of my labor, I saw Mrs. O'Breen and Manus standing in a shadow across the room. After the sex of the infant was announced, they both disappeared. In my own heart I succored a secret joy.

While I relished the early, harmonious months with Caitlin, Manus grew more distant and anxious over his work than ever. I became used to his absence at dinner. There were still disagreements between himself and Duncan Brady, and he was bucking to leave his apprenticeship and begin his own career.

And though he was preoccupied, I saw each tiny daughter steal her father's heart. I would find myself moved by his soft manner with his children, the easy way they could melt him.

Over the next few years after he left his apprenticeship, Manus took on the design of two wealthy homes, both in the smarter suburbs of Dublin.

But after that, he accepted an offer to work again with Duncan Brady and the Dublin Building Association.

I asked him about his choice, and he told me that he'd been haunted for years by things that he'd seen in the tenements. One mem-

ory in particular had stayed with him. In an unventilated, one-room
flat where a family of eleven lived, he'd seen a little girl on the floor in a
pile of clothes sleeping with a dead cat in her arms.

It confused me when Manus befriended John McMartin, the red-haired
man whom he'd had such vehement differences with. He knew how little I liked McMartin, so when the man began to come around often,
Manus said to me, with a note of defensiveness in his voice, "I've a high
opinion of McMartin. He's a good judge of character and a reader of
faces."

One night McMartin waited for Manus for an hour in his study.
When Manus came in he was exhausted, his clothes covered in plaster
and paint.

"You're the master, for God's sake, O'Breen! What are you doing
the donkey work for?" I heard McMartin ask.

"I like to get my sweat and breath into the mortar," Manus said in
response.

"Christ! Sweat and breath! You should have been a bloody poet!"

It was in McMartin's company that Manus began to drink heavily,
and here I mark the deepest, most extreme change in him.

I repeatedly asked Manus if we could move to a different house. He
refused, but I fought with him over it. To placate me he said that he'd
think about it. One day, walking a circuitous path home from the
market, I discovered a large, empty flat near Fitzwilliam Square. Men
were inside painting, and when I asked how I might contact the
owner, I was given an address a few streets away. I spoke with the land-
lord, expressing interest, and he showed me the flat. For weeks I visited the site where the men were working, and Manus came with me
once. But in the end he said it was not possible, that we did not have
the money at present, that I didn't understand how finances worked.
They were asking too much.

⚶

We were in this house for eight years when I gave birth to our third child, a boy. Manus sat in the room and watched me in agony as the infant was delivered of my body. He held the boy himself for the few minutes it lived, before expiring in his hands.

The midwife had to give me sedative doses of belladonna to calm me and help me sleep. The second day after the baby's death a neighboring woman with whom I had a congenial aquaintance, Colleen Bell, came by and sat with me and held me. She'd lost an infant five years before, and because of this, I found comfort in her arms and in her company.

That night after Colleen had gone, I heard Manus railing and crying in the other room, and I knew that he was drinking.

Still bleeding heavily the following night, I heard Manus calling out in the hallways, "Flowers for the forty hours adoration! Holy Mother of God!" The door flew open and he came in, closing it hard behind him.

"I'm going to put another child in you," he said.

Weak with the belladonna, I rose unsteadily, trying to get away. He grabbed me by the hair and threw me back onto the bed.

"Manus!" I cried. "For the love of God!"

He climbed over me, pressing one hand to my mouth so I could not speak or move my head. I struggled but may as well have been a bird fluttering under his iron hold, the panting of his heart and his hoarse breathing amplified at my ear.

As he pushed into me where I was raw and birth-ravaged, it felt as if I were being stabbed with a steel blade, each stroke keener than the one before it, like he would kill my sex if he could.

"Bitch!" he snarled until a change went over his face, a stinging of tears in his eyes. "Bitch!" he cried and winced as if he were also causing himself physical pain, his head flashing up as he choked back a sob in his throat.

Panting, he took his hand from my mouth, his eyes open but without focus. He rolled off me and fell into a drunken sleep.

In the light of the next dawn it looked as if a murder had been committed in our bed, blood on every sheet and blanket. I lay exhausted and crying, agonized and unable to move, terrified that it would be one of the girls who would find us so. Fortunately Mrs. Daley arrived early that morning and found us. Manus was asleep on his side, blood on his naked skin and his face. Blood dried in his hair. Mrs. Daley contacted the doctor, who, after attending to me, took Manus aside and admonished him. Even with the injury he'd inflicted upon me, I gloated and cried with satisfaction at his terrible shame, red fury with him deepening my grief for my dead baby.

He came to me that night and stood before me weeping. "Deirdre," he cried. "Please forgive me, for the love of God. It was the drink."

I refused to speak, my jaw tight with hatred against him.

Weeks passed, and even in my stillness as I struggled to heal I could not let go of my outrage.

I had taken to the little bed in the spare room, a cold, drafty part of the house.

When two months went by and I still refused to speak with Manus, the priest, Father Finbar, came to me and told me I must forgive him.

"He is your husband," the priest said.

"He hurt me," I answered.

"It was his grief!"

"What of my grief?" I cried.

"It was a son. He's been waiting for a son."

I said nothing, but moment by moment, Father Finbar was deepening my resolve against Manus. Every muscle in my body and mind felt in revolt of his authority, and of the other, more subterranean authority that directed our lives.

It was a week or so after my words with Father Finbar that Colleen Bell visited. Mrs. Daley served us tea in the front sitting room.

"I heard you were doing poorly for a while, Deirdre," she said in a soft, empathetic voice.

"Yes," I said.

She fixed her eyes very carefully upon me, and I saw that there was a purpose to her visit. "I hear that Manus is doing very poorly even now."

A tightness came into me. "Did Father Finbar dispatch you here to speak to me?"

"He's very concerned about Manus," she said.

I began to shake with anger and grief at what felt like a betrayal on her part. "I don't know what Father Finbar said to you, but Manus brutalized me, Colleen."

She winced faintly.

I began to shake with anger. "Colleen," I said. "He *raped* me!"

She froze at the word, silenced for a few moments by it. But watching her face I could see that she held hard to the mission the priest had entrusted her with. "He was drunk with his grief," she ventured meekly.

I stared at her. A spasm of nausea moved through me.

"He's stopped drinking," she said.

I was soaked with sweat, the room adrift with moving lights. "I think you should go," I said.

"Will you come and see me?" she asked as she stood.

"No," I said quietly.

She hesitated, then before turning to the door, she said, "I'm sorry, Deirdre."

I shook my head, and when she stepped outside, I closed the door.

Everything changed. If I had forgiven him as he had repeatedly begged me to those first months after it had happened, perhaps we would have gone on in the strained unhappiness we'd been living before that. But fury and outrage had changed me and given me a nervous determination.

And I began the most profound rebellion I could have made against the established order of the house. I made my room permanently on the third floor. I locked my door at night.

This time was also marked by another important change. The girls were old enough now for school, so three months after the death of the infant boy, they began their studies. Though St. Alban's was not very far from Merrion Square, I could not bring myself to go home after seeing them through the massive doors. At first I paced up and down Kildare Street, overcome with anxiety, rarely taking my eyes off the brown arches and iron gates of the school for the seven hours that the girls were stationed there. But as the weeks passed I began to wander further off, never discouraged by inclement weather.

I dared myself into lanes and narrow streets, made curious by the facade of houses and buildings; by a half-drawn lace curtain or the broken glass of a porch lantern; sometimes drawn by the smell of burning turf in a city of coal fires. Discovering little refuges from the weather, I watched the gypsy women with their bands of children, barefoot in the cold, wandering the streets in search of a few pence. They managed, I thought. They managed in the unsafe world.

There was something wildly liberating about wandering the city. Up until this time I had hardly veered from the roads that led to the market and to the church, cloistering my daughters and myself in the house on Merrion Square. Now I looked forward to losing myself in congested Dublin. There was an eerie privacy to moving among crowds.

Walking downwind of the river I welcomed its charred and molten smell. I gravitated to the bridgepiers, where the gulls were fidgety and territorial, their white feathers made gray with soot. I spent hours sometimes watching the rowboats rock at anchor, or I'd watch the faces of passersby over Halfpenny Bridge, some careworn and unseeing; others with bold, unheeding stares.

A year went by so, and I softened a bit toward Manus, exchanging cordial words with him regarding the affairs of the house or the children. One night I walked into the front parlor, where Maighread was writing her letters on a slate.

"Look, Da!" she cried to Manus. "I've written my name."

He squatted next to her where she sat and held the slate, studying the spindly characters she'd drawn. I could see that she'd left out a letter, but Manus didn't remark on it. He smiled. "You're getting on like a house on fire!" he said with great animation, and she smiled with pleasure.

A warmth flooded me for him. He turned and saw me there, registering the feeling in my face.

That night, having turned the gas off at the main, I climbed the stairs to my own room on the third floor. Manus stepped out of a shadow on the landing, startling me.

"Deirdre," he said, and pressed me to him. He was not drunk, but I smelled whiskey on his breath. For a moment I did not move, but when his mouth hungrily found mine, revulsion filled me, everything in me seizing up against him.

"No!" I cried and pushed him away.

He stepped back from me. In the shadows I could barely see his face. He said nothing, but I could hear his troubled breathing as he made his way down the stairs.

After that night he began again to drink heavily.

He attached himself to McMartin, and I was stunned to see him pick up McMartin's mannerisms and expressions. He grew a beard and, like McMartin, began smoking a pipe. I stared at him, which irritated him and caused him to blush with self-consciousness. Always sensitive to the expression in my eyes, he began to avoid looking into them. At night the two of them caroused.

I was certain as time went on, and I would not open my bedroom door to Manus, that he went with McMartin to the prostitutes on Leeson Street.

Once when it was very wet out I left my boots in the vestibule, and when he came in he kicked them aside with vehemence.

And though I disliked the behavior intensely, I found myself paying close attention to him, trying to fathom him. I watched him when he was unaware of it.

One night, two years after the infant's death, I saw Manus sitting alone in his study, his door ajar, mouthing words and gesticulating with his arm as if McMartin were still there, then affecting a laugh, the color up in his face. Was he reimagining an interaction with his friend or practicing for a future one?

He contorted his face at his invisible companion and smiled, shaking his head up and down. Speaking with McMartin's cadence, he cried out to the air, "You guttersnipe!"

He seemed to tire of the charade and sat forward, rubbing his face. He stared at the floor, disheartened.

Only now was it clear to me how lonely he was. He could not bear it that I would not forgive him. I felt moved but still conflicted. I wondered if we would ever be able to find our way back to each other.

He stood and went to his desk, looking distractedly through his papers. I was about to go upstairs when I saw him pick up the picture he kept of me in a white china frame on his desk. I watched, reluctantly moved as he gazed at my image, a kind of wistful seriousness overcoming his weary features.

Had I not known it always, I wondered, what I knew in this moment? That it had not been me he'd meant to injure that terrible night. It had not been me.

Two or three nights later, I sat with the girls before bed, reading to them from an old book we'd taken out of the library, illustrated with black etchings. They'd chosen a story of a mermaid combing her hair. When they were both asleep I took the book with me to my room and found myself intrigued by an etching of what looked like a woman's hands holding an infant in fire. The story was called "A Terrible Rite."

I sat in the chair in my room reading the tale, which was about a mother who held her child in fire every night for a few minutes so that he would learn to endure it.

"Eventually," the mother told her friend, "he will become a god."

After surviving each rite of fire, the infant felt cold and lay shivering in the corner while his mother went on with her business. I closed the book and kept trying to dispel the story from my thoughts, but having deeply unnerved me, it occupied my imagination.

I tried to sleep but found myself starting suddenly with an irrational worry over Manus. I went downstairs and saw him in bed, asleep.

Illuminated by the streetlight through the open curtains, he lay on his side, arms around the pillow, chin lifted. His expression open, the muscles soft across his brow. Sleep rendered him innocent. My heart quickened, and I sat in the chair and gazed at him.

He was not gone, the Beloved one, Manus's true self. Here he was, lying before me.

Though I would not show it in my gestures for years to come, I was seized with tenderness for him, and visited by euphoric memories of the passion that had once been between us.

For four more years life went on so for us, and there were times I wanted to go to him, to break through the revulsion that seized me when he touched me. But he grew more and more remote with alcohol and anger.

And so there were two of him, and it was the lost one who I was in an intrigue with; the one who was only visible to me when he slept.

When the girls were in bed at night, Manus left the house and didn't return until two or three in the morning. I slept fitfully in my room on the third floor, waking at the creaking of the stairs when he got home, and the noise of his footsteps on the second floor as he prepared for bed. I would wait a while until all was silence, then creep down into his room while he slept. If the curtain was closed I'd open it quietly that I might gaze at him in the light from the streetlamp below.

Now my girls were fourteen and thirteen. They were off to Kenmare and soon to school.

The fourth day they were gone, I wandered out toward the familiar landmark of the Customhouse, jostled once by two people avoiding an ambulance car that galloped past. As I approached O'Connell Bridge, the river carried with it an unnerving stench. I moved far away from the water, going south on Grafton Street and then to Stephen's Green, where I sat on a bench in the park.

It was the urchins with no shoes who drew my attention that day, selling the *Dublin Penny Journal*. Though they strutted and shouted, I felt afraid for them, small and motherless and half naked.

When the afternoon grew dark with the promise of rain, I started home. Under an arch on Baggot Street I saw a man in fine Donegal tweeds and a ragged woman pressed together in a doorway outside O'Donoghue's Public House, the woman panting with soft laughter. The spectacle of this upset me, and I rushed home, where loneliness issued from the walls.

I could not bring myself to go out again the next day. I began to keep to my little study, afraid to move, autonomous existence a precarious and unbearable condition. Nothing weighted me or tied me to anything. All I could do was give myself to the quiet that opened the senses.

If I stayed very still, remembering the days I'd spent with Manus in the hidden garden room, would lichen grow on the glass? Would the little draftsman's table grow a branch, find roots in the wood of the floor? Would my Love return as he had been that final night of childhood, just before dawn; just before we went back into the house of his mother? In his ruffled cuffs, his torn, crushed silk jacket, its tatters flailing in the wind?

Every physical thing has a spiritual counterpart, the *Secretus Secretorum* had told us. *There are two suns: the outer, natural sun and the bright spirit sun, the vivifying fire.*

And two kinds of architecture. *Terrestrial and Celestial.* That all houses had their celestial counterparts, just like each human being had a body and a soul. And where was the counterpart of this house? This is where he must be hiding from me. I would wait. I would slip through the seam when it opened. When the curtain of air parted, I told myself, I would meet him there.

THIRTEEN

For one week I sat from dawn to dusk in my small back room. It felt as if something shimmering awaited me in the corridors, on the point of appearing, something both beautiful and terrible, threatening to sweep in like a belt of weather from across Ireland.

On the seventh day after the girls had gone, the postman brought three letters. I watched from a shadow near the turn of the stairs while Mrs. Daley received them at the door, leaving two on the side table for me and taking the other into Manus's study. I heard a drawer open and close. When she disappeared again into the kitchen I retrieved mine, one from each of my girls. I tore them open and read, relieved and amazed by the mundane contents of each: complaints about days of rain, requests for me to send certain articles of clothing, various books.

I went quietly into Manus's study, a room I rarely entered. It was originally meant to be a parlor, but Mrs. O'Breen had decorated it with lithographs of priests and generals. An artillery infantryman's jacket was displayed on a wicker bust in one corner, next to a trooper's tunic. The heavy suite of furniture made the air smell of leather. A delicate chair covered in crimson velvet stood against one wall, neglected, out of its element in a room meant for a man.

I opened his drawer. The letter was postmarked Kenmare, from his mother. I slipped it into my pocket, and when Mrs. Daley went upstairs to dust, I took it to the kitchen and steamed it open over the kettle. It was a thick letter, five pages in Mrs. O'Breen's florid, but compact, hand. She said that the girls were happy, busy swimming and riding the mares. I raked the pages looking for more news of them, but much of the letter belabored properties and family business. I was about to fold it and put it away again when I saw my own name.

> It is Deirdre's duty to give you children. You must not forget that. Be diligent with her, gentle but firm. There are more children meant for the two of you. With the girls gone she'll focus more on you. There is a boy to come to you yet, Manus. It is a sin for her to refuse you. If she goes on doing so you must have Father Finbar speak to her again. She's good to bear children for another ten years. Thirty-three is a good age for a woman to bear a child. I was thirty-three when you were conceived.

I listened for Mrs. Daley, then returned to Manus's study, where I put spirit gum on the envelope, sealed it, and put it away.

That night when Manus came home I stood in the shadow of the stairwell, listening as he opened his top drawer and read the letter. I walked past his door, haunting the vestibule. He quieted, as if he heard me there.

At the meal he was pensive. I knew his mother's words were in his thoughts.

When he finished eating, he put down his fork and knife and sighed. The tightness at his jaw was not there. He stared at the window and watched the trees moving in the porchlight.

In that moment the Beloved flashed in his face. It was a moment that passed in the blinking of an eye, but such moments I had learned over the years to memorize, to keep alive inside myself. The Beloved managed to appear when Manus was tired, and he seemed tired now in a way he had not seemed to be when he'd walked in the door. I wished then that there was no wall between us; no animosity. He inclined his head into his hand, and I sensed the Beloved here in this moment, ajar of Manus, causing the light to change at the window. He was the shadow cast from the soup tureen on the table. The gust that rushed by the side of my face as Mrs. Daley passed me with the water pitcher. Manus stared now at the table before him. The Beloved moved closer and closer to him, hungry to return, as in exile from him as I was.

Feeling my eyes on him, he broke from his daydream, tension coming back into his jaw. "Mrs. Daley," he said. "Can you bring the whiskey in to me?"

She placed it on the table before him, and he poured half a glass and drank it down, the color come up on his skin. After a second he looked at me with a certain baffled determination. The whiskey was fortifying him, driving away the vulnerable presence of his true self.

Any moment he might have stood and taken me by the arm. Fearful over his clenched jaw, I left the table and went into the little back room and locked the door.

I remembered the first time I'd seen the Blasket from Ventry Harbour, the distance of it; how strange it had looked to me, as if I had not lived on those rocks my entire life. That same feeling of hopelessness seized me in that dark hour as I thought of my girls. I could not conjure their faces clearly.

I found myself filled with a pervasive sense of loss, and of the tides raging at the rock. The great uncertainty of the world.

I opened the *Secretus Secretorum* and read.

> Where is this golden Mercury, this radical moisture which dissolved in sulphur and salt becomes the animated seed of the metals? He is incarcerated and held so fast that even nature can not release him from the harsh prison. . . . An intervention is what is required. Radical moisture. Dew that appears like a miracle.

Every night for five nights Manus and I went through the same routine. He drank at the evening meal to strengthen the oppressor, and always, before Mrs. Daley left, I eluded him, locked him out of my small back room. He usually knocked, tried the door; then swore at me and left. I knew that he was, in a sense, relieved, or he never would have stood for it each night. The Beloved within him could not bear the violence he had once committed against me; could not bear the prospect of hurting me again, and I knew that was why he suffered.

But on the fifth night Manus leaned on the door and wept. That time I was standing pressed to the other side of the door and I almost opened it, but the anger rose up in him suddenly and he punched the door with his fist so I felt the shock of the blow in my shoulder. After that I heard him on the landing, his breathing drunk and confused as he climbed the stairs.

Very quietly I unlocked my door, following him at a distance. From the darkened stairs I could hear him in the bedroom undressing. He threw one of his shoes against the wall, and I heard the noise of metal against metal as he unhooked his belt and dropped it, with his pants, to the floor. For a moment it was quiet, and I imagined him struggling with his shirt buttons. "Bloody hell!" he sighed, and the bedsprings sounded.

It was only moments before his breathing grew long and drawn in sleep. I peered in. The curtains were wide open, and it was just beginning to rain. The streetlamp threw its colorless patina over part of the bed and floor. He had gone down now like a shipwreck, dismantled, broken apart, the hard mortar that had held him in place having disintegrated with alcohol and exhaustion.

I stepped in and stood at the foot of the bed, gazing at him. In the strangeness of the light, I saw him in his earlier incarnation. The boy I'd married with the intense, vulnerable face. Memory of all intervening years seemed, in that moment, insignificant, and I felt a paroxysm of love and excitement wash over me. The real Manus, the Lost One, murmured, and I wanted to know what he was saying. I moved close. "What is it?" I whispered. "What is it?" He sighed as if he were in pain. Tears crowded my eyes. He threw his arm back across the bed, turning from one side onto the other. He flailed his arms, fighting the cover irritably, and a shudder ran through him as he shifted posture again, ending on his back. The drunken sleep would set in soon. The sleep from which the Oppressor was forced to submit for three or four hours at least. The sleep of helplessness.

The Lost Manus was here, closer to the surface. He turned his face uneasily. A furrow of emotion crossed his brow.

I took candles down from the shelf, casting glances at him as I lit them and placed them around the room until seven or eight of them burned. I knelt on the floor at the bedside and kissed the air around his face. I was very close to him now, struggling to control my breathing and my whispers, struggling not to touch my lips to his skin and to his mouth, which was open slightly. I rose and went to the foot of the bed and pulled the blankets away slowly. He had mananged to unbutton his shirt but not to get it off, but his body below was bare.

I sensed the awareness of the Beloved as I got on the bed and knelt between his open legs. As if with anticipation, he stretched a thigh further open and my heart raced. With very gentle fingertips I touched the sinuous stretch of muscle on his inner thigh, grazing his skin slowly up toward his velvety parts. I bent over him and breathed warm breath over his cock, the thick hair that surrounded it like a mat of fragrant silk thread. It began to harden, and under its velvet sheath, it twitched and tensed. His own breathing quickened, his naval rising and falling. With a few gentle touches of my hand, his cock was transformed. Tight and hard like a ripe fruit about to burst its skin. A single droplet appeared and gleamed on its head. I remembered the way he'd weakened when I used to suck and furtively lick him, while rubbing my spit softly over his balls. I restrained the urge to take him into my mouth, afraid that my tongue would jar him awake. I kept touching him softly with my fingertips until they burned.

The rain intensified outside, hitting the window like a wall of water. I remembered the days we'd spent in the hidden garden room, the way he'd watched my face as he'd made love to me. His aggressive, physical candor, his tireless athleticism. "Call me Stag," he had said. "Call me Mercury." There was an entire list of virile gods and animals he'd wanted to be called. And I'd whispered the desired name, and he'd gritted his teeth with pleasure.

In an impulse I bent over him again, a loose strand of my hair tickling his thigh, and he stirred suddenly and opened his eyes and I started, terrified. But it was the Beloved who gazed back at me, as if from somewhere hopelessly far away. He did not move, still under the dominion of his captor.

"My love," I said to him. "My Stag. My Eagle. Manus of the Ruffled Cuffs."

His eyes closed slowly. If only I could have put him inside me without waking the other.

But I couldn't. I knelt there and looked at him, holding back my caresses, my breaths singeing the air. After a few minutes he stirred and caught the sheet with one toe as he turned, pulling the humid train of it over him as he went on his side, facing away from me.

I lay all that night in bed beside him. When dawn came into the sky, the darkness tinged with pink, I heard the clatter of horses leading the milk lorries in the street below. Manus turned toward me in sleep, one of his arms falling at an angle over my stomach, the other arm up over his head, that hand in a fist.

I shifted a small bit under the hand that lay heavily on my belly until it lay between my legs, only the satin of my slip between his skin and mine. With subtle, concentrated movements, I brushed against his hand.

I managed to pull the slip up from between us and pressed his hand gradually, irresistibly, until he cupped me with his palm and two fingers slipped inside me, a sound escaping on my breath. I moved twice or thrice and came.

I put my fist to my mouth, struggling to quiet my breathing.

Through the tears in my eyes he appeared to be looking at me.

A few minutes later he awakened, stirred from sleep, sensing something. He turned and looked at me lying there, curled into myself, my eyes only partly open. I was humid, breathing, recovering from the tremulous night of yearning, which had been relieved at last by the burst and wash of love. It had not been random, I told myself, Manus having turned, his arm having landed upon me. It had been the Beloved, the gargantuan effort of the repressed soul to come into union with me.

Manus sat up, looking at himself, the sheet in a twist around his hips and thighs, his shirt hopelessly wrinkled. I saw the thought come to him. He lifted his hand to his nose and smelled me on his fingers. He looked faintly stunned. He dropped his hand to his lap and seemed to be considering, imagining. After a beat he turned and faced me thoughtfully, and I saw something soften in his expression. I struggled to read the look over a course of moments in which it underwent nuanced shifts and changes.

He stood and looked at me again, and I sensed him opening further. I lay perfectly still as he moved about the room, gathering his things for work, then went into the lavatory, the sounds of him pouring water from the pitcher into the bowl, the opening and closing of the cabinet soothing me, the rapture having effected a peacefulness in me, though in the course of the day with Manus gone, I would start again and again from sleep, exhilarated, sensing the coming of the Beloved, the presage of him like the coming of summer, the wind sending its message, exciting the trees.

I believed that I had brought him back.

In the afternoon I hid from Mrs. Daley. I walked quietly and purposefully through the halls in silent communion with myself.

When I closed my eyes I saw my parents standing thigh deep in the sea, embracing. My father's back and arms articulated with muscle. My mother gracefully reposing her head on his chest near his neck, her long hair blowing slowly like the tail of a comet. A boat went by on the waves, and I saw then how tall they both were, high as Skellig Michael, gulls screeching and mewing, circling them like small white flies, the curragh of men going past, small and insignificant. The music, Donal na Grainne.

But late in the day I fell from the heights of elation. The night before and the early morning hours took on the aftertaste of a potent dream. I felt exhausted and afraid of the intensity of my feelings, and of what I had done.

When at last Manus came in late that afternoon, he was with McMartin, who went ahead of him to the study while Manus went to hang their jackets in the vestibule closet. Congenial from his interaction with McMartin, there was light in his face. Turning and finding me watching him from the bottom of the stairs, I saw the memory of what he'd realized this morning come to him; a spark of the Beloved. On his way back in to McMartin, I moved toward him, stopping him and embracing him. Surprised, he kissed my forehead and was breaking the embrace when I clasped him hard around the waist, holding him back.

"Send him away, Manus," I murmured.

"For Christ's sake, Deirdre," he said, grabbing my wrists and thrusting my arms aside. "Christ!" His eyes were stern under the dark brush of his brows.

He went in to McMartin and closed the door.

I stood panting with fury, poised to knock, my knuckles white. I smelled the pipe smoke, heard the low boom of McMartin's voice. I picked up the framed photograph of Manus's father, prominently displayed on the long marble side table, and threw it to the floor.

Manus came out at the crash.

"What happened?"

He stared at the picture, then bent down and turned it over to find the glass cracked over his father's face. A hurt look passed over his features.

I immediately regretted having broken this particular picture. Why had I not picked up some useless piece of bric-a-brac placed there by his mother? I breathed hard, gritting my teeth. Instead of sternness, it was the Beloved that flashed in Manus's face. I remembered, in that moment, that the days we'd spent together in the hidden garden room had been preceded by a fit of my anger, when I had broken the bottle of attar of roses.

"We'll get a new frame," he said.

I stared at him, still too upset with him to answer. My anger a forceful thing, streaming hot, an indication of a passion held too long in abeyance.

He picked up the pieces carefully and placed them back on the marble side table. He remained, seeming forgetful of McMartin. I watched him closely, knowing that in this moment he could have gone in and dismissed McMartin. "Maybe in the attic," he said, arranging the pieces with a shaking hand. "We might find one that will suit."

He tore his eyes from mine, stared hard at the shine on the floor, and went back in to McMartin.

For a protracted amount of time, I did not move from the hallway, until the afternoon light began to dim and the gloom became a strain on my eyes. When at last I knew he was not sending his friend away, I retreated to the back room.

❧❧❧

In my memory I was following her as she paced a hill on the island, her eyes a glassy, fevered blue, watching every bit of flotsam riding the backs of the waves like it might be the remains of the man she was waiting for. If she spoke it was not to me but to the air. I followed her breathlessly to the sacred precincts of the screes, where they had made a bed in one of the grotto caves. After this, we visited every marriage bed they'd made on the island, each one marked with blue stones, and it seemed to me at the time that I could discern the impressions their bodies had made in the grassy furrows where they'd lain.

His leaving had always hurt her, and the longer he stayed away, the more certain she was that the ocean had taken him from her.

She swore at the uneasy sea, or into the haze, a sky threatening rain that would not come. She swore that she would not forgive him. She swore her undying hatred of him, that she'd tear him limb from limb, leave bits of him all over the island. She foamed at the mouth and she cried, spat and almost choked on her own breath. I hid my head in my arms and turned wild circles. How old was I?

And at the hour we saw him coming again in his own time, striding easily up the hill from the White Strand. You'd think he'd only been taking a stroll. She stood, staring, afraid to look away, as if he might disappear, and when she was sure that she was not hallucinating, her body racked itself with tremors. She ran at him, beat him; she tore hair from his head. She was like a vicious bitch dog; he defended himself against her. She rent a gash across his temple with a stone, and there was blood on everything and he was off, stumbling, holding his wound with his hands. I ran away toward the crossroads where men were returning from the sea, and I heard them talking about the man and the woman, saying that neither was full human.

I heard her weeping that night behind the yellow curtain and knew she was waiting for him. And in the middle of the night he came in and she took him, all vulnerable, into her arms and into her bed again.

I was afraid. He'd gone too far in courting her suffering. I heard them breathing together. No one should ever taunt that soft, hopeless place in her. Why did he not know that? I fretted in the dark over it. Fretted and shivered because he did not know.

I detached from the memory and struggled to move away from it. They had done such things one to the other, and it was part of the passion between them.

I stayed in the back room, unmoving, afraid to go to Manus; afraid if I opened the *Secretus Secretorum* it would be to the image of the dead couple, blackened by the flames of the alchemical oven.

It was dark when I heard Mrs. Daley leave. In the kitchen I found soup on the stove and a fresh loaf of soda bread on the board, now gone cool.

I heard Manus saying good-bye to McMartin at the door. I waited and listened. When McMartin was gone, I stepped out into the light and faced Manus.

He looked at me and then at the picture, which I had left, along with the shards of glass, on the marble side table. He weaved slightly on his feet, then turned and went back into his study, closing the door.

I went and gathered the shards and the picture, carrying it all carefully upstairs in search of a new frame.

FOURTEEN

❧

I awakened in the morning when the downstairs bell rang. Reaching the stairhead, I saw Manus below, still wearing his clothes from the night before, his shirt untucked, receiving a letter.

My heart rushed. "Is it about the girls? Is anything wrong?"

He was standing quite still reading it, his brow furrowed. He shook his head vaguely.

"From St. Dominic's," he said. Bairbre had left Enfant de Marie seven years before to join a cloister of Poor Maries at a convent in Kilkenny.

Manus stared at the letter a while longer, then folded it.

"Bairbre's dead," he said.

In the coach on the ride from Merrion Square to Kilkenny, I could not keep it clear in my mind that Bairbre was dead. Manus's face had taken on an urgent melancholy. I touched his arm, and though he did not move, I felt him start inwardly, a sensitive shiver. With the pull and jolt of the carriage hypnotizing me, I was thrown back in time to the coach ride with Bairbre and Manus from Enfant de Marie to Kenmare, when I'd experienced for the first time the silent, unfathomable history between the two of them. For a few intense moments, Bairbre's soap and tallow smell filled the carriage with a stunning immediacy. I let myself go back to that time: the feeling of the veil oppressing my heavy hair, calluses on my knees from praying, the hunger from a perpetually empty stomach.

"I was thinking of her last night," Manus said suddenly, breaking me from my daydream.

"You were?" I asked.

"I had an urge to see her."

"How strange," I said.

"No," he answered, his eyes meeting mine for a moment. "I think of her often."

"You do?"

He turned his face away from mine.

When Manus and I had been married for one year, I had written to Bairbre and had received word back from the Reverend Mother that she had chosen to be fully cloistered and had no correspondence with anyone but her mother. I had tried several other times over the years, but to no avail. Manus had little attended my upset over this at the time and had seemed to accept it silently.

"I didn't know that you thought of her," I said.

His eyes remained fixed at some point above the passing fields.

🙰🙰🙰

The convent was nothing like Enfant de Marie, but a much smaller stone building half covered with ivy.

Inside we were directed up a cobbled hallway, where we ascended a flight of rickety stairs. Cold air met us at the threshold of the dead room. We paused in unison, uncertain if we should proceed. Bairbre was laid out on a narrow bed, and another robed and veiled figure attended her, arranging a spray of violets between two of her fingers.

Once the nun had succeeded with her task, she moved suddenly away from Bairbre's body. Manus grasped my hand in his, squeezing it so I thought he'd break it.

An old nun knelt at the foot of the bed, her head bent, eyes in a stupefied doze. The nun who had been attending Bairbre approached us and, looking up into Manus's face, asked, "Are you Manus O'Breen?"

He gave a nod. She perused both of our faces. "We'll leave you alone with her," she said, then stirred the older nun out of meditation, and both left the room.

The figure lying on the bed looked only vaguely like Bairbre, a darker, thinner version, like a poorly replicated waxwork. It was the hands that I kept looking at, familiar to me, having retained a girlish grace. I remembered her fingers delicately working the threads and pins of her laces, but each time I looked at the face, a cold sensation of shock moved through me, distancing me from the reality of the situation. Manus went to his knees and began to weep. I knelt beside him, but, unable to take in the gravity of the moment, the tears in my eyes were more in response to Manus's sobbing than to the loss of Bairbre.

We remained a long time in the room. I was pensive, distracted by details, wondering about the funeral and about when Mrs. O'Breen might arrive. I debated with myself whether she would bring Maighread and Caitlin with her. I thought it most likely that she wouldn't, and I felt both disappointment and relief at the thought.

Manus suddenly put his arms around me, buried his head in the hair at my neck, and began again to sob. When he withdrew, he stayed close to me, head bowed. I dabbed his eyes with my handkerchief, took his face in my hands and pressed my lips to his temple and forehead by turns. The purity of his grief inspired in me both a maternal solicitude and a wave of carnal feeling that confused me, and for which I admonished myself for having here in his sister's dead room. Perhaps it was because Manus's grief was so strong that I could not find my own. But the figure on the bed was not her. It felt as if Bairbre, as I'd known her, was alive and that she would reveal herself to us at any moment.

When the nuns turned on the gas downstairs, the sconces on the wall bloomed slowly with light. We got up then and left the dead room.

Manus spoke to a nun named Sister Clair. "My mother has definately been notified?" he asked.

"Yes," Sister Clair answered.

"What illness did my sister have?" Manus asked.

The nun paused, then spoke hesitantly. "She was ill for a few months. It was a bronchial infection that she finally died of."

Manus looked expectantly into the nun's face, waiting for more from her, but she changed the subject, suggesting a rooming house down the road where we might stay.

It was a gaunt old building with feudal arches, and after we paid for a room for the night, we sat in a tea shop across the road from the convent, watching for Mrs. O'Breen to arrive. The tea shop closed at half eight and we remained standing outside the convent until half nine, no sight of Mrs. O'Breen.

That night in our room, Manus told me that once, after Tiernan's death, he'd gone into Bairbre's room and she had been staring out the window, looking up into the night sky. He had asked her what she was doing and she'd told him that she was holding up the stars, making certain that they did not fall.

"She said she had to do it because she was afraid everything in the universe might go wrong. With the magical way children believe, she stared vigilantly and with great concentration as if that might stop the stars from falling.

"I had begged her to let me do it too, and I managed it for maybe ten minutes before I asked her why there was all this milky light streaming around the stars and she told me that it was because I was tired that it looked that way.

"I had already closed my eyes when I heard her cry out because she had seen a star fall. I fell asleep, and when I woke hours later she was still staring out the window.

"Before Tiernan died, Bairbre was different. But after, she wasn't like a child anymore. I remember missing her, like she was the one who had died, not Tiernan."

The service had been set for 10 A.M. but Mrs. O'Breen still had not arrived by half twelve. Sister Clair approached us where we sat in the nuns' reception room and said that we needed to go on with the burial.

"You're certain that my mother was notified?" Manus asked.

"Yes, Mr. O'Breen," she said slowly and took a seat beside him. "Even yesterday I was not altogether certain that your mother would come."

"Why not?" Manus asked with quiet alarm.

"There was a break of some sort between Mrs. O'Breen and Sister Bairbre. It happened after your mother visited here. I'm not certain what was said between them, but Bairbre stopped writing to her, and no letters came from Mrs. O'Breen. Five months ago it was. Mrs. O'Breen stopped sending us her regular check. That made things very hard for us," she said as an aside, her eyes meeting mine a moment. "It was about three months ago that Bairbre . . . well, she stopped leaving her cell." The nun was silent but seemed to be trying to find a way to go on. Finally she said, "Bairbre mortified herself."

Silence took possession of the little room.

"How did she do that?" Manus demanded.

"A nailed shirt, an infection she would not allow to heal."

I had heard of such torture devices at Enfant de Marie.

"Is this a common practice here?" he asked.

"We try to encourage limitations on this, but it's difficult. Nuns cannot be stopped from following the examples of the saints. . . ." Her eyes grew large in her face, her pupils dilated. She was a strange, owl-like creature.

"You have no infirmaries?" he demanded and stood up.

"Yes," she said, also rising, "and she was attended to there, but her wounds would have only begun to heal when she'd apply the shirt again."

"Outrageous!" he cried.

"Let me assure you, Mr. O'Breen, this was Bairbre's choice alone to mortify herself. No one told her to do this."

Manus and the nun held each other's eyes. Gradually the fierceness against her went out of him. He was perspiring heavily, and as his gaze fell to the tiles, his eyes began to lose focus.

"Manus!" I cried, guiding him to sit. The nun put a vial of spiritous ammonia to his nose, which made him start and sit forward.

We stood with eight or nine nuns in the churchyard, all holding their veils against a blistering wind, that knocked the heads off the morning glories so they swept in over the coffin.

After the service, the priest threw the first handful of dirt onto the lowered coffin, and a man in dark clothes came and shoveled in the sod. We were approached by Sister Clair, who reached under her bib, drawing out a letter. "Bairbre asked me to give this to you, Mr. O'Breen." She held it toward him, but he only stared at it, so I took it for him. It was warm and sent a frisson of sadness through me.

"Mrs. O'Breen," she said. "I wonder if you might deliver something to Bairbre's mother when you see her next. I was meant to give it to her myself, but under the circumstances . . ."

I accepted from Sister Clair a bag stitched together with rough fabric. Whatever was in it weighed very little. I guessed that it was one of Bairbre's lace workings.

We traveled back to Dublin that afternoon.

At home Manus put the letter in a drawer in his study and I placed the gauze bag meant for Mrs. O'Breen on Manus's desk. We climbed the stairs together. He got into bed while I moved about putting things away, seeing to things, but, exhausted, I lay down next to him and fell asleep.

I awakened to the sound of Manus softly repeating my name. Grief had brought his pure self back to him, had driven off the harsher other. I turned and put my arms around him and we lay entwined. He fell asleep in this position, and I drifted between sleep and waking, every subtle modulation in his breathing sending washes of feeling through me. It was in these hours that I shed my first tears for Bairbre, the reality of her death slowly dawning upon me. Gusts of air coming through the window smelled of a coming storm.

When I awakened again, it was after six in the evening. I whispered to Manus that I would go down and see to supper.

I gave Mrs. Daley instructions and sat without helping as she methodically placed the napkins and cutlery on the table. The early evening light was deep through the shutters and spattered the table-cloth. Rain had come and gone while we'd been sleeping.

As I heard Manus coming down the stairs, a front of shadow over-took the late Dublin afternoon, subsuming the room all at once, the dressers with the dinner plates going crimson and amber. The quality of the air in the room changed, growing cooler and damper.

Manus came in, and Mrs. Daley set the whiskey and a glass down near him. He eyed it, then looked at his plate. I did not breathe. My heart beat in jaunts.

Mrs. Daley moved past us to leave, turning the flame up in a small lamp on her way, which did little to cut the strangeness of the light. It seemed to me that she was moving very slowly toward the hall, echoes rising from her footsteps. My own chair sent a vibration into my body, the entire room in a tumult of vibrations. I touched my fork, and removing my fingers from it could still feel the buzz of it, and every cell of me starting to open like I was being dissolved into a wet mist. My love hung his head and did not move as the shudders and the faint hysteria of the room gradually quieted, and I could hear my own breathing and his. I stood and went to him, kissing his face, his neck. I sat back on the floor and reached for him and he came down to me, embracing me, moving with me, our breathing growing heated and insistent. When he lifted my dress and pushed into me, I saw, in my peripheral vision, the glass of the window spontaneously shatter, a tumult of silent glitter.

I held his hair, kept his face above mine, the moon peering at the sun.

We moved together with waves of a slow, aching pleasure. The light in the room went gradually purple, and the descending sun glinted on the cutlery and ignited the gilded edges of the dinnerware; everything metal and gold in the room bright as the bars of a furnace.

Afterward, we remained there on the floor. The window resumed its unbroken state. When we stood, it looked as if there were dew on the dinner plates, beads of humidity having gathered on the water glasses. There were conditions to this enchantment, and we were cautious.

We held hands and walked through the hall, past the armoire and up the darkened stairs, dampness on the railings. The house like a dangerous woods, night leaking in everywhere through windows left open.

I lit candles and watched him sleep.

His own childhood was as unapproachable to him as mine was to me. I had never understood this because we lived in proximity to Manus's childhood. So much heritage and legacy present; so much that directed our lives, allotted our roles.

Gazing at my sleeping husband, I remembered my mother's vigils for my father, and I felt her panic and expectation of loss; afraid he would drift from me, afraid he might return to the mundane world. I watched over him, guarding him against the deadening air of the house, thinking that if his soul fled from him I might see some sign, and that I might deter it, open a fuller dialogue with it.

⌒⌒⌒

I had fallen asleep during my vigil and awakened that night to find Manus was not in bed. The clock said half past nine. I went downstairs and saw the light coming from under the door of his study. I knocked softly, but he did not answer.

"Manus," I said and opened the door.

He was sitting forward on the leather sofa with his head down, the opened envelope on the cushion beside him, the letter hanging from one hand.

I moved into the room and stood before him.

"What does it say?" I asked.

He waited a while, then finally looked up at me and asked, "Do you remember the story of the Three Fates from Greek mythology?"

"Vaguely," I answered.

"After Tiernan's death, when I was six and Bairbre was eight, my aunt Ethna told us the story. She said, 'There is Clotho, she who spins the thread of life, and there is Lachesis, she who assigns each child a destiny. And the other one.' She quieted and said, 'The one we won't speak of now. The one whose attention you don't want to draw to you.' She pressed a finger to her lips and said, 'Ssssshhh.' "

" 'Who is she? Who is she?' " I had begged.

" 'Atropos. She who cannot be turned. She with the abhorred shears, who cuts the thread of life.' "

"Bairbre and I didn't sleep that night.

"From doorways we watched my mother and her sisters moving restlessly about. The three all wore the same kind of heavy nightgown. Their faces looked stern. Looking at them that night," he said and winced, "I was confused as to which one was my mother.

"We heard the word *intercessor* again and again. The hiss of that word, ricocheting along the walls.

" 'What is an intercessor?' I had asked Bairbre. And she had told me that it was a 'go-between' for someone with God. There were arguments among them. I heard my name and Bairbre's volleyed back and forth. But it was my name whispered in the worst heat between them.

"The next night they lit a fire outside and they told us our fates. Bairbre was given a linen veil to play with. She would be a nun. I would grow up to marry, have a career and many sons.

"Once everything was decided, the three of them, who had been walking most of the night, casting shadows in the vestibule, all fell into a heavy sleep. And I don't know if I dreamt this part or not, but I remember seeing the three of them all asleep side by side in the matrimonial bed, and they were whistling in their sleep, 'Intercessor! Intercessor!' "

He grew quiet. Two pages of Bairbre's letter were on the floor and he was stepping on them with one foot. I took the last two pages from his hand and read:

Our mother and I had kept up a steady correspondence. I lived for her letters. In mine to her, I kept a kind of diary, charting my prayers and indulgences, drawing for her a picture of my life as a nun. We had maintained a kind of heightened expectation in our letters, as if we were reaching together toward some shared goal.

I had been waiting for her to come here. I had been looking forward to it for a long time. She'd been sending her usual checks to the nuns here as she always had at Enfant de Marie, and they wanted to meet her.

I had placed so much hope in seeing her. For so long I had cut myself off from everyone but her. When she came I was exultant, but I did not find the satisfaction I'd hoped to find being with her. I don't know how to describe what I had built up in my hopes about her. She was here. We went for long walks. We prayed together. We sat in the nuns' reception room and talked. The days passed and I knew she would leave again. I didn't want her to. I was afraid of what it would be like when she was gone. I didn't understand why I was not fulfilled being with her. Every day that passed, I grew more nervous at the idea of her leaving. My neediness set her on edge, but I couldn't curb it. I begged her to stay. I wept and held her, and this wore on her. I felt her pulling away from me. She told me then that she was dissatisfied with the way

things had turned out; that you and Deirdre still had no sons; that
perhaps my having become a nun had not redeemed her in God's
eyes and because of that the sin of her leaving the sisterhood had
not been forgiven. I felt as if she were saying that there was something missing in me, some flaw, some way in which God had not
accepted me in exchange for her. Like Tiernan, I had turned out to
be a terrible disappointment to her.

Since that day that she left me here, I have not stopped thinking of our brother, Tiernan. I have been revisiting the last days of
his life.

You were small, Manus, but do you remember the end of Tiernan's last school year when he had been sent home for throwing a
rock through the chapel window? Our mother had met with the
priests and had settled things with them by offering them money
until they agreed to let Tiernan return in the fall. Anyhow, that
summer at home, he was prone to fevers, a frailty that had stayed
with him since recovering from the typhus. The fever had come on
him one night that summer and our mother dispatched a servant
to get the doctor, and she and I were with Tiernan in his room,
cooling his brow with a cloth, helping him to sip water. She was
adjusting the sheet on his bed when a letter fell out from under the
mattress. It was a letter from the seminary, addressed to our
mother. It was dated weeks before.

I went with her into the front drawing room where she opened
it, finding the check she had written to the seminary returned to
her. The head of the school wrote that after much consideration the
priests had decided that Tiernan's presence was too disruptive for
the other boys, who were struggling to come to terms with the sac-
rifices that a religious life demanded of them. And he said that it
was clear to them all that Tiernan did not belong there; that he
had no vocation and was desperately unhappy.

Our mother was stunned. She began to drink. After a long
silence she said with a terrible finality in her voice, "He's dead to
me now, Bairbre. He's dead. You no longer have an older brother."

I had never heard her say such a thing.

There was a storm that night, which must have been the reason that it took so long for the doctor to arrive. Our mother continued to drink, and eventually fell asleep in her chair. I waited calmly in the vestibule when the servant arrived with the doctor. I told them that Tiernan was fine now; that he was sleeping peacefully and that my mother had asked that they not wake him. And so they left. The following afternoon, Tiernan was dead.

What have I told myself about this over the years? I hated him because he made her unhappy. And she had decreed that he was dead. She had already decreed it. All these years, Manus, I have been thinking about this in the same childlike way: My mother had told me that my brother was dead, so I sent the doctor away.

I've lived in a dream all these years. Tiernan had not redeemed her, but I would. The dream is over.

You may not remember this, Manus, but when we were small, after Aunt Ethna told us the myth of the Three Fates, you asked me if our mother was Atropos, the third fate. She who cuts the thread of life.

I said no, that our mother was Clotho, the Giver of Life. Ethna was harsher, so I decided that she was Atropos, even though I knew Moyna had the least say in decisions that were made between the three of them, and could not have been Lachesis, the Decider of Fates. It bothered me that you had asked that, and one day, not long after, I asked you about it. You said that Atropos was the strongest one, so that's why you had thought it. It was you who actually put that thought into my head long ago.

That day, here at the convent, before our mother left me, I told her that when you were only six, you had asked me if she was Atropos. I told her to hurt her. Her beloved boy, the one she would not demand the terrible sacrifice of, had said this of her. I told her because I knew she was leaving me for good.

We've been afraid of Ethna and Moyna. We've hated them, but the truth is they have always been only her shadows. Our mother is all three fates. She is the giver of life, the decider of destinies, and the one who cuts the thread. She cut the thread of Tiernan's life, but in reality it was me who killed him. And I cannot live with that.

Here the letter ended abruptly and without a signature.

I slowly read and reread the final three sentences, until tears rose in my throat. I put the letter down.

"Christ, Manus!" I said softly.

He sat in silence. Finally he said, "I hardly know what to think of any of it right now."

"I want to get our girls from your mother's house!" I said.

He shook his head.

"They're all right, Deirdre!" he said.

"I want them. She can be cold to them sometimes. . . ."

"I'm certain she's pampering them."

That night I read and reread all the letters I'd received from them. They were riding horses and swimming, having tea in fancy shops and in the hotel on Henry St. in Kenmare, being ushered around like princesses, and feeling their independence from me for the first time in their lives.

As I lay sleepless in bed, the terrible revelations in Bairbre's letter haunted me. In the middle of the night I got up and packed a bag. But when I went downstairs to tell Manus what I had decided, I heard him crying. I went in to him.

At dawn I penned a letter to the girls, asking them if there was anything they needed; if they wanted me to come sooner. The reply I received a few days later reassured me that all was well and that I should wait until the appointed time.

I sent back a letter, telling them that if they needed anything at all, or if they changed their minds and wanted me to come sooner than planned, to please let me know and I would be there immediately.

A few days later, an offer came in for Manus to head a restoration project of an old house in the Liberties. He accepted it immediately and threw himself headlong into the work. I saw very little of him then.

We began again to live separate lives in the house. Slowly over the weeks I realized I was with child.

FIFTEEN

Leaving by train for Kenmare just before August, I had Bairbre's gift to her mother in tow.

Moving through the center of Ireland, I saw things on the roads and passing fields that startled me. A dead cow in high grass. A gorse fire out of control, a child running from it. Another hurling sticks into it. My brain felt misty. Each time I closed my eyes, I imagined the infant inside me through a curtain of membrane, a rainbow shimmer to it.

This pregnancy had taken, almost immediately, a strong visceral hold of me. My breasts ached and my stomach was queasy. I had a powerful need for sleep. But every now and then, my heart would hesitate and, as if it were a sentient being in its own right, seemed to be listening for something, as if some signal from the womb was not forthcoming.

I did not know how to read these pulses of uncertainty in my blood and feared that the child might be delicate or malformed. I sensed a soft precariousness to the condition. But the stronger the pregnancy took hold of my body, the fiercer my desire for this child. I told myself, in an effort to reassure, that it was my tendency to worry, always to fear the worst.

Arriving at the big house I had to struggle with my demeanor, barely able to contain the wild excitement to see my girls. "I must behave as if I'd seen them yesterday. Not let them see the loss of breath in me, the vacuum in me," I told myself. As I ran up the flight of steps all I heard was my banging heart. They watched me come in from beyond. I stopped and there was a hush as all three, the girls and Mrs. O'Breen, looked at me. For a terrible moment it was as if they did not know me.

Then Caitlin stood. "Mammy," she said. She came and embraced me.

"Love," I said, gratitude in my voice, moved and stunned by the feel of her, silken as a flower, a sensation from a far-off time. I was seized with guilt and incredulity that I had not fought harder to keep them with me. They looked small, girlish.

Mrs. O'Breen stood next and, walking toward me with open arms, said, "Deirdre!" She searched my demeanor, reading the hue and lights of me like a fortune-teller, and was about to speak when I said, "I'm sorry about Bairbre."

Her pupils dilated for a moment and then grew small again. "It's very sad," she said.

"What happened?" Caitlin asked.

I looked at Mrs. O'Breen, surprised that she had not told them.

"Your aunt, Sister Bairbre, died."

Maighread, who had remained in her seat across the room, met my eyes. "How?" she asked.

I paused. "An infection . . . not properly healed."

"No!" Caitlan cried out softly. They had both always been fascinated with their invisible aunt when they were smaller, romanticizing the fact that she was cloistered. They had drawn pictures of her and had played games where they each had taken turns pretending they were her.

Mrs. O'Breen had been looking away from me. When silence prevailed, she seemed to be counting in her head for what she thought might be an appropriate time to pass before saying, "Your skin is like alabaster. And there's a bit of rose in your cheeks. Do you . . . are you?"

A vague smile lingered at the corners of her mouth. She could see it. My hesitation seemed to answer her.

"It's not yet confirmed," I said.

"But you believe it," she said. "You know, don't you?"

I hesitated. "Yes."

"Well then," she said and drew a restrained breath in which I sensed the ferocity of her excitement.

Immediately I regretted not outrightly denying it.

"Really, Mammy?" Caitlin asked, softly startled at the news. "A baby?"

I nodded.

I looked at Maighread, waiting. But she did not get up. She stared off in the other direction and out the window.

"Look how choppy the sea is!" she said.

I went to her and leaned down, looking into her face. "Hello, Maighread, Love." Her eyes were ringed in shadow, and I recognized her exhaustion. She looked away from me, proud, lonely, and angry. I understood that she'd been having a bad time but knew she would never admit to it.

I looked at Caitlin and saw by her dismayed expression that I was right. I wondered at what point things had grown difficult.

I sat down next to Maighread.

"Tea, Deirdre?" Mrs. O'Breen asked me.

"Yes," I said. My hands trembled, and the cup rattled on the saucer. Maighread noticed it with irritation and I felt her bucking to strike out at me somehow, to hurt me. She held back, but the minute Mrs. O'Breen left the room, she started. First it was bragging about how important she was to her grandmother, a brash insistence to her voice. I sat nodding vigorously, but that further irritated her.

"Why do you look sad?" she screamed.

I shook my head, struggling to cast it off me.

She clucked her tongue. "You're weak as water!"

"What's wrong, Maighread?" I asked, confused by her fury.

"I hate the way you look at me like we're all victims of something! I hate that look on your face. I despise it!"

Caitlin banged her spoon down onto the table and yelled, "Leave Mammy alone!"

Maighread quieted, eyes wide. She struggled to catch her breath, as if she had been running.

I sat in the stunned silence, aware of the sweat on my face. I longed for sleep, a somnolence to the house in summer. I was at a loss as to what to do for Maighread.

Caitlin followed me to my room and helped me unpack. She touched my hair and held me. "I missed your smell," she said. "No one smells like you."

"What do I smell like?"

"Like macaroons."

"But I don't eat them," I said.

"But you smell like them."

I left off my unpacking and sat down on the bed. "Lovely, lovely," I said, brushing my face in her hair, drinking her in.

"What happened with Maighread?" I asked her.

"About a fortnight ago, Maighread woke up screaming for you. Nanny came into the room. Maighread asked her to write to you and tell you to come. Nanny got angry about it."

"What did Nanny say to her?" I asked.

"She told her that you were busy in Dublin and that you couldn't come right now and to go right to sleep. Nanny has no patience at night."

"Nanny drinks at night," I said half to the air.

"Yes, she drinks whiskey."

"Why didn't Maighread write me?"

"She did write you! The day after."

"I didn't get the letter!" I cried.

Caitlin and I exchanged a meaningful look. Mrs. O'Breen had likely not sent it on purpose.

"Tell Maighread to come in here to me, please, Caitlin," I said softly to her, taking her hands.

"All right," she said and went off to fetch her sister.

A few minutes later Maighread's shadow appeared in the doorway. She stopped there and would come no further. "Come in here to me, Love," I said, holding my arm out to her.

"What do you want?"

"I want to see you."

She remained where she stood, her eyes on the wall. She put her hand over her face and looked ashamed, as if her outburst had confused her.

"Caitlin tells me that you sent a letter asking me to come. But I *never* got that letter!"

She blinked and shifted her posture but would not meet my eyes.

"I wish I'd gotten it! I missed you something desperate! I didn't come sooner because this was the appointed time and I knew you wanted your independence."

She remained silent, staring at the floor.

Since she'd come into the world, I'd had less of my own anger, as if she'd had a direct vein to the place in me where it had resided; as if she had nurtured herself on that red richness before she'd left my womb and now had almost too much of it for one soul to bear. And it was as if it was all she'd had to live on those early days of her life when I had not known what to feed her. I felt an empty spot in my body from where she'd come.

She'd been very temperamental as a baby but had evened out a bit at the age of four. Since the onset of puberty, she'd been touchy, her fury easily roused.

"It's this age," Sarah Dooley had said to me once, talking of her own daughter. "If we can get to the other side of their nineteenth birthdays, we'll know we've lived through the worst."

Maighread's face looked softer now, and she sighed.

"Come here to me, Lovely," I said. Her expression grew slightly petulant in response to my summons, yet she came and stood a few feet from me. "Can I not have a kiss from you?"

She allowed me to kiss her but held her forearms protectively in over her chest, bowing her head, her brow nettled.

At the meal that evening Mrs. O'Breen held court, talking about all the things the girls had been doing. Maighread sulked but seemed less prone to lash out. She did not stare, looking to find fault. By the time the pudding was brought out, she was too tired to eat it.

"I'll take you up," I said to her, and she threw down her napkin and stood.

"I can go by myself," she said and was up the stairs.

I watched Mrs. O'Breen's face. She had washed her hands of Maighread. She was tired of the demands on her; though Maighread did not lash out at her as she did me, it was not good between the two of them. I sensed Mrs. O'Breen having tired even of Caitlin. I suspected the girls knew this and must have been hurt by it.

That night when I was sleeping, Maighread crawled into bed with me. She was shaking as she clutched me. I felt her relief to be with me. She fell asleep tangled in my arms, my tears spilling quietly onto the pillow.

In the morning when I awakened, she had already slipped off.

In bright morning light Maighread forgot her nightmare. Was her night self so divided from her morning self? Or was it that way with all of us? I felt that I was, at once, the source of all her unease and the balm for it. How would she reconcile with night and aloneness at Enfant de Marie?

I thought of Sarah Dooley's words and how right they felt. Maighread wanted me to break her out of the places where she got lost, set some limits on her terror by curbing her fury.

By midmorning I was already tired. I told myself it was the pregnancy. My breasts smarted; my eyes lost focus.

"Deirdre, are you all right?" Mrs. O'Breen asked.

"A bit tired," I answered.

I fell into a heavy sleep and woke when the early afternoon air was tender and hushed.

Downstairs they were praying. Mrs. O'Breen warbling about the purity of the saints and the two girls, her chorus, mewing in answer, their faces raised, their necks long. Being led like lambs.

In that moment, fresh from dreamless sleep, I saw everything with a supernal clarity. I saw them distinct of her; their subtler selves facing away from her. Each had experienced the chill of her limitations.

Everything bubbled up in Maighread when she saw me. I knew she was angry at me for sleeping so many hours. She was looking to stir me up. As we ascended the stairs she stopped on the landing and lingered before a tapestry of a nude, allegorical couple. She pointed at the man's naked hips and giggled with a shrillness younger than her age.

"You're acting the fool," I said. Caitlin and Mrs. O'Breen both looked at me, taken aback by my uncharacteristic manner. But my attention was on Maighread, the way she froze for the hair of a moment, the hesitation even in her step and her breath.

I felt strangely sure of my authority.

"You'll not want to behave that way at Enfant de Marie," I said calmly.

She did not breathe a word.

Later when we sat outside in the garden, I found her looking at me, her expression reassessing, surprised.

It was only a shift, I thought. Just the shift in my understanding, and the air between us was changed.

That evening after the girls were in bed, I took Bairbre's gift to Mrs. O'Breen, where she sat alone in her parlor.

"Bairbre left this for you," I said, holding the parcel out to her.

She hesitated to take it. "Do you know what it is?"

"No. I assume it's one of her lace works. It's light in weight."

She took it from me, and without opening it, set it down on the table beside her.

"Thank you," she said, and her eyes dismissed me.

In the morning the girls led me through hedgerows and field paths, wanting me to see what they'd found in the woods. The turf shed looked haunted, the door half off. The nearer we moved toward it, the more redolent the air was with rot.

They'd found the rusted remains of a child's wagon, two wheels missing. It had been under the loam and the leaves. A light rain began suddenly, and we sheltered under a canopy of the branches.

"Look," Caitlin said, pointing. It was the rain that illuminated a tiny porcelain hand near the shed, a little flexed hand, dirt in the fingernails, palm to the sky.

"Someone played here once," Maighread said. When the rain stopped, both girls went to it, squatting over the loam, moving leaves and earth aside, unburying a broken doll, cracked and disfigured, her chest cavity open and full of peat, one eye clouded over and the other wide open and blue, her perfect teeth along the porcelain gums edged with grime. The remains of her dress were decomposed, a silk that crumpled stiffly, mulching back along its edges into earth.

I held the doll and saw that under the dirt there were rhinestones pinned to the soft canvas where the hair, entrenched and matted, was woven.

"It must have been our aunt's. The nun."

"Bairbre," I said.

"She looks like an old child," Caitlin said, clearing earth from the doll's face.

"She looks like a tinker girl with jewels hidden in her hair," Maighread said.

"What kind of an infection did Sister Bairbre have?" Caitlin asked.

"They're very secretive, the nuns," I said. "They don't tell us everything."

"Nanny didn't act like anyone had died," Maighread said. Caitlin stared at the grass.

"No, and she didn't attend the funeral. Your father is very upset about that."

"Poor Daddy!" Caitlin said. They both resolved to write to him that evening.

"Our poor aunt," Caitlin said.

I took off my shawl and wrapped the doll like a baby.

"Let's bury this poor doll," Maighread said suddenly.

In the shed the girls found a little spade, and together they dug a hole in which they placed the doll, and the three of us covered it over with earth and leaves, then we knelt gravely around the little mound.

"Sanctus, Sanctus, Dominus, Sempiternam Requiem," Caitlin uttered, making the sign of the cross.

"Kyrie eleison. Christie eleison," Maighread whispered.

We wandered further, daring each other forward like three wayward children into the embankments and the trees.

We lay on the overgrowth.

"We'll get leaves in our hair," Caitlin said.

"I don't care," I said.

"Are you really going to have a baby?" Caitlin asked. She listened at my belly.

A quiet held the air, and I knew their thoughts were filled with their baby brother who had lived less than an hour. The night he was born and died the girls had been on the stairs peering down through the rails. "Like a puff of wind had put him out," they'd heard the midwife say to Mrs. Daley as she'd left the birth room.

"I know this is a girl," Maighread said. "She should be named Bairbre."

She had collected daisies and sat up now, weaving them into a chain.

A humid heat fell from the yew tree above us. Caitlin cut hazel sticks, and when we got up we hacked through the overgrowth and trespassed through high grass beyond a fence, where cattle stood watching us.

A single cow approached us like a horse might and allowed Caitlin to pet her. Maighread hung her daisy chain around its neck. She was a sweet cow, her udders heavy and beautifully veined. I wondered when she'd last calved.

It struck me suddenly that there might be some plan hatched to take the child from me. My heart racing at the thought, I walked ahead of the girls until I could collect myself. No, I said inwardly. Mrs. O'Breen did not do things that way. Yet the thought nagged at me. I felt the child asleep and present within me and knew in that moment that it was a boy, the little frond of him tucked close.

Near evening, making our way home, I pretended not to see Mrs. O'Breen there watching our return from a high window, her face pale and only half visible, like a waning planet.

At the meal I sensed a kind of weakness from her, her staunch excitement over the child within me less steady, the high curve of her chest now sunken. The gift from Bairbre must have affected her, I thought. For much of the time at table, her thoughts were far away. I was hopeful that at some point during the visit, I might see some display of grief from her over her daughter's death.

Once when Caitlin burst into laughter at something Maighread said, Mrs. O'Breen looked up from her plate, startled. She seemed confused by the affection among the three of us, the way we'd disappeared and returned with our dresses dirty, our hair undone; how we'd come in holding hands, and the wonder of it wounded her, threatened to dismantle her.

"We found an old doll," Caitlin said.

"Yes. It must have been Bairbre's," I said and watched her. She looked down at her plate and seemed to be studying her food.

"We gave it a proper burial," Maighread said, a faint tone of admonishment present in her voice.

In the quiet as we drank our tea, the lamps lit now around us, I imagined Mrs. O'Breen was watching me with one eye, like a blackbird.

For the rest of that late summer my daughters and I spent our time together, restored to one another, walking the tide. Stormy sunsets we breasted the rain at the beach. On dry evenings we carried oil lamps out toward the tide, letting the water run over our ankles.

Only at the ringing of the Angelus did Mrs. O'Breen preside, though we laughed behind our praying hands at the way she huffed when she fell to her knees, the dramatic way she held her arms open when she prayed.

Some nights we stayed up late, Caitlin playing the piano, Maighread playing bells or singing. Or we read. The happier we were, the heavier Mrs. O'Breen, the earlier she withdrew to her parlor to begin her drinking.

Mostly she stayed clear of us, and they were days of wonder. It was like exploring the grounds of a castle, whose watchful, discontented queen was temporarily usurped. The back of the house was a maze of neglected gardens partitioned with walls, some pristine, some ruined.

One day we wandered through an unlatched door in a high garden wall and found a crowd of statues clothed in mist and up to their thighs in creeper. Some had fallen into thickets, harebells growing around them. All were women, similar of feature, heavy white stone,

Greek looking. Many were broken or half destroyed, as if deliberate violence had been inflicted upon them.

Clearing creeper from around the feet of one figure, Maighread cried out, "Look at this!"

The word *Valor* was carved into the stone below its feet. They were allegorical figures. Reason and Justice were both tumbled, broken from the knees down and tangled in the thicket.

Chastity was shattered at the breast and thighs, as if beaten with a hammer or some kind of mallet. Justice had no arms, a crumbled waist and shoulders. Forgiveness's face was all but gone.

"It must have been a group of boys who did this! Only boys would do this sort of thing!" Caitlin said.

"There might be a girl who would do such a thing," Maighread said with a defiance as if called upon to defend the potential for fierceness in her sex. But her comment faded into the background.

Whoever had done it, had done it long ago, the breaks overgrown with lichen and stained brown where rain had run in rivulets, streaks running from eyes or the curves of hair, the wells of collarbones.

"Look at all the damage," Caitlin said.

Death and Despair were the two figures that remained untouched; Despair with lowered head, one large, graceful hand covering her face. Death looked upward, emotionless, staring into the light of the heavy afternoon.

Late in August we brought Mrs. O'Breen's victrola out on the grass. I clapped as the girls danced a *ceilidh*. The late-day sun suffused every flower and leaf, and ignited the blue in Maighread's hair, the copper in Caitlin's.

A deep vernal smell on the wind reminded me that summer was coming to an end. I closed my eyes and heard my mother weeping, a memory from early in my life. Something that I had not remembered until this moment. I was sitting on my father's knee, and him saying to me, "Your mother loves you so much that she's afraid the faeries will take you." And my mother looking at me in the light of the embers, her face and eyes bright with tears. "She's afraid to take her eyes off ye, for fear of losing ye."

It stunned me to recall this, for that fear in her had passed as I'd gotten older. But it was the same raw pain I felt for my girls now.

I opened my eyes and watched them dance, memorizing the graceful jump and turn of their limbs, their laughter and high, pealing voices. "How fragile," I thought, my heart beating swift and soft. "How fragile the connections between all of us."

Manus was supposed to come to Kenmare to help me see the girls to Enfant de Marie, but on the appointed day a message arrived that he could not leave the job site at present but that he'd arrange a special trip down soon just to see the girls at school. They'd been disappointed but too excited to dwell on it, with all the preparation and packing; with all the anticipation of what their new lives would be like.

I had the sense that Manus was avoiding his mother. He was still stunned by Bairbre's death and her letter, and was escaping through work.

The last night before they were to leave for Enfant de Marie, Maighread flailed in her sleep and let out an uneasy cry.

I turned the flame up in the lamp and tried to wake her, moved and guilty, thinking somehow that it was my own upset that she was attuned to and that possessed her. I gently shook her.

She sat, wide-eyed and blinking, unable to remember her dream. I gave her water and sat with her.

"Will you be all right at Enfant de Marie?" I asked.

"Yes!" she said impatiently.

"But when you have those dreams?"

She squeezed her mouth tight. "It's worse for you than it is for me!"

I sat in wonder over her words.

"If I wake up, the dream is gone! It isn't so bad! Stop making it worse than it is!" She seemed determined to move into the next stage of her life.

I sat quietly for a moment, searching her face. Her anger was right this time, her defiance. I nodded my head slowly.

"All right, Love," I whispered and kissed her softly on the temple, leaving her to herself.

SIXTEEN

*Hide the unborn child in the womb
of the North Wind.*

—FROM ATALANTA FUGIENS

With the girls settled into Enfant de Marie, I felt again as if I were floating, nothing weighting me to the ground. Distressed at the idea of being so far away from them, I could not bring myself to go back to Dublin. I told Mrs. O'Breen about the weeklong break the girls had coming at the end of October, and that I was already thinking ahead to that day.

She seemed to vacillate between discomfort at the idea of my staying and a kind of purposeful excitement that she could keep an eye on my developing pregnancy. My condition elevated me. My wishes had to be honored now. Her authority over me had thinned since midsummer, and she seemed a little afraid of me in my insistence and looked at me as if I were sacrosanct.

I had come to sense in the last weeks that the ordered elegance of her carriage was not something she was able to sustain for long. Some days she dressed plainly and did not bother with her hair. She gave a scattered, vulnerable impression, and seemed to thrive on long hours of isolation.

She usually left the house early to see to her various businesses and properties, and I was left to myself. I got up at dawn the first morning without the girls, and moving through the rooms at that early hour, everything seemed significant, a glow to the bric-a-brac, crimson and amber, reflecting on the vases and cut glass. A deepening other than a season's change of light might effect.

I had only inhabited one small area on the second floor in the west wing, but this morning the familiar corridors became complicated for me, a maze leading to dead ends. Taking a few turns in a passage to get to the descending staircase, I found myself back at the hallway outside my room, trying to trace the mistake I'd made.

Not once while the girls had still been here had I gotten lost. I resisted a feeling of panic, the familiar walls emitting a suffocating anxiety.

After making the same mistake a second and a third time, my heart was racing. I gave up easily that morning, unwilling to confront the house, half blaming my confusion on the vicissitudes of pregnancy, yet I had the uneasy feeling that the house itself was against me. By midmorning I was unable to keep my eyes open. I woke with the first shadow of late afternoon and the feeling that I should not have slept.

When I awakened anxious again the next afternoon, I resolved that I needed to get out of the house in the morning each day, before sleep pulled me under. So I made it my routine to take air early after a light meal alone at the vast, polished table.

I walked long distances, sometimes into town, drawn to the train station. Over the days the urge to go to the girls, to make sure of them, grew stronger. I resisted, knowing how much such a thing would anger Maighread. But I kept thinking about how she had needed me in the summer and I hadn't come. I went back and forth, telling myself there were new tests I had to pass with her, pacts I had undertaken to keep. My deepening weakness was a disappointment to me, yet I found myself increasingly lost, and one day, not even a fort-night after they'd gone, I purchased a ticket to Kilorglin.

I took a coach from the Kilorglin station to the outskirts of Enfant de Marie. The trees all around the cloister and the battlement were going yellow, an early leaf fall on the grounds. For an hour or so I walked near the back walls, hiding in the bracken, listening for voices. When the Angelus bell sounded I said the prayer automatically to myself, and just as I finished, I heard girls laughing and chatting, com-ing out into the courtyard where I myself had once walked as a novice.

I looked through a break in the stones of the wall, my eyes raking the little cliques of girls, some standing, others strolling. I saw Maighread in a group of four under a yew tree.

I watched her intently, trying to read her gestures. It seemed a seri-ous discussion, but one of the girls said something with great anima-tion and all four laughed, Maighread nodding her head vigorously. A little later they drifted apart and Maighread walked alone to a bench, where she sat, crossing her arms and gazing off reflectively, until a red-haired girl joined her and the two exchanged friendly banter.

In a few minutes another group of girls came out, Caitlin among them. It was like nourishment to me. I drank it all in, hardly breath-ing, full of joy to see them so easy with their friends. I heard a gate close but could not discern from which direction the sound had come. I rushed from my hiding place, thinking I might slip from the grounds unseen. As I circled the wall to the path that led down the hill, I saw a figure coming toward me, as surprised to see me as I was to see her.

The creature I met with was a soft avalanche of a nun with a slop-ing bosom and a pink face. I was startled to recognize the face, though much changed. It was Ann Carey, who had been a novice in the battlement with Bairbre and me; someone I had taken little interest in at the time.

"Is it Deirdre?" she asked.

"It is," I answered.

She seemed happy to come upon me, smiling and praising my daughters, saying that I'd been very much on her mind since they'd come.

This reception made me want to confide in her.

"I've been worried about my daughters. I just had to make sure of them."

I explained that Maighread had nightmares from which she could not awaken, and that it was me who she called out for. It was a precarious thing for some to be alone, to be adrift and disconnected, I explained to Ann.

"Yes," she said in a soft voice, and squeezed her lips as if she were moved. "If such a thing occurs, Deirdre, I'll take the tenderest care of her. I may not be you, but I'll be second best to you, I promise. But let me reassure you about both of them," she said and went on about Caitlin's kindness to her friends and that Maighread was admired for excellence in her schoolwork, and how each was popular in her own way among her peers.

"Such fine girls could only be the results of a devoted mother," she said to me. "Ah sure, girls like yours know they are loved!"

I squeezed her hand, moved and amazed by her generosity.

"I always remember you, Deirdre. The way you were so fervent. I used to wish I had your fire."

"Ah, no, Ann. You couldn't have wished such a thing!" I said in wonderment. She smiled at me, and I tried to understand how I'd been so oblivious of her. What else in all the world was I so blind to?

"Please don't tell them that I was here. Maighread would be furious. She'd say I was weak as water and she'd be right."

"I'll not tell them, Deirdre, but I'll keep special watch over them."

When I returned to Kenmare, Mrs. O'Breen and her two sisters were sitting together at the dining table. "Behold!" cried Moyna Furey, rising to her feet. "The handmaid of the Lord!"

Mrs. O'Breen pressed at her sister's forearm, and Moyna sat again, looking away from me, then hid behind the lilies at the table, which leaned and seemed to peer like nuns from under their white hoods.

At the meal, her eyes kept darting up to mine as she bent over her plate, furrows between her brows as she trimmed fat off her meat.

"It was Deirdre's idea to stay here," Mrs. O'Breen said, "and now, well, I want to keep her here!" As always in her sisters' company she was highly animated, though I had come to recognize the falseness of that ebullience.

"What have you been doing with your days, Deirdre?" Ethna asked.

"Walking," I said. "In Kenmare."

"Have you walked yet up the Cashel Road? A mile and a quarter to the south. Saint John of the Cross, the seminary school."

"No, I haven't."

"The grounds there are lovely! A little bit of woodlands surrounding it. And peaceful."

"I'll have to go that way," I said quietly and sipped my tea.

A conversation ensued among the three of them, and as I had witnessed before, Ethna and Moyna were called by their Christian names, while Mrs. O'Breen was addressed as 'Madam,' though, as always, they made no deference in their behavior to her, and she seemed to be posturing for them, holding her head high and her face at an angle, displaying the stretch of her neck. I wondered why she always dressed up for them when they came. Why she took pains with her hair and painted her eyes.

Blighted early on in the wish to call her "Mother," I had never asked Manus what her Christian name was.

That same night, sensing something afoot, I came out of my room and stood at the end of the corridor, looking toward the wing the aunts occupied when they visited, the same wing in which I knew Mrs. O'Breen's room was located. I heard a clatter and low voices. One door was ajar, and I could see shadows moving within.

I went back to my room and waited an hour or so before venturing out again and back to that wing. I opened the door where the shadows had been moving. Inside I found a kind of nursery filled with religious objects. A Sacred Heart lamp had been left burning before a statue of the Blessed Virgin Mary. Against one wall stood a rack of unlit votives. I approached the strange, dark cradle at the center of it all. It was oddly shaped, unlike any cradle I had ever seen, its black wood canopy elaborately carved in a kind of medieval-looking detail, and set with a band of discolored green velvet, overly embellished with pearls. The sight of it upset me. I touched it and it rocked with a dissonant squeak that made tears start from my eyes. The bolts issued an unsettling odor, as if made unctuous and bloated from overoiling.

The next day at the afternoon meal, Mrs. O'Breen asked me if I wanted to accompany the three of them on a visit to the grounds of Saint John of the Cross.

"It's a wonderful school for boys who will eventually enter the Jesuit order," Ethna said.

When I remained silent, they all looked expectantly at me.

"This child might not be a boy."

A collective cloud passed over the three of them.

"But if it is, this particular school is best for him."

The oily smell of the damnable cradle came to mind, sending a wave of nausea through me. "If this child is a boy, he might not want to be a priest," I said.

Again there was a dark silence before Ethna said, "You must assign your child his destiny."

My heart battered at my chest. "I would never do that," I said.

"How will he know who he is if you don't help him? You don't come from a strong, established family. Your circumstances are cut off. But if you'd come from an established family, you'd have had your role in life directed for you."

"No," I said. "I would not do that to my child."

The three exchanged looks.

Ethna gazed at me almost placidly, though her cheeks were suffused. "Then you leave him adrift in the world. You fail him as a mother."

"You're being harsh, Ethna," Mrs. O'Breen said, but I had the sense that all of this had been discussed and that Mrs. O'Breen's role was to modulate, to soften, to seem to take my side if I proved argumentative.

Suddenly, as if she'd been containing a wild vehemence, Moyna cried, "One of your girls, Caitlin I think, surely could have been a nun!" Immediately she seemed startled by her own inappropiate ejaculation, sat back, and retreated against the silent tide of disapproval from her sisters.

"Nuns are supposed to have vocations," I said.

"Did you have a vocation?" Ethna asked me.

I looked away.

"It's painful not to know what one is supposed to do. It's painful not to have direction," Moyna said.

"My children should have choices. I had nowhere else to go but to the religious life. But my children have both their parents living, and there is money." There was a long silence in which no one much stirred. A penumbra grew on the air, effacing the room of its opulence.

Moyna's voice broke the silence. With a more controlled impatience, she said, "You behave as if you think there is something terrible about what we want for the child. As if there's something wrong with encouraging a vocation, as if it isn't a wonderful thing!"

My skin burned. The food on my plate looked gray in the ill-colored light.

"I'm tired," I said and stood, leaving the table.

"Deirdre," Ethna said, and I turned to face her. "You shouldn't be contrarian. You knew what was expected of you when you married into this family."

That night I came out of my room looking for them so I might listen to what they were saying. I heard them in Mrs. O'Breen's parlor. Though I kept hidden and at a distance, their voices were not subdued.

"It's all taking too long!" Moyna said.

"The child in her will be a boy," Mrs. O'Breen said with a faint note of hysteria in her voice. "I know it!"

"What control have you over her? Very little, it would appear," Ethna said.

"A thousand things could go wrong."

"I know it will be all right," Mrs. O'Breen said.

"As you've known everything else, Madam . . . ," Moyna said resentfully.

I thought of leaving, of going to Dublin, but something polarized me; an odd conviction that I was safer in Kenmare, as if I were in the very eye of a storm and moving away from its center I might get lost again in its force, swept away. And I felt my resolve deepening against Mrs. O'Breen and her sisters, as if observing them helped me build strength against them.

It wasn't much longer until the girls' October break. I knew I would not bring them back here. I counted the days until I could see them. I remembered Sarah Dooley telling me about a little hotel on Inch Strand, the Elen, westerly along the Dingle Peninsula, not at all far from Kilorglin. She'd taken her children there on holiday a few years back; a simple place but comfortable, away from everything. The next day I went to town and posted a letter to the Elen, making arrangements, and then I wrote to Manus asking him to meet us there.

A few nights later, joining me at the dining table, Mrs. O'Breen looked a little unsteady, struggling for poise, and I suspected that she had been drinking since her sisters had left earlier in the afternoon.

In the middle of the main course, I asked her suddenly, "What is your Christian name?"

She looked up from her plate, surprised. She blinked, and in a gossamer voice, answered, "Esmerelda."

"Why don't your sisters call you by your name?"

"Since I was a child, they haven't called me by my name. They always called me 'Sister,' because I was supposed to become a nun. Only my mother called me Esmerelda."

She continued eating for a few minutes. My question had made her thoughtful. She put her fork down and with a small, wistful smile, said, "My mother said it was a name for a beauty. You could never name a plain girl Esmerelda. My mother was interested in the effect of my physical beauty on the world. She brought suitors to the house for Ethna and Moyna, and I always felt their eyes on me. They often spoke to her about me, but she told them I was destined for the convent. And though I had to pray more than my sisters, she dressed me up, she cultivated my beauty. My sisters have never liked me, Deirdre. Not only was I our mother's favorite, all their suitors fell in love with me. My mother liked that, that she could show me to them and then tell them that they couldn't have me."

"Why?" I asked.

"So God would know what an extraordinary offering I was," she said as if I should have figured that out.

"Our mother seemed to take pains to make my sisters less attractive. Ethna could have been a handsome woman." She was quiet for a few moments, then looked directly at me. "You were a lovely offering to God, Deirdre. There have been times I've wondered if perhaps He's angry at me for having taken you. I saw something in you all those years ago, Deirdre, in your veil in the choir loft, wearing the same white novice robes I'd worn at your age. 'Be it done unto her according to Thy word,' I'd whispered that day." She took a sip from her glass, then said, "You offered such a malleable face. There wasn't a spark of rebellion in you."

I waited for a few moments, my heart going hard at the insufficient, idealized way she'd once seen me.

"You don't look deeply enough at people, Madam," I said.

Her face froze.

"You don't bother to look into anyone's heart but your own."

Color shot slowly into her skin.

She put her napkin down and, without looking at me, got up and walked out of the room.

That night as I was preparing for bed there was a knock on the door. I opened it to find Mrs. O'Breen standing there. She seemed sober as she said in a controlled voice, "You're a part of this family. You don't want to be responsible for its downfall. You've married into a kind of royalty, and the royal are responsible for those who came before them."

It was an odd, irrational thing to say; something she had once said to me before. How could anyone be responsible for those who'd come before them? What did that mean? Yet it rang a deep note in me, not in relation to her family but to my own, and I tried to fathom it.

She must have seen the effect of her words on me, because when I looked at her again, she was searching my face.

"You'll see the sense of your child studying at the seminary," she said softly. "You'll come to know that it's the right thing to do."

For the remaining days before I was to leave for Kilorglin, I avoided Mrs. O'Breen. I had my evening meals sent to my room on a tray.

Some mornings I'd find things left for the baby on the shelf outside my bedroom door: soft blankets and little sweaters; children's books illustrated with corpulent angels, a sweet-faced, haloed Christ shepherding lambs. I put them into the closet in my room, where they accrued.

Often, awakening in the middle of the night, I sensed her somewhere in the house, listening for me.

The night before I was to leave to get the girls, I went into one of the downstairs drawing rooms to return a book to the shelf where I'd found it. I opened a desk drawer in search of a piece of paper to make a list of things I wanted to get for the girls, when I saw the gauze bag I had delivered to Mrs. O'Breen for Bairbre.

I hid it inside my robe, took it with me up to my room, and closed the door. Sitting on the edge of my bed, I slowly untied the cords and opened the cloth bag, then carefully unwound successive layers of cloth until what was revealed was hair, gathered like a loose stook of barley, tied like a broom lengthwise and bound in three or four places with coarse thread. The hair cut from Bairbre's head the day she took her vows. The hair meant to be buried with a nun at the end of her life; the nun's bridal gift to Christ.

Stunned, I lifted it slowly and held it before me. A few loose strands, drawn to the wool of my robe, clung to my chest, softly crackling with electricity.

"Bairbre," I said softly, as if in response.

I lay it across my lap and touched it with my fingertips. Tears stung my eyes.

It still maintained the dark gloss and blue highlights I had once admired. I could hear again Sister Vivian's shears sighing like a scythe, and see it falling to the altar floor in drifts.

Seventeen

I took the girls by train to the Elen hotel. The first day there it rained. The owner of the hotel, Mrs. Ross, was very friendly to the girls and gave them a box of chocolate. She helped us send a message to Manus in Dublin, reminding him that he should come and meet us here.

We had tea brought to the room. Caitlin read to us, poems by Kipling about setting out to sea, and a poem about horses. *"Where run your colts at pasture? / Where hide your mares to breed?"* All morning we nibbled wedges of cold, buttered toast and ate from the box of chocolates.

In the afternoon we stood outside under the awning, watching the rain on the sea, the sky to the west, broken with areas of brightness, evoking a misty incandescence. I felt as if I were breathing for the first time in ages.

The second day when we came downstairs into the hotel lobby, Mrs. Ross presented us with a message from Manus:

Impossible to come now. I am sorry. All love to my girls. I promise to make loads of time at Christmas.

Both girls were disappointed. Caitlin started to cry, and Mrs. Ross, moved by Caitlin's tears, rummaged through her desk, looking for something to give her to distract her, as if Caitlin were a small child.

"Oh, Love! Oh, Love!" the old woman said softly and pleadingly, handing her a map of County Kerry. "Ye mustn't cry on your holiday!"

Caitlin thanked her, wiping her tears, and, as we climbed the stairs, both girls exchanged looks, suppressing their laughter over the old woman's earnest manner.

A serving woman came and stoked our fire while the three of us lounged on our unmade beds and ordered more tea. I soaked in their company, listened to the stories of their friends and of the nuns, struggling to rest and to forget Kenmare.

I was waiting to feel the baby's first movement. I had felt my other three babies move by four and a half months. It was coming on five now, and this delicate one would begin anytime.

I told the girls I was going to nap and lay on my side on my bed facing away from them as they unfolded their map.

"Seo é léarscáil," I heard a familiar, girlish voice say, startling me as if from a dream.

I sat up and looked. It had been Maighread speaking.

"I think you said, *'This is a map,'*" Caitlin said.

"Seo é léarscáil," Maighread said again. "Now you try it."

"Seo é léarscáil," Caitlin repeated with less confidence.

"You're speaking Irish," I said.

"It's compulsory now in school, Mammy," Caitlin said.

"It isn't . . . ," I said.

"It's an ancient and beautiful language," Maighread said defensively, interpreting my startled reaction as some form of disapproval. She shook her head dismissively, and the two continued unfolding the map of County Kerry.

"Here's where we are: Inch Strand," Maighread said, her finger tracing the Dingle Peninsula.

"Here's the Great Blasket Island! An Blascoad Mor," Caitlin said, and they bent their heads over the map.

"Sister Elizabeth says that island Irish is the purest. The Blasket Island in particular. Preserved there. Medieval Irish, it is! Unruined by English invasion."

"An Blascoad Mor," Caitlin repeated, struggling to make the syllables smooth in her mouth.

"It's where I was born," I said.

They both turned and looked at me.

"And where I spent my childhood," I said.

"You're from Ballyferriter," Maighread protested.

"No."

They both turned expectantly toward me.

"I wasn't allowed to speak the Irish when I first went to Enfant de Marie. I was made to be ashamed of it."

"But Sister Elizabeth says the Blasket Islanders speak it with great dignity. And that they all speak like poets!"

"Well, the nuns are singing a different tune now than then. They thought islanders as common as ditchwater. There was one nun in particular hated the Irish language. Sister Dymphna."

"She's still there, Mammy!" Caitlin cried.

"Is she? She must be an old one now."

"Ah, that one! I know her," Maighread said. "All withered up in her iron chair."

"She has a sad story behind her," Caitlin said. "When she was small she lost her entire family to the Famine."

"Sister Elizabeth, the history nun, says that that's how the Irish language was abandoned to begin with. After the Famine it was identified with dire poverty and humiliation," Maighread said.

"And that's what it must be with old Sister Dymphna. Hearing the language must bring it all back to her," said Caitlin.

"She was dreadful to me. You'd think that someone who has suffered so would be compassionate to others."

"Pain turns some people into monsters," Maighread said.

I looked at her in wonder. Where had she heard this, or was it her own observation?

There was a moment of silence before I said, "Sister Elizabeth sounds like quite the popular teacher!"

"Oh, she's lovely. And fierce!" Maighread said.

"Yes!" Caitlin broke in. "She's young and has a grand, low voice and speaks like an actress."

"She says that the Irish are heirs to an ancient civilization," Maighread said, "and that we should again make our own language the national language!"

"There was no such talk in the convent in my day."

"There are great changes in the air, Mammy!" Maighread said.

They both gazed expectantly at me. An interval of thoughtful silence followed.

"Say something to us in Irish," Caitlin said.

I thought a moment. "Tugain grá do m'iníonachta," I said.

I could see that Maighread understood immediately. It took Caitlin a moment, and then she said, "Did you say that you love your daughters?"

"Yes," I smiled.

"Wait until we tell Sister Elizabeth!" Caitlin said.

I felt their sudden new pride. They looked at me, marveling.

They each took a turn saying something in Irish, the other trying to translate.

"Cuir sin faoi d'fhiacail agus cogain é," Maighread said.

"Something about smoking a pipe," Caitlin said.

"I said, *Put that in your pipe and smoke it,*'" Maighread said.

"Ba cheart thú do cheann a scrudú."

"Something about my head being painted," Caitlin said, making a face.

"I said, *'You ought to have your head examined.'* " Maighread cried, and both of them burst into laughter.

I sat back listening, and for a little while they spoke only Irish, broken with laughter.

"Ta an fharraige ghlórach," Maighread said. *The sea is loud.*

"Ta an fharraige chiúin." *The sea is quiet.*

"Ta srón dearg ag Bean Uí Rós." *Mrs. Ross has a red nose.*

"Ta srón Bean Uí Rós as alt." *Mrs. Ross's nose is out of joint.*

That night in the dark as the girls lay sleeping, I recalled the sound of them speaking the Irish. Caitlin with an odd, unpracticed cadence; and Maighread like it was her own low, ululating tongue. She could have been of the island itself. And lying there I knew that I had always associated Maighread with the Blasket. With fierce yearning and squalls of wind.

As I began to fall asleep a phrase surfaced, and I half awoke speaking it: Ise a bhí liom go deo. *She who has always been with me.* I seemed able to identify things; the odd patterns of connection between us like drawing lines between the stars of a constellation. I felt Maighread tuned to something of mine that I dared not look at myself. I had bequeathed to her my inconsolability. It was her legacy from me, I thought. All that I would not bear or feel, I'd left to her.

And I wondered if it was that mute pact between us that she had always bucked against.

How deeply buried the things are that drive us, I thought. How remote we each are from ourselves.

The next three days were temperate, and we walked on the strand. The girls often ran ahead of me, long gandery strides trailing their petticoats, to gather shells or look at things washed in with the tide. I'd watch them, grateful for the high winds on the shore, which could be blamed for the tearing from my eyes.

The third day there I opened the girls' map, and looked at the Great Blasket Island. The mental picture I had always kept of it was that it was a great distance out to sea. But there it was on the map, so close to the lip of the Dingle Peninsula.

The wind blew down from the west and on it I smelled my girlhood.

The late sun shone mildly, the blue of Maighread's black hair almost purple like the wet shells of mussels. "Uair an tréadaí," my father had called this time of day. *The Shepherd's Hour.* I saw his back, his big hand pulling mussels from the rock. I saw him walking thigh deep in the tide, where he hunted out the creatures with jellied tentacles, things with no faces, soft and quivery but with sad eyes, like humans enchanted by the hags or the faeries and biding their time in the tidepools.

And I saw my father's face suddenly as I had not let myself remember it, his near direct gaze at the sun, the whites of his eyes red, the irises almost milky blue.

And I searched the memory for my mother's face because I knew she was there, too. I felt her there but I could not fix her with any clarity. I could only breathe her like weather.

Our plan had been to leave Inch on the fourth day and spend a night in Killarney, where we might visit the castle, but as we sat at the depot waiting for the eastbound train, Maighread said, "Let's not go east, Mammy."

"Let's spend the extra day on the Great Blasket Island," Caitlin said.

"Oh, no," I said. "I won't go there."

They badgered me a bit more, but I was firmly against the idea. They exchanged disappointed looks.

The eastbound train would be a while, we had been told. I sat on a bench looking seaward, a watery sun out, while the girls walked toward the beach and seemed to be conferring. When I heard the train arrive I felt the little child within me undulate like a fish. I waited, not breathing, not moving. A heartbeat later there was another tiny shiver. Instead of joy, my heart plummeted. I'd felt in those tiny convulsions how precariously he held to me. I told myself to calm, to bide with him.

"Sta-a-ay," I said inwardly, drawing out the word, my senses tuning themselves, straining to catch any tiny flutter. "Sta-ay."

The girls had turned at the sound of the train and watched me from the sand, but I made no move to get up and I did not call them over.

When the train was gone the girls remained in the distance. The wind was high and had a cold edge to it. I felt their eyes on me as I stared at the wrinkling waves.

I was thinking of my father. Of sitting on his knee by firelight while he talked about the rough justice of the Fenian warriors. What my grandmother called "the stars of irony" gleaming in his eyes. In the right mood, my father could talk a blue streak.

It was the romances I loved to hear him tell. Particularly Cuchullan's enchantment by the faery woman, Fand; talking about the nature of love when one is under a spell, how terrible it is the way it gets into the skin and hurts: raptures and agonies by turns; fevers and shivers, a kind of illness that makes one capable of desperate feats.

"You miss the Great Blasket Island, don't you?" Maighread asked me.

They pressed at me with questions:

"Were you really fourteen, Mammy, when you left there?"

"Yes."

"My age!" Maighread said. "Ah, then, you weren't such a child."

"I was a child. You're both children," I said.

They wanted to know more, and I told them about my mother losing her own father to the sea when she was small, and about her first love, Macdarragh the mute boy, and how he was lost to the sea as well. And about how she met my own father and how she would come to taunt him over Macdarragh.

"And how did they die? Was it as you told us once years ago? Were they crossing the bay when their boat went down in a storm?"

I watched the light off to the west. "No," I said. "That isn't how it goes."

"Tell us."

I looked at them both. "It's not something I've ever told," I said.

They peered at me, yearning to know.

We heard the whistle of an approaching train, soon grinding slowly to a halt. A train facing westerly.

Caitlin whispered something to Maighread, then approached one of the porters, whom she spoke with. He nodded and waved us over. "There's room for us on this train, Mammy," Caitlin called. "He says we get out at Dunquin and there's passage across to the island."

I looked with agitation into Maighread's face.

"They were our grandparents," she said. "It's our own history you've been keeping from us."

I felt the magnet of the sea and the wind. Where else in the world was there really to go?

The porter led us to one of the finer passenger cars, but the girls wanted to sit in the back, where we were among an older trope of people who smelled of sheep and dead fires and where we heard the bawling of calves. Each girl in her elegant clothes, reverent and quiet, taking in everything she saw.

When the afternoon sky went black with rain, the porter lit a lamp in the train car. A woman and a sallow-faced child leading two calves by ropes boarded our car. The woman bedded her child down between the two calves for their warmth. My girls stole discreet glances at the child, keeping a wide-eyed silence. Everything shimmered with the smell of seal oil, of animals and damp alfalfa. I could hear in the next car pigs in creels.

Moving west I recognized place names on the signs: Slea Head, Smerwick Harbour. The girls, familiar with the names from their map, whispered them to one another as if they were in church.

A ragged ballad singer got on when the train made a stop. He moved through the cars singing a song about English treachery and deceit.

Maighread gave him a few coins, while Caitlin offered a toffee to the sallow-faced child who had sat up from her bed between the calves to listen to the singing.

The red sky deepened to crimson. When it went dark, it was like passing through a curtain. We had moved from a lit century to a dim one. We had crossed into the past.

The train was up the gap through Croagh Martin and moving to Slea Head when we stopped and I saw the Great Blasket herself, breasting the waves, a vast, dark creature.

In Dunquin we moved toward Mrs. O'Leary's, the nearest bed-and-breakfast to the pier and the train. It was a gray house that faced seaward. I had a terrible longing to lie down and close my eyes. I knocked and a short, bent woman let us in, squinting through cloudy glasses, sussing us up in our fine clothes.

"Have you only these bags?" she asked.

I nodded. I heard a gannet shriek, turned and saw it circling, and had a sudden wish that we had not come. "Do you have a room that does not face the sound?" I asked.

Her eyes stopped briefly on my face.

"Mammy!" Maighread said. "Don't you want to face the sea?"

"No," I said, feeling the sting of sudden tears.

"You're white to the lips!" Mrs. O'Leary said.

"My mother's with child," Caitlin said.

"The sea makes my stomach want to rise," I said.

The girls supported me as the old woman led us up a narrow staircase. If a room could be pitied, it was this room that she'd brought us to. A room in need of air, with curtains faded and gray. Mrs. O'Leary went straight to the casement, and a bit of dust rose as she pushed it up.

"No one ever takes this room," she said apologetically. "It's always the rooms over the sound they're wanting."

She brought us water in a basin, then said, "Breakfast is at half seven. If you're looking to visit the island, the ferry leaves at nine. If you're hungry, there's a shop still open up the road." She nodded at us and left the room.

That night while the girls slept, I went outside and found a bench near the harbor, where I looked toward the island in the darkening light, trying, for the child's sake, to eat a currant bun we had bought earlier in the shop.

Centuries had passed and would go on passing and the water would remain as mad for that rock as ever, as crazed in love with it, attending, attending. Shamelessly throwing itself, crashing at it. And that both moved me and put a pain through me. I stayed out until I saw the dim paraffin lights quenching in the dark and distant windows.

Crunching along a gravel pathway, I made my way back to Mrs. O'Leary's and up the creaking stairs.

"No one'll be crossing to the island this day," Mrs. O'Leary said to us early the next morning. "Look at the sea."

While the girls finished their breakfast I wandered out toward the pier, where a group of fishermen were securing their boats to the dock. I recognized Seamus Fehan, my father's crony. He looked the same but more deeply weathered, his hair gone gray. To my relief, he didn't recognize me, and how could he have; a full-grown woman I was now, in tailored clothes and fine black boots. No one might know me for an islander. He spoke to the man he was with, and the sound of his voice for a moment confused itself with the memory of my own father's, sounds tasting of salt and brine.

I remembered Seamus Fehan, younger and with darker hair, smelling of wind and fishing, drinking warm milk near our fire, from a cracked majolica bowl, while my grandmother boosted the fire with dried heather, the swish and gusts of her skirts causing the cinders to bloom.

I could not move. I stared at his shoes and saw them caked with the soil of the Blasket. He smelled of that peat, of those fires. I was afraid of the beautiful, dovetailing sounds from his throat and how they gored me with longing.

I kept a step behind Seamus Fehan, my head bowed, smelling the air around him, listening to him. He turned and held my eyes, but I could see he could not figure out why I looked familiar to him.

I tore my eyes from his and watched the waves indulging a chaotic mood, working themselves into a dark boil.

Wandering back into Mrs. O'Leary's, I found my daughters sitting before her fire.

I stared into the flames. "Seamus Fehan," I uttered, the name hurting in the craw of me. I meditated on the fire, and seeing me communing with my past, struggling under its thrall, the girls moved close to me. I felt Caitlin's kiss on my temple.

"Tell us, Mammy," Maighread whispered.

In my mind I moved through the details of my story, searching for the place to begin.

Eighteen

The spring I was twelve, the cottage floor was perpetually damp, muddy in places with all the rain, and my mother and I brought bag after bag of dry sand up from the beach to spread over it. But she tired of doing it one day and left it to me, dailiness wearing away at her.

My father watched her that spring. He saw her clutching the little sculpture of the centaur that Macdarragh had given her, the one she'd promised him she'd tossed into the sea.

Once I'd heard my father ask her, "How can I ever compete with the two of them, Macdarragh and your own father fused together in your heart?"

He hated the little brass centaur. How many times as a child had I heard him ask her to throw it in the sea? Wanting her back from the distances her mind went when she held it, my father prepared to go out in a curragh with Seamus Fehan and Padraig Scanlon to harvest the mackerel. This brought her focus back to him, wild as she was against the idea, for they'd be out at night with their nets. But my father set himself on it and she could not change his mind, even though she threatened to keep him from her bed so he'd have to sleep on the hard stone of the hearth.

She said he did it purposefully to rouse the suffering in her so he could see how much she needed him. He shook his head and told her that it was for food.

"I'd rather eat poorer than the rest than have the sea swallow you and keep you from me. I'll eat the rocks and the kelp," she pleaded.

I saw him close his eyes, gratified that she needed him so. He wanted to relent. I saw the thought move again and again across his face. But for something else in him, measuring, always measuring some level of devotion in her. It wasn't the pain in her voice that he hungered after but the intensified focus he suddenly had in her eyes, his way of switching her thoughts from Macdarragh to him. He tried to weigh her feelings like so much oats or flour. If he paid close enough attention he thought he might navigate my mother's moods. He took terrible risks to bring her back to him.

She waited as he held his breath, considering what he might do. When he stood and took up his net again she screamed, "Then I'm on a deathwatch! I'll get ready for your wake!" She cleared the table of plates and cups with the side of her arm, banging down the twelve long candles in bottles. And every night before he left they went through this, the candles set out in preparation each time. The twelve candles representing the disciples of Christ, eleven lit and one giving no light in memory of Judas the Betrayer.

Sometimes I thought he did want to meet up with death; that he might usurp the place her dead kept in her heart.

I felt the unbearable burden of his leaving. Some nights I woke to her keening and thought she'd received the anticipated news.

"The stars have gone missing, Deirdre," she'd said one night, her eyes on the weather. "The way they did the night the sea took the little boat." The two boats that had taken her father and Macdarragh down had become one boat.

She tried to draw comfort from me, holding me and rubbing her face in my hair. Such a touch always inspired in me a terrible hopelessness: I could not soothe her.

Seamus Fehan arrived at our house at dawn explaining that they'd been in the curragh and the sea had risen over them. Seamus had been able to clutch at a shelf of rock, but Liam had washed under.

Three days after, a dead man came in to shore. Three men followed by a band of women brought him up to the house, where the table was ready in preparation. "The sea is a jealous woman," Kate Beg uttered under her breath. "She selects the best men, then takes them for herself. And just look at them when she gets through with them!"

"Does the sea shrink a man as well?" I asked, this body a head shorter than my own father.

"The sea distorts and changes the features so you'd not recognize your own but think him some man from the far reaches of blackest Africa," Seamus Fehan explained.

It was because she couldn't bear it any longer that it was easier for my mother to believe this was him.

First her father, then Macdarragh, and now Liam. Was it God against her? she asked, and the women silenced her, looking around them as if God were a man who might be eavesdropping at the door.

The three men who'd brought him set off that very hour for the mainland to get a coffin, so he could be borne again across the sea and buried in the Ventry churchyard.

One could reduce the danger of a haunting by touching the remains. But I would not. I did not believe it was my father, and in case it was, I wanted him to haunt me.

A beautiful placard was carved: "Liam O'Coigligh, Beloved husband to Molleen Mohr." I painted flowers around it. My mother and I stayed behind as the boat went off and the body was buried in the Ventry churchyard.

So, a day later, when my father walked up from the pier, a battered man, his clothes so shredded they hardly covered him, his hair plastered to his forehead with streams of blood, people, hushed and terrified, followed behind the walking dead.

It was a good half hour before my mother was convinced that he was not a ghost. She tended him for days then, cleaning and applying seal oil to his many wounds. He lay in the great iron bed while she pampered him. He told her how the sea had thrown him this way and that, taking him down very low into its deepest chambers. How he'd died there and then, but that in death he'd ached for her. "For you, Molleen Mohr. In death I could not let go of you." He told her that he'd washed up onto a shelf in the craggy rock, and his spirit had floated and hovered there until it had found its way back into his body. Finally he'd gotten enough strength when the sea was easy, to swim across from the cliffside back to the island.

He began to shiver with emotion. "I'm the one that won't leave you, Molleen Mohr. Even dead I come back to you."

When he was strong again, my mother and he walked linked on the roads and pathways of the island. Mo Roí, she called him. *My king.* The island women followed, moved by the romance of my father's condition. A man with a body in this world, and one in the next. *The dead man who walks*, they called him and wanted to be near him, my mother proud that he was coveted, his cuts and bruises decorative like badges. Girls and women murmuring awe, throwing flowers, carrying lamps at dusk and lighting their way. And I trailed after, among the adoring, the other girls coming up and touching my hair or looking into my eyes because I was his daughter.

He did not go out again trawling that spring. Everyone brought us fish and helped my grandmother harvest her potatoes and cabbages.

But as the world settled again, I saw that something had come ajar in my mother. At first she was confused. Once my father walked in the door, and she started, as if he were still dead and his return had been only a dream. I saw her have to remember everything. I saw her breathing hard, agonized and bewildered. I saw her hold her head in her hands. And for a while there was a strange ring on the air. A dead man could return. The dead came back.

When the thrall of his return had worn thin, she watched him mistrustfully. She believed in her heart that he'd tortured her so on purpose. I watched her eyes, the way she snuck secret looks at him at night when we sat around the fire eating our potatoes and fish.

Slowly, she ebbed away from him.

'Twas the following spring when the French boat was anchored in the sound, the island men crazy to gather their lobster pots from around Beginish. The boat blew its horn, and the curraghs were hurrying about, hauling in their cargoes.

All the men were excited. The sea harvest was great that year. The French offered whiskey and porter and tobacco. The women insisted the men get money instead, but the men went wild with the celebrations.

Padraig Scanlon, the islander whose pots had brought in the greatest load of lobster, decided he would buy a horse with his money, horses being a luxury, expensive creatures. There'd been none on the island for over a hundred years. Padraig had the biggest plot on the island and wanted a horse to pull his plow.

The entire population of the island stood on the pier watching the boat coming across the sound, the waves lifting and dropping it. The docking facilities for a ship that size were inadequate, so the horse was tethered, held aloft in a high harness, and swayed a while in the air before being lowered by rope from the boom into the sea. The islanders, up to their necks in the waves, drove the poor creature up onto the sand.

It was golden, sandy colored, fifteen hands, Padraig said, its voluminous mane and tail riddled with briars. Frills and strings of saliva flew from its lips around its bared teeth, the women all whispering to it and stroking the nervous giant as they might calm an upset child: *"Wisha! Wisha!"* and kissing the side of its face. It was, from that moment, between the horse and the women of the Great Blasket, love at first sight.

The horse's peculiar attraction to my mother could have been taken for granted. Some creatures took naturally to one person over another. But Kate Beg, who remembered the day that the schoolmistress and her tall, beautiful son had come to the island and how the son's eyes had only been for Molleen Mohr, saw that it was just the same with this creature. And didn't he look like Macdarragh himself with his long face, beautifully boned, and the same sandy-colored mane of hair.

"The devil if it isn't himself!" Kate Beg cried.

And so the horse was called Macdarragh. And my mother stood before it wistfully, almost afraid. The horse nodded and moved close to her. She touched its face and took in her breath ever so softly. It flicked its ears, and with its mouth closed made a low, guttural neigh. "You're like the mute one himself," she said to him, "with the sounds from the depths of you."

The women laughed softly, moved, remembering the other, uttering about the truth of it. He was Macdarragh to a *t* they said, the closest article imaginable; mute and larger than life, nervy but gentle, full of restrained power.

"He said he'd be back to you, Molleen Mohr, and if this isn't himself before us, then I've not lived a day. The shape-shifter!" Kate cried and touched the animal's flank gingerly and devotedly with her palm.

Macdarragh refused to pull a plow, though the men hit him with switches, the horse up on its hind legs screaming. The men who'd already come to dislike him.

"It's too fine a creature to break its back on work!" Kate Beg scolded, running in among them, scattering the men like boys.

"It's got donkey blood in it, stubborn as the doost!" cried Padraig.

"No donkey in this fine creature!" Kate Beg screamed.

"We've been duped because we're island men and they know we don't know horses. Look at the twist of its back leg. A gimp leg. You've been bamboozled, Padraig. This horse'll do nothing for you but eat and shit."

The men talked about transporting the horse back to the mainland, filling themselves with riot and severity, but the women took shifts guarding Macdarragh where he was put to graze in Glenagalt.

In his company the women could do naught but utter his praises. "He's a creature out of the old stories. Look at his lovely long tail! The sweep of it!"

I was among the women and girls gathered at the fence to gaze and to feed him flowers, and he nuzzled us with his velvety nose and the soft breath through his nostrils. Better than any dog Macdarragh was for affection.

Before he'd even see my mother come into view, Macdarragh would throw his head up and sniff at the air, then move side to side in anticipation. He'd raise his mouth to the side and screech. When she was close, he rumbled softly and held her eyes, besotted.

One night the men watched warily from the cliff while the women gathered around Macdarragh on the beach and lit a fire, feeding him directly from the home grain sacks, the oats that would have made the next morning's porridge. We plaited his mane with fuchsia and ferns.

The men drank the whiskey they'd gotten from the Frenchmen, and as the night deepened, the tinier children were bedded down in blankets in the sand.

"Godless heathen lot!" one of the men cried.

"We're all cuckolded by a horse!"

"Hey Cathleen!" Padraig cried to his wife. "That one's a gelding and'll not give you what you're after."

"Hah!" she cried.

"He's got a good dangle on him, but it'll not be standing up to you."

"Listen to the filth they're speaking."

I went alone with my mother to visit Macdarragh one day, feeding him the leaves of an entire cabbage so that we might feel his warm breath on our palms and fingers. We played a game with him, taking turns, standing in front of him with our backs to him, and he would push us between our shoulder blades with his great head, propelling us forward. A kind of thrill in the jolt of it that made us laugh and feel both dreamy and giddy.

Once we visited him with our own hairbrush to free his mane and tail of the briars. That day I saw my father watching from a distance, standing very still, a tension all about his figure.

The French boat returned to the sound, anchored near the causeway on a night when the water was still. Preparations were being made now for the mackerel harvest.

When my mother saw my father repairing a net, she knew he had it in his mind to go after the fish. She was angry, the sight of the net always rousing pain in her. When she asked him not to go, he went on repairing the net.

Instead of fighting him she withdrew and sat before the embers, lost in her own thoughts.

The first night of the fishing my father went out in the boat but returned early because of a storm, and found the horse weathering the rain in our cottage. It stood beside the bed, its twisted back leg bent and at rest, its head lowered. My mother was sleeping, the curtain partly open, one bare arm hanging from the bed as if she'd stroked the horse's leg until she'd fallen asleep. My father lay on the stones in his coat near the fire. Throughout the night I looked over to him, his eyes always open, like the pale golden eyes of my grandmother's ewes watching Macdarragh from their bed of damp straw in the corner.

The next night the men went out again.

Near dawn, Brighde Donnely and a band of women came to the door and said, "Come up with us to Black Head." We followed them and saw the French steamer with its lights on, drifting at anchor near the causeway, the men carrying on. "They're after bein' stinking drunk!" Brighde said.

"Is Liam there?" my mother asked.

"He is," Brighde said. We sat on the rocks and listened to what was going on, the laughing and the music and the carrying on, some the voices of Frenchmen, each woman picking out the voice of her husband, some of the men fighting like they were ready to murder one another, and then we heard the woman's voice, piping up in French.

"Jayzus God! They've got a slut on the boat!" Brighde Donnely cried in a loud whisper.

"He'll see his patron saint!" a woman whispered breathlessly.

We could hear music playing, the voices of the men rising in laughter and jesting.

My father was dancing hard, lifting the woman in the air and carrying her about.

The men all laughing, dancing with her, some veering into the light, kissing her. There were loud cries in French and in Irish. Padraig Scanlon and Michael Dunne got into blows as if they might murder one another. Padraig picked up a wooden crate and broke it over Michael's head.

"Jayzus!" Mary Dunne cried. "Your Padraig's after cracking my man's skull open!"

"The devils," the women murmured one to the other.

As rain began to fall, I followed my mother, who was moving back toward home. When we got to the cottage, Macdarragh stood at the door waiting and my mother brought him in against the dark, covered him and boosted the fire, then kept to him all night.

Very early in the morning the men came back talking about the grand time they'd had of it, Padraig and Michael now with their arms around each other, sporting their bruises and cuts and broken bones.

The women gathered in a band near the Way of the Dead, but my mother was not among them, and my father's eyes raked the rocks and paths for her.

I went with him, looking for her. It was the soft sloshing that we heard, that drew us down the slippery rock and around to the estuary in the tide pools.

The horse was standing knee high in the water, the sound of the tide riding in and away in minimal wind. My mother was naked, washing Macdarragh. She poured a bucket of water over his back, rinsing away the line of foaming soap. She dropped the bucket in the water and embraced the horse, kissing its nose, both woman and horse oblivious that they were being watched.

The color rose on my father's face and he held in a breath. A moment later he was moving away over the hill at a fast pace.

"The storm will be over by nightfall," Mrs. O'Leary announced, coming in to us where we sat, the embers in her fire having gone low. "You'll be able to cross tomorrow. After such a storm the bay will be easy."

I was tired and promised the girls I'd finish the story the next day.

Nineteen

———❧———

In the morning a single boatman stood at the pier, and as we moved toward him, our boots clacking on the boards, I imagined that he was waiting exclusively for us.

He helped us in, smiling and nodding at us, and we crossed the bay without exchanging a word.

Except for a few chickens pecking at the white sand, the beach on the Great Blasket was deserted. The girls stayed close to me as we ascended from the pier. I looked above at the houses sheltered by the mountain, a few figures passing between, shadowy and half familiar.

When we reached the rocky path we were still a few yards from the first house. From this point I could see the cottage I'd once lived in, poised there at the summit and facing off away from the rest. "There," I said to the girls, pointing to it. It looked different than I remembered it, smaller, and the green felt roof had grown decrepit, dingier and weather darkened, edged white in salt, but still holding. The prospect of it disoriented me, and I felt a wave of fear, as if I were walking on ground that might suddenly shift and dissolve beneath me.

A woman's voice pierced me through the side. "Deirdre, is it? Deirdre O'Coigligh?"

I stopped and faced her. I knew her right away in spite of her weathered skin and the streak of gray hair visible under the hood of her dark cloak. My childhood friend.

"Eileen, is it?" I asked.

"Yes, yes. I'm glad I'm not so changed that you don't know me. You look lovely yourself, Deirdre, like a grand lady of society."

"Not at all," I said, shaking my head.

The wind came up suddenly, the particular noise of it here on the island catastrophic and achingly familiar.

"These are my daughters, Maighread and Caitlin."

"Lovely to meet you both."

Both girls nodded politely.

"Come in and I'll give you tea," she said, and led us in to her own hearth, boosting the fire and starting a kettle.

"You're with child," she said as I removed my coat.

I nodded as I sat at her rough-hewn table.

"I married Sean," she said. "You remember him. The three of us were grand together as children, were we not?"

"I thought you would one day marry him, Eileen," I said. "How is he?"

"He's off in Dingle too often, drinking. I don't even see the back of him much these days. We haven't been happy. We've no children."

"I'm sorry, Eileen," I said.

I struggled to relay my experiences. When I told her that I'd almost become a nun, she said, "I often wish I'd become a nun, Deirdre. It'd have been a happier life for me, I'm certain. I've dragged my way through life, as it is now. God's Son and his Glorious Mother my only comfort."

Each girl warmed her hands around the cup she was given, nodding gratefully, awed by the roughness of the little abode.

She strained toward me yet seemed in my presence tremulous with hesitation. "What's brought you here, Deirdre?" she asked.

I held her eyes but found it difficult to speak. Finally I asked, "Does anyone live now in my childhood cottage?"

"No one at all but Mrs. Herlihy's cows and chickens."

"I'll go and have a look at my old home," I said.

A quiet moment passed between us, and she said, "I go now and again to the island graveyard, Deirdre, and put flowers on your parents' grave."

"The island graveyard," I said to the girls, "is for the wayward and the unidentified. For unbaptized children and unknown sailors who washed up with the tide . . . for those not fit to be buried on the mainland in a churchyard."

The girls peered at me, their eyes wide. Caitlin touched Maighread's arm. They looked stunned, afraid.

Eileen bowed her head and looked away from me.

"Might I borrow a lamp from you, Eileen? I'm sure the place is all shadows. I'll bring it back to you."

The lane between the houses was barren now in the rain, and as we ascended I pulled my hood far over my face, shying from a few old faces looking out of doorways at the strange sight of my girls and me bearing the light under an oilcloth.

Only one soul had needed to spot me from a distance for the entire island to know within minutes of my presence. They were afraid of me, I told myself, staying back from me so, as they had when I was fourteen.

⤍⤌

The elements had softened every edge of the cottage, and it appeared to be sinking into the ground. The crooked door pushed against the earth ground. It was dark and wet smelling inside, chickens starting up from their roosts, clucking nervously at our arrival. The lamp reflected back at me in two points of a cow's eyes.

The iron headboard was gone, but its presence remained, having worn off the whitewash of the wall it had once pressed at. It had left its shadow, a replica of itself in all its dovetailing curves. The old bed's springs were still there, mortared, with earth and hay and chicken droppings, to the floor and stone wall like a great and elaborate fossil, struggling to mulch its way into the structure of the decaying house.

The bar from which the yellow curtain had hung was still there, too, and a bit of the curtain itself, which I walked up to and touched. It was hardened and cold, the weave of it broken down.

A driftwood chair my father had made leaned against the hearth wall, its seat collapsed, one leg crooked. Two chickens roosted in straw beneath it.

I moved close to the hearth, amazed to find, sitting on a small protrusion of rock in the wall, my grandmother's majolica cup with the periwinkles painted on it, a stub of ancient candle stuck within. On the wall, the rotted husk of the basket she had once kept dried heather in to revive the dying embers of a fire. I stared at the bare area of the hearth where my father had lain when he was banished from the iron bed. I closed my eyes and saw him as he'd once stood at his great height, and I felt his eyes on me and his tender regard for me. It was as if he were there again. I felt him holding my hand and smelled the food from the tidepools. Dulse and sea lettuce and murlins. And the girls seeming to hold in their breath as if they sensed him, too.

And the presence of my mother, a saline smell and a terrible stillness.

Everyone had said that the horse would fall, the way it climbed the windward side of the rocks, down the slick descents to get the tether grass that flowered yellow between the limestone ridges. He was, in spite of a twisted leg, adept and strangely sure-footed on the cliffs, like the black-faced sheep. When he came up missing that's where the women went to look.

He was dead far below, stuck between rocks. No one knew how to retrieve him, and it would only be powerful, exploding waves that might rise up and free him from the rocks and carry him seaward. But none strong enough came for days, and the women gathered at the cliff around the site, keening and throwing flowers down to his broken body, lighting votive candles, leaving them on the shelves of rock, a high wind coming in now and again, sweeping the lot of them off so they shattered and the bits of glass flew.

In the days before the sea finally lifted Macdarragh and carried him off, my mother stayed among the women, her face hidden, anonymous in her black shawl, her own grief mingling with the rest. But when the days of vigilance were over and the horse's remains were lost in the ocean, she disappeared. I felt the pressure of fear in my stomach, the sense that the universe had come loose of itself.

I walked with my father looking for her. We camped the island. It may have been only one night we slept under a hedge of stones, but it seems to me it was a long wandering the two of us did, so it could have been a fortnight, every second so vivid. We were under a strange spell and pulled by a dangerous enchantment. The animal grace of my father, a febrile brilliance to his eyes, the tension of the search and the cold blasts of western wind made us light-headed, even euphoric in our quest, as if we were following after a glimmering promise.

We'd gone full circle around the island when we came back to Macdarragh's Cliff and found her there below in a rock pool, a few yards from the rocks where the horse had fallen.

She floated and bobbed with the shifting forces of the sea, suspended about a foot below the surface. She was bent slightly at the waist, looking down, her face hidden in her dark, softly rippling hair. The dress, thin and white and translucent as a membrane around her, shredded at the hem, moved in different directions like the tentacles of a sea jelly.

My father squatted on his haunches and let out a wild, yet restrained, moan, then with sudden fierce energy jumped up and made me stand behind him. He tied me to his back with the rope, coiling it around us both again and again so that I was painfully pressed to him. He hooked the end of the rope to a jutting rock, then lowered us both down, him managing the rope with all his might and me so meshed to him I felt every strain and ache of his muscles as we descended.

At the bottom, with me still bound to him, he pulled her up to a narrow ledge of rock, forcing her head back and breathing into her mouth, pressing at her chest, groaning between every attempt. He sat back, unwinding me from the painful tie of the rope.

Eventually, the day darkened, the wind cold, both of us with our eyes pinned to her, waiting for her to cough and wince or sit up suddenly. But the wind had dried her and the salt from the sea glowed where it had gathered in her eyebrows and around her nostrils; thin clumps of her hair salted and quivering stiffly against the face, her eyes half open, empty.

"I can get her back, Deirdre," he said. "I can bring her around." And I believed he knew something about living and dying that I did not know. He had been drowned and returned himself.

My father made me wait with her while he crept along the under-ledges of the cliff and came back eventually with a curragh. He lay her in it, and I sat behind her and he in front, and he rowed south and easterly to the skellig.

It was a low cave there where we went, and inside he lay her carefully in a shallow basin of rock, then made a small fire, and we warmed ourselves.

"'Twas I, Deirdre, who drove the horse off the cliff," he said to me.

He told me to go back, to take the curragh, that he had another hidden there on the island, and that this is where he might bring her back and the two would return to the Blasket together.

As I set off he said, "Say you forgive me, Deirdre," and I thought he meant forgive him for driving the horse from the cliff.

I did not want to forgive him for that, or for the way he'd taunted my mother to try and bring the love out of her. But he looked at me with his eyes so sad and pale. "Say you forgive me."

I nodded.

I crossed back to the Blasket, but I did not go home. I weathered the night half frozen and chattering under a ledge of rock, never taking my eyes from the firelit cave. In the deep of night, huddling into myself, I opened my eyes once and saw that the fire had gone out.

I must have fallen asleep, because when I awakened the sun was bright. I rowed back. The tide was high and washing into the cave where I'd left them. I rowed back to them, navigating the little boat to its entrance and, standing knee high in the water, beached it on rocks.

"Da," I called. "Da."

There was no answer. Then I saw them, in the basin where he had lain her. They were together, pressed face to face, the ropes coiled around and around them, chest and waist and hips, their arms free, her face to his neck. The water all around them was red. I stared at him. "Da," I said, thinking him still alive and just beside himself with grief. I took the redness of the water to be a trick of minerals or iodine from the rocks. But the longer I looked, the closer I grew to knowing. A forceful tide washed in and spilled over into their pool, stirring up the red water with clear, and that's when I saw the clear water going red around his wrist and I saw the gash there, and came to understand the source of the redness.

As the three of us descended the hill back to Eileen's, the girls sobbed softly.

I had neglected to put on my hood, and rain was coming down hard and streaming freely over my face and hair.

"Deirdre," Eileen said as she opened the door. "Come in out of the wet for the Love of God."

She extricated the lamp from my grasp, took my coat, and wrapped a blanket around my shoulders. I stared at her fire.

"How did I get back that day from Skellig Michael?" I asked, watching the gently lapping flames around the turf.

"Deirdre, why do you want to dredge up such sad history?"

"Please, Eileen," I said softly. "I need to know this."

She paused. "There'd been a search party. I was there. Sean, too. Padraig Scanlon and a few others. 'Twas bright sun that morning, the bay as calm as new milk, and there you were below, crossing.

"No one could have known, Deirdre, from your manner, that there was a thing wrong. But I knew, the two of us sharing secrets since we were small girls. 'Twas an unnatural calm on your face. You told us that you'd been at the neck of sand where Ossian had been called away to Tir Na Nog. But you weren't coming from the direction of the legendary site.

" 'Where is your father?' Padraig kept asking you, but you hadn't an answer.

"Padraig and Mairtin took the curragh back in the direction where you'd come from. And no one could have guessed what they were about to find in the skellig cave."

"How long after that did my grandmother and I stay?"

"Holy God, Deirdre, I don't know. A month at most, I'd say." She paused and said, "And after you left, Kate Beg said that every time she passed the cottage, she could hear the bars of the iron bed ringing within, so a few of the island men, fearful of a haunting, crossed the bay and fetched a priest from the Ventry church, looking for some way to purge the cottage of damnation. The priest prayed in the house and said that the bed of two suicides should be destroyed, so the men burned the bag of stuffed straw and feathers, and they carried out the iron headboard and tossed it down into Macdarragh's rocks. And Jesus God, if the same thing that had happened to the horse himself didn't happen to this headboard, stuck there in the rocks where the horse's body had been stuck until a great wave had carried it off. But the headboard remains there to this day, a sad monument. I don't go down there," she said, and her eyes filled. "But I'm told that in the spring the kelp winds round the bars of it, knotting up in its curves and eddies and it still hums with the tide."

"I want to see it," I said.

"Ah, you don't."

"I do."

❦

When the rain stopped, the girls and I walked across the headland to the cliff and the rocks and looked down together at the site. And there, stuck at an angle between the jagged rocks, the headboard of my parents' bed, black and corroded now by the waves, eaten away with the salt water.

"We came and lit candles here," I told the girls, "when the horse, Macdarragh, lay in those rocks."

"In such a windy place?" Caitlin asked.

"How did they stay lit?" Maighread asked.

"They didn't for long, but we kept lighting them anyhow."

"I wish we had candles now," Caitlin said.

Gradually the dark washed from the sky and we descended to the pier where the boatman was waiting.

The two girls slept with me that night in one slim bed. We did not speak much. Now and then one or the other would press a kiss to my arm or cheek or wind a finger through my hair.

After I said good-bye to the girls at Enfant de Marie I felt an issue of blood. I took a coach to a doctor's house in Kilorglin, and that afternoon I was admitted to the local hospital. The nurse posted a letter to Manus in Dublin. The bleeding, which remained light, stopped that same night, and the doctor told me that the baby's heartbeat was steady.

Early the next afternoon, Manus walked into the room, two or three days' of growth on his face and jaw.

"Jesus, Deirdre," he said softly and earnestly. "Are you all right?"

"Yes," I said, "and I think the baby's all right now," I told him.

He held my hand and stood at my bedside. "I only got word a few hours ago," he said. "I was at the building site until this morning."

"I can see that," I said.

He looked self-consciously down at his rumpled clothes, then back at me, passing a hand through his uncombed hair.

When the doctor came in, Manus shook his hand. He was an older, white-haired man with a kind face and a quiet, reassuring voice. He explained to Manus that there'd been a slight rupture in the membranes at the cervix. He recommended that I take no chances and stay in bed for the rest of the pregnancy.

"When should I take her back to Dublin?" Manus asked.

"Not for a week at least," the doctor answered, looking at me. "And I'd be very careful about that as well."

The doctor's hesitation filled me with caution. "I'll not go back to Dublin then, until the baby is born," I said.

They both looked at me, and there was a pause before the doctor nodded and said that if that were possible it would be the best thing. He told Manus that his sister, a widow, Mrs. Donovan, had extra rooms nearby, and Manus undertook the arrangements and hired a private nurse.

Mrs. Donovan's was a modest but well-kept house, and the room I was granted appealed instantly to me, papered pale green, with a raised darker green foliate motif. Often those months, lying there in repose, I would study the curves and patterns of that design and muse that if it were red, it would have a distinctively Eastern character. But the green and the bit of knotwork portrayed as leafy vines and inhabited by rabbits and birds gave the impression of an old Celtic forest. An arched window, deeply set into the wall, faced the bed, and through it I could see the branches of a pear tree and an area of garden. When the casement was open, the curtains, broderie anglaise, billowed toward me, catching and brightening the daylight.

Manus was intrigued by the thickness of the walls and the Baroque character of the window. He had remarked more than once that it was a very sturdy little house, and that was something I came to feel immediately: the safety the room offered with the fire going at night and the wind blowing outside.

The winter months would prove an extraordinary time in my life. Everything and everyone was at service to my determination that this baby live. It became for me the focus of the universe. Though I had books at my disposal, I preferred to daydream, gazing at the garden through the window, charting the slow changes in daylight and weather, whispering to the baby within me, "Sta-a-ay," my repetitious interior chant.

As I lay in my room in Mrs. Donovan's house, trying to see my mother's face in my mind's eye, I remembered the story she used to tell me about how, when I was three or four years old, I had run from her out onto the edge of a rock that overhung the sea, a far drop below. I'd stood in bare feet at the very precipice of that rock and raised my arms. The wind had blown me back, back, away from the edge. I'd turned again, happy and ignorant of the danger I'd been in, and run to her.

The first time she'd told me that story I'd been eight or nine years old, and she'd said, "I stopped fretting over you after that day, Deirdre."

"Why?" I'd asked her.

"The wind'll always rescue you," she'd said, looking into my eyes, "and the water'll never swallow you."

I had marveled over that then, wondering what it meant to have the elements looking out for me so. But as I'd grown older, what she'd said about the wind and water made me angry.

And one night when I was twelve, she'd told the story again near the fire.

"You don't want me to need you," I'd said to her.

She had not replied but had colored, as if ashamed. She had stared into the embers.

As I recalled this, my mother's face became vividly clear to me: her wide eyes and wind-burned skin and the vein that stood out on her forehead, that ran from one eyebrow up at a slightly broken angle and lost itself in her hair, the vein I had forgotten about until this moment, that appeared when her feelings were roused.

❦

There would be nights in Mrs. Donovan's house when I'd awaken in the dark and feel my mother close to me, hesitating at my bedside, bringing with her an ineffable fragrance, something like bog-lilies and guttering candles.

One night, the baby's turning and rolling awakened me. I lay there for hours in a protracted joy with a new certainty that he would come. The world slowed down around us. Thunder sounded outside, and I felt the room brace itself around us to receive the downpour.

How bold and comfortable he was, a little watery acrobat. I felt his first flurries of independence, sensed the daring in his nature, so that I asked him, "When did you stop being inseparable from me and become your own mighty little self?"

Sarah Dooley, who had four children, two of them sons, had told me that her boys had been distinctively different from her girls. "More physical," she said. "More rough around the edges and when you've got two of them," she said, "they pound each other." I sensed it even now, the subtly different nature of his energy: slippery and mercurial, testing his muscles as if he were feeling his potential. His excitement charged through me, so different from the slower, calmer twists and turns of my girls.

I had told Manus the first day when I was moved into Mrs. Donovan's house that I didn't want him to tell his mother where I was.

"I have no contact with her. I haven't been answering her letters," he said.

"Well, she will contact you, wanting to know how I am."

"What should I say to her?" he asked.

"I don't care what you tell her, Manus. Just do not tell her where I am. And tell the girls not to as well."

After a moment's thought he nodded his head. "All right."

On the weekends Manus came down from Dublin and brought the girls to visit. After he'd taken them back to Enfant de Marie, he and I spent long hours talking, as he stoked the fire, keeping it going.

He had no access here to his drawings and his study. Here, he could not, on an impulse, rush off to whatever he was working at.

On one such weekend, when I'd been here about a month, I learned that the girls had told him of the trip to the Blasket. I told it to him again in my own words.

"There was a time I wanted to tell you. When we were first married."

"I always knew there was something sad in your past, but I never pressed you to tell me."

"Why, Manus?"

"I've hardly been a brave man, Deirdre," he said.

There was a long silence.

"A letter came yesterday for you from my mother." He took it out of his pocket. "Do you want to read it?"

I shook my head. "No, Manus."

He looked at the sealed envelope, turning it over in his hand, then threw it suddenly into the fire.

"She has no rights over this baby," I said.

"No."

"You'll have to tell her," I said.

He was silent a while and looked troubled, as if imagining the confrontation.

"Yes," he said. He watched the flames blacken the envelope until it curled. "I'll have to tell her."

That same night Mrs. Donovan brought our tea to the room on trays. She took the glass globe off the lamp and lit the wick, then left us to our meal.

When Manus put down his fork, he went and knelt before the fire, blowing at the turf with the bellows until the cinders glowed hot.

"Since Bairbre died," he said, still on his knees, "I've been day-dreaming a lot. Thinking about things I haven't thought of since you and I were first married."

He stared a while at the little flame coming up on one of the sods, before he stood and returned to his chair.

"I want to colonize the sky, Deirdre," he said in a soft voice. "It's always the skyline I look at in Dublin. I'm always staring at the spires and the towers. I want to build up there. With many of the architects I know, immensity is a dream. But for me it's always been height.

"When I was little I used to climb trees, and being as high as I could go only made me hunger to go higher. It's like a physical urge to rise up into the sky; to be nearer the clouds. And to make something beautiful. You know the green dome of the Four Courts, how it stands out on the skyline? I want to gild the tops of buildings . . . the pinnacles of them. To catch the light up high.

"Remember how I once thought I should have been born in an earlier century because of the principles of aesthetic beauty, which seem less important to architects now? I've come now to believe that I should have been born at a later time, when Ireland isn't so polarized that it can't move forward into the new century."

That same night Manus, who ordinarily spent the night in a room down the hall, took off his shoes and lay down on the bed next to me.

"We should leave Merrion Square," he said. He closed his eyes and fell asleep.

Manus was with me the night I went into labor. The midwife sent him into the adjoining room, and within three hours I gave birth to my boy, who seemed so tiny at five pounds, both his sisters having been more than eight pounds when they were born.

He was blonde and very pink, with graceful little hands. Manus was afraid to hold him, the memory of his first son's death fresh this moment in his mind. But he came in close, and the baby studied his father's face with half open eyes.

"I want to call him Liam," I said to Manus, "after my father."

❧

When Liam was three days old, Manus went to Kenmare. He was back two hours later, sitting in the chair at my bedside, looking thoughtful.

"What happened?" I asked.

"It's over," he said vaguely.

"She's going to keep after us," I said.

"No," he said. "I told her that we have a son and that he will not be sent to a seminary."

"What did she say to that?"

"She argued, I hardly know what she was saying to me. On and on about how we are beholden to our pasts. I told her that the past she talks about is nothing more than an ancient grudge, heavy beyond all comprehension. She said that I was speaking too sharply to her. I got up to leave at one point and she threatened to stop sending money each month into the Dublin bank account. I told her that if she did send money I'd send it back. She came after me and said she was sorry for having said that and she started crying. She talked in a halting voice, repeating things she'd already said about responsibility and about ancestry. But when she was finally quiet, I told her that the ecclesiastical family had died with poor Bairbre.

"She didn't move. And I left."

It was not Mrs. O'Breen I thought of all that day, but the house at Kenmare. I imagined odd things: snow falling in the rooms; toadstools growing in the cushions of the sofa. I imagined the statues stirring from their pedestals and wandering confused through the corridors.

PART FOUR

Aqua Mirifica

Miraculous water brings about the albedo, *the white state of innocence, which, like the moon and the bride, awaits the bridegroom.*

—Aurora Consurgens

TWENTY

1914
Dublin
Merchant's Quay

Three days of the week I taught Irish to a group of fifty girls at
the Star of the Sea Convent on Dollymount Strand.

It was the last Friday afternoon before summer break and they'd
all gone sleepy with the repetitions: *"Seacht a chlog ar maidin; Ocht a
chlog ar maidin . . . Tagan se ar an Luan; Tagan se ar an Mairt . . ."*

Shoals of girls faced me in the afternoon light, their faces lifted,
peering up from a sea of tremulous blue uniforms.

Nuns in the back listened, staring beyond the horizons of the
room, the old ones uneasy at the language's resurgence, like Sister

Dymphna at Enfant de Marie, who could not disassociate it from agonies of the past.

The sun set in the western sky as I took the tram back toward the
quays, passing lines of dark stone houses, three and four floors high,
some with water towers, the nicer ones with terraced doorways, and
set back behind iron fencing. The church spires of north Dublin were
slowly becoming silhouettes beyond, the city at that hour still shivering with life, coaches galloping past, harnesses jingling; the scorched
smell of grain from the Guinness factory permeating the air. I got out
of the tram and walked along the river wall looking into the Liffey.

Clouds moved in, dimness coming on suddenly like a thousand
candles snuffed out in the sky, a penetrating smell of rain. I was anxious to get home to three-year-old Liam, but I had to stop first to see
the local seamstress. As a gift for Maighread's upcoming graduation
from Enfant de Marie, I had commissioned new bed curtains for her
room. I moved toward Merchant's Quay, past the haberdasher's and
the pawnshop and the wine and spirit merchant's until I reached the
silk mercer's. The proprietress's name, Olga Leary, was stenciled in
small gold letters on her shop door. Two signs were displayed in the
lower corners of her window: ALL FABRICS WASHED IN RAIN WATER
and IRELAND—A FREE NATION UNTO HERSELF.

I knocked but there was no answer from within; then I tried the
door and found it locked. I was about to go when I heard thuds on the
stairs. It was Eoin Flaherty descending, the big man from Achill who
drove the coach for the bottleworks, with its crates of chiming glass.
He lowered his head when he saw me through the window, a blush on
him, supressing a little smile at the corners of his mouth. He opened
the door, brushed past me, and crossed out to his delivery wagon,
adjusting the harness on his horse.

Olga Leary appeared on the stairs, a curl of hair stuck to the
dampness at her forehead. She was older than the big man out the
door, and voluptuous, giving the impression that she was about to
spill forth from the stays of her dress.

Her mother had been an actress, she'd told me, and had received her greatest praise for playing the role of Olga in *The Three Sisters,* thus her Russian name. "But I'm as Irish as you are, Mrs. O'Breen," she had said to me before we'd been on a first-name basis, as if it were important to her that this fact be known.

Feeling in her pocket for her hairpins and not finding them, she made a face, trying to think where she might have put them. In the wake of the man who had just left her, she was all scatterbrained softness.

"Deirdre," she said. "You've come about the crepe de chine."

"Yes," I said. "It's about to deluge."

I followed her up four flights of stairs and out onto her roof, a black, lesser-known city up there: charred spires and towers, ascending plumes of smoke from distant chimneys.

"Rain adds a certain texture to silk," she had explained to me in the past. Now she showed me the five yards of crepe de chine I had chosen pegged to clotheslines, spread in a sheet facing the sky. Lightning rent the clouds, the thunder following close after, a comforting rumble, presaging soft rain. From the awning of the door we watched as the sky opened, pelting the fabric, saturating it.

"Something in rain not found in terrestrial water," she explained to me again, as she had before. "A purity in it. Encourages lustrousness and resilience. The cloth less likely to devour itself over the years as fabric is wont to do."

This new silk was twilight color, "Arabian blue," Olga called it, and beautifully detailed with flowers and leaves in fine silver thread. I hoped to have the curtains ready and hanging for Maighread by the time we returned from the west after the upcoming ceremony.

Since I had first come to Olga Leary for fabric to upholster a sofa, a vermillion jacquard silk mottled softly and textured by a winter's rain, I had been drawn to her with her unorthodox ideas. She wore skirts of great amplitude, impractical in the sooty puddles of Dublin streets, her hems discolored and in flitters because of it. On every one of her window ledges, large-mouthed bottles caught precipitation. She kept and dated rainwater, making notes if it was a morning, after-noon, or evening shower. If it was light or heavy.

After a few minutes she put on an oilcloth coat and hood and fetched the fabric, rolling it up, bringing it in to her garret, where again it was stretched out and pegged to clotheslines.

"It's better if we can air-dry it. Let's hope for a clement day tomorrow," she said, "and breakers of clean wind from the sea."

She went to the window, her eyes raking the street below for Eoin Flaherty's Bottleworks coach. It was nowhere to be seen, and she lifted her eyes to the sky.

"Te se dorca," she said. *It's getting dark.*

I smiled and gave her a nod.

Relatively early on in our acquaintance, Olga had asked me to teach her the Irish. "Every citizen'll be speaking it soon enough," she'd said. She belonged to a secret nationalist society, the name of which she would not tell me. "Suffice to say, Deirdre, we want nothing at all to do with Westminster. We want to take back what's rightfully ours. And we will."

It had been Olga who'd shown me the ads in the *Evening Telegraph,* two years before, wanting teachers of Irish.

The big man from Achill Island, most likely married, I thought but wouldn't ask, was more handy with the Irish than the English. Since she'd been rendezvousing with him, the phrases she'd asked me to teach her had taken a turn for the amorous.

Standing at the window, her eyes on the street below, she asked, "How do you say . . . *the little death?*"

"An bás beag," I answered.

"An bás beag," she repeated.

When Liam was ten days old, we'd traveled back to Dublin. We were only a few days at Merrion Square when Manus came in to me early one morning and asked me to get dressed. There was a house he wanted to show me.

The coach took the three of us to Merchant's Quay. "Four stories over a basement," he explained, a curious excitement in his voice. "On one of the original streets of medieval Dublin."

He'd procured the key from the owner, who had not bothered to sweep or to clear away the cobwebs, which hung from the fixtures and lintels like swathes of fine gray mesh.

I carried Liam in my arms, supporting him against me, cupping the back of his head with one hand, stroking lightly his fine blonde hair.

"Manus," I said and laughed. "What is it about this house that you like?"

He led me up the stairs to the second floor. "Angled chimney breast," he said excitedly, showing me the edifice around the mantel. He strode across the room to the window, beckoning me to follow, and pointing out the cross sections of the exposed wall. "Like looking at ancient layers of sediment," he said.

"I'd like to do with this place what my father was trying to do with the back rooms in Kenmare. Strip it down of all the festering paper and plaster," he said. "Tear away the extraneous and expose the medieval walls, study it, satisfy my curiosity. Then we could finish it anew, the way *you* would like it finished."

Out the back door there was a garden, a quagmire of tangled briars; ivy tightly embracing a larch tree.

The stairway down to the kitchen, which was situated in the vaulted spaces of the basement, was all mustiness and rot.

"Christ, Manus!" I said. "It's probably filled with ghosts."

"If there are ghosts here, they're neutral to us," he muttered.

We spent an hour or more ascending and descending staircases, moving from room to room, sometimes together, sometimes separately.

I gravitated mostly to the third floor, easily imagining the rooms there for the girls. Liam had fallen asleep against me, his little head just beneath my neck. The sun shone suddenly and, shielding the baby's face from it, I peered out at the brightening water of the Liffey, which was visible from the front windows of the second-, third-, and fourth-floor rooms. Manus joined me, and in the brightness I saw how his hair was streaked now, a tarnished silver.

He opened the window to the horn of a passing steamer; the bustle and commerce of Merchant's Quay.

"We're in the heart of it all here," I said uncertainly.

"Yes," he said. After a pause he asked, "Do you think you might see your way clear to it, Deirdre?"

I laughed softly at the question. "I think I've already begun to claim the place," I said.

He held my eyes.

"I don't think you know . . . ," he said, ". . . how much your life reaches into mine."

He pressed a kiss to the top of my head, then, without looking at me, turned and wandered into the corridor. I stayed where I was, unshed tears defracting the empty room into numberless rooms.

Over the next months Manus laid bare the walls, revealing a pastiche of color-washed shadows and petrified mildew, which he affectionately called "glacial fauna."

We moved into the house, with its roughened walls and piercing drafts. Manus had tried on three occasions to wire some of the rooms for electricity, but the bulbs never worked, flashing with nervous indecision, a strain to the eyes.

"Do we really need it, anyway?" he asked.

"It's too wet a country for electricity," I had replied and he laughed.

"Yes," he said. "It's a miracle the modern-day Irish aren't electrocuted by the hour."

We burned coal in the fireplaces, kept gas in the wall sconces, and late every night I turned it off at the main.

Manus and I made our bedroom on the fourth floor, where the worst drafts rose up from the floorboards. Heavy curtains were required for around the bed to keep out the chill. I padded Liam's cradle in fleece and swaddled him at night in thick layers of silk so he never felt the blasts of cold.

Bats lived in the rafters in the attic above us. From the window at dusk I showed Liam three or four of them slipping out and taking to the air, mewing like kittens and flying north across the river into the spires beyond, the smoke from a northside factory, a dark wash on the sky.

In the middle of the night Manus cursed when they woke us, bumping and settling themselves on their return. But I wouldn't let him drive them out. Delicate winged mice, satiny soft, I have been told. Creatures poised between the terrestrial and the aerial.

Black cracks of thunder could send charges through the very groynes and pediments of the house, and the wind shook the windows in fits. Crows got into one of the lesser-used chimneys. Yet I felt safe here. It was ours, and, though shaky and old, and noisy with the commerce of Dublin leaking in the windows, it felt like a shell in which it was safe to dream.

We'd brought very little with us from Merrion Square, only the things the girls were attached to. It was their rooms I labored over the most, worried that they would not like the house.

I pushed the pram through the winding cobbled streets of Temple Bar, looking in the shops, selecting an occasional piece of furniture or a lamp to be delivered to the house, or soothing myself by gathering little delicacies for the girls' rooms: white eyelet runners for their dressers, porcelain ewers and basins, dried rose petals to put in bowls beside their beds, cream laid paper and peacock plumes for pens. And candles in parchment; pale yellow, poured by the nuns of Christchurch.

Manus plastered and painted their walls, and finished their floors in palid red marble stones and Turkish rugs, and I commissioned and hung bed curtains, double layered, from Olga Leary: the first layer heavy wool for warmth, the outer layers watered silks. And all of it ready in time for their return home at Easter break.

I was relieved that they liked their rooms, the house a kind of novelty for them then. They planted zinnias and marigolds in the back under the larch tree.

The day after the girls left to go back to school, I sat upstairs while the baby slept, listening to the rush of the wind and the steamers; a carriage galloping past, its driver blowing a whistle.

I saw each of my daughter's faces in my mind, tracing back the events of the days that had just passed. The wind blew hard and the house moved in response, leaning slightly forth.

I had, in that moment, a strong impression of being home; that I had returned from a long and difficult journey; that I was as well traveled as the Liffey herself. This house was like a barge, docked at last at the quay.

And so it is in such moments, the way we remake ourselves in dreams.

We'd been moved in for six months or so when Manus began to disappear for long hours into his study. He seemed to have lost the urge to continue with renovations. Rooms and big areas of hallways were left in unfinished states. Something had taken his attention.

If I'd have pressed him about one thing or another, I think he would have undertaken it. But I liked the walls and floors stripped down. There was a look to it, an earthiness that put me in mind of the more elemental habitats of the Blasket: stone and sand and raw faded wood. When I came across a painting I liked in one of the shops, I put it up myself directly on the roughened wall. I placed rugs on the unfinished floors.

TWENTY-ONE

S ince we'd moved, Manus had neglected all the bills and papers, and while he was spending long hours working in his study, I decided to undertake them myself: balancing the accounts, updating ledgers, my mind absorbed by the challenges of the ordinary.

The house on Merrion Square was in Mrs. O'Breen's name, so Manus had dealt with her solicitor when we'd vacated it. A good portion of what Manus had saved over the years went to the purchase of the house on Merchant's Quay. We certainly would not starve, but I could see by looking through ledgers from years gone by that our circumstances were greatly reduced from what they once had been.

I'd intrude upon Manus in his study to open a window or fill a lamp. Once when he was not there, I read through the writings he'd left on his desk.

> *Transforming nature is nothing but driving the elements around in a circle.*

And on a separate page:

> *The goal is to make a house with a mineral life; a meteorological life . . . a house that lets in the universe.*

I asked him once what it all meant, and he said that they were musings related to something he wanted to build; something that still existed in the realm of dreams.

For months, again and again, I read his scribblings to himself. Eventually thoughts and questions gave way to drawings, the beginnings of a sketch of a building, and in the margins various notes and questions to himself.

> *What is the tension between the visible and the invisible?*
> *Ether, charged by fire and water, has the power to suspend matter on air. How much fire? How much water? In what measurements of each might fire and water support each other?*

Questions reminiscent of the ones he'd pondered long ago in the hidden garden room; his father's notes related to the Celestial Mansion.

One night he did not come up to bed. In the morning I found him asleep in his study. On his table, a completed drawing of a house, delicate and intricately detailed with turrets and towers, floating above the earth. In the margin he had written:

Angels? Might angels be the lambent servants of air . . . bear the Celestial Mansion above? Three orders of angels: Purifying order. Illuminating order; Perfecting order.

The naive purity of his quest troubled me, as it had in the hidden garden room.

He awakened and found me looking at the drawing.

"It sounds like a faery-tale house," I said.

"What is it for? I ask myself," he said. "What purpose could such a building have? I can feel it there, but it seems impossible. How can one build something that has such an amorphous nature?"

For months he remained obsessed with the shifting, evolving idea of the Celestial Mansion, struggling to give it form. He drew details, corners, and cross sections. But mostly he resorted to ideas.

The lower world is cut off from the divine world of love and light. How does one bring the glowing air down to the coarse matter of the world.

The stone must pass from one nature into another. Mercury must come down and charge it with divinity.

He seemed possessed by a medieval way of thinking, like an alchemist in his den, intent on making gold.

To achieve the suspension of great weight on air, one must study the four compass points and the winds.

Near each wind he had drawn a small face blowing blustery gusts of air through its lips, images done in soft, smudged pencil.

The rough North wind is cold and brings snow. Supplements of this wind are called "circius," which brings snow and hail, and "aquilo boreas," which is frosty and dry.

*The East wind is moderate. To its left blows the drying "vul-
turnus." "Eurus" on the right waters the clouds.*

*The South wind, Auster, a symbol also of the holy spirit, brings
heavy clouds and light showers and encourages the growth of
plants. "Euroauster" on its right is warm. Austroafricanus on the
left is warm and mild.*

*The Western wind, Zephyrus, is the gentlest wind. It blows
away the cold of winter. Africus to its right brings heavy storms.
Coros on the left brings clouds to the east.*

He found me in his study one day pondering his notes. I read
aloud to him: " 'The house that shimmers above on air like a
thought.' "

He held my eyes.

"This is poetry, Manus," I said.

"It isn't meant to be," he said. "It's meant to help me with what I
want to do. I want to build something beautiful."

"But stone is heavy, Manus. It cannot float."

"I know . . . ," he said distractedly. "I know."

The more he suffered over the unreality of his idea for a Celestial
Mansion, the more fantastical his drawings became, and more seem-
ingly impossible to realize. In one, the building was depicted carried
on the back of a giant gull, in another, it housed an aqueduct,
labyrinths of water running through the rooms.

He was working on a rich parchment paper different than the thin,
crisp sheets he had used before, and using a pencil that made ghostly
blue lines.

He would not come to bed but sat up all night struggling, afflicted
with the dream. He left Masonic texts open on the floor, the sofa, the
desk; pages were marked with feathers, with handkerchiefs. I opened a
large volume, which seemed to exhale each time I turned a page. What
was he searching for, I wondered. Everything I read struck me as indecipherable until I stopped on a drawing of a wheel.

"Turn the wheel, make the effort, until the heavenly mixes with the earthly." It was the image of the wheel that made me suddenly understand. He did not trust that he could bridge his passion with his craft, having always been engaged in a duller, more utilitarian kind of architecture. He was stuck, unable to make the wheel turn, to move from one place to the next. He was lost in dreaming.

The next day while walking along Dawson Street, I found an odd little box composed of crystals and amber. There were five lids like small doors that opened into compartments. It was an elaborately imagined construction and reminded me of Manus's drawings.

I gave it to him at home, and he studied it a long time before he set it on the window ledge. Light refracted through the crystals, casting rainbows on the ceilings and walls, and white, incandescent specters that traveled with the movement of the sun, over the furniture and floor.

He spent the next few days drawing the plans for a particular structure. The following week he met with the contractors who had been building a great museum in southeastern Dublin, and they awarded him an extraordinary commission.

"A kind of pavilion," he said. "On the roof of the museum. Something no one's ever imagined before in Dublin, and they leave the entire design to me."

"A pavilion?" I asked.

"I hardly know what to call it. An atrium, perhaps."

The next day he visited the quarry and the glassworks, and the wheel was set in motion, the dream brought forth out of ether.

It was that September that I started teaching Irish at the Star of the Sea, and hired a kindly woman named Mrs. Flanagan, heavyset and red-faced, who panted as she climbed the stairs, to help me with Liam. That Christmas when the girls were home, the house was, much to their consternation, in the same state it had been in the previous summer.

Maighread complained about the lack of electricity, that it was "positively medieval" with the gas lamps and the candles.

"We can certainly afford electricity! Even the nuns use some electricity," she said. It was a particularly cold winter, and wrapped in shawls and blankets, we kept close to the fire.

Mrs. Flanagan cooked a goose on Christmas, and as we sat to eat, Caitlin begged Manus to take us to the pavilion he was building.

"I'm going to take you to it as soon as it's finished, but not before."

"Please, Da!"

"No, Love," he said.

He set his cup down and stared into the black pool of his tea.

"Da, I was chosen to sing the 'Salve Regina' to Sister Frances's piano accompaniment at the Christmas party the night before coming home," Caitlin said.

He struggled to focus on her but seemed unable to tear himself from some thought that occupied him. He nodded at her.

I asked her to sing it for us, and while she did, in a tremulous and self-conscious vibrato, her eyes flit back and forth from the cut glass centerpiece on the table to her father's face. At first his eyes brightened at the sound of her, but halfway into the song his gaze grew distant. He toyed with his spoon, touching the filigree of the handle. I saw Caitlin's face fall and heard volume draining from her voice.

Maighread and I clapped. Liam on my lap squealed and mimicked the clapping, crying out, "Caitlin! Caitlin!" That brought Manus back, but only for a moment.

For the rest of the meal he remained far away, Caitlin's eyes fixed to him.

Manus said he had to go out to the site; that he'd not be long.

As I helped Mrs. Flanagan clear the plates, I touched Caitlin gently on the shoulder.

"He's distracted lately," I said. "I don't think he hears half of anything I say to him."

"Da needs a haircut and a clean shirt," Maighread said. "He has tea stains on his cuffs!"

෴

Later I found Caitlin in Manus's study at his desk, rifling through his papers.

"What is all of this?" she asked, taking out his drawing of the celestial house on the back of a cloud, carried by dozens of gulls.

She read aloud, " *'Might angels be the lambent servants of air?'* What does all of this have to do with constructing a building?"

Maighread came in behind me.

"He was just musing . . . ," I said.

Maighread looked at the page Caitlin held, then made a sound of incredulity. "I think you're *both* mad, living in this house the way it is."

When I kissed the girls good-night, Manus still had not come home.

"I'm going to wait for him," Caitlin said.

"Don't, Love," I said. "You'll see him in the morning."

"All right," she said, but kept her lamp burning.

I awakened in the middle of the night and went down to look in on them. Maighread was asleep, but Caitlin was not in her bed. Downstairs the light was on in Manus's study.

Peering in from the doorway, I saw the two of them sitting on the sofa, his arm around her. Manus looked like he'd just come in, still wearing his heavy shoes and a sweater, his coat draped over the back of his desk chair, Caitlin in her nightgown resting her face on his chest and pressing a palm to one of his shoulders.

There were times now I felt invisible to Manus. In my company he mused and whispered as if he were in dialogue with his pavilion, whose double I sensed at first, tingling above him, chandelier-like on the air. Now it had become a more carnal presence: sphinxlike. Chimerical. It had taken on a female quality.

The claim it had on him hurt me. He was all devotion to it, inexhaustible, his passions for it surging and resurging.

ᴄᴀᴇᴏꙋᴀ

One winter morning I awakened to find that he had not come home at all. I waited distractedly for him until dusk, and when there was still no sign of him, I left Liam with Mrs. Flanagan and went out to find him. The museum was locked, and though I pounded on the doors, no one heard me. Faintly and from far above I heard noises of building; boards breaking, distant shouts.

It began to rain, and I made my way home. I lit the fire in his study, searching through all of his papers, trying to penetrate this pavilion's mysteries. But most all of the drawings with their lines and graphs and numbers were indecipherable to me. When every folder was opened and searched, I went to my knees on the floor, pages spread out everywhere.

Gazing benevolently down at me from the mantel was the photograph of Manus's father; the man who had sailed so far north in search of fire marble that he'd dissolved into whiteness.

Jealousy turned to worry. Afraid to leave the house again, I waited for his arrival or some message. I walked circles through the rooms, feverishly cursing him, begging him to come home, imagining all sorts of tragedy having befallen him.

A few hours later he walked through the door.

"Where were you?" I cried.

"Working," he said, surprised by the question.

"You didn't send a message to me!"

"I'm sorry, Deirdre, I thought you'd just know."

"How could I have?"

"I've worked through the night at job sites before," he said. He touched my shoulder and I stiffened. My breaths came fast with emotion.

"What's wrong?" he asked in a quiet voice.

"I'm tired of your not being here," I said.

"I'm sorry," he said helplessly and sat down. He sighed and leaned his head back so he looked up at the ceiling. "I'm lost in this thing. . . ."

The night before Manus, Liam, and I were supposed to leave for the graduation ceremony in Kilorglin, Olga Leary finished the Arabian blue curtains for Maighread's room and I hung them up.

Manus surprised me in the corridor.

"I got a letter. Actually, it's been in my pocket for weeks, but I only opened it today. My mother is selling the house in Kenmare."

"Why?"

"It's too much for her to keep up. She's moved to Dungarven with her sisters."

"Was the letter from her?"

"No, it was from the solicitor. They're auctioning off most of the furniture and things."

There'd been times in the recent years when Manus had thought about certain paintings or pieces of furniture at Kenmare, things he'd left there that he'd wished he could get again.

"Were you thinking of going by there when we're in the west?"

He shook his head. "Ah, Deirdre. I'm not going to be able to go with you."

I stared into his face.

"I'm literally days away from completing the pavilion."

"You choose this thing you're building over your own children," I said quietly, stifling my fury.

"No!" His eyes were so set upon me, so vividly blue in that moment, that it startled and unnerved me.

"You're a bastard," I said softly as I turned. I scaled the stairs to my bedroom, then closed the door, unpacking his things roughly and tossing them onto his dresser.

That night after I'd gotten Liam to sleep, Manus came and stood in the upstairs doorway, watching me comb out my hair.

"Deirdre," he said tentatively. I looked away from him, but he remained in the doorway, and when I glanced again at him he gave me a nighttime look that sent a shiver of nervous excitement through me. I felt in that moment how deeply I missed him.

He approached, and the sensation of his fingers on my hair caused me to sigh. I closed my eyes, my reserve breaking down.

He brought me to my feet, but as he pressed a kiss to my temple, I saw my daughters faces in my mind as I explained to them that their father could not come. The disappointment I knew they would feel, flooded me, and I recoiled from Manus.

"I want to be on my own," I said.

In the middle of the night I got up and opened the window, thinking that a draft of cold air might help me sleep. I was surprised to see Manus below, standing at the river wall, looking at starlight shivering on the Liffey.

TWENTY-TWO

After the commencement ceremony, I took Liam and the girls to the Elen hotel, and they gave me all their news. Moira O'Hare, a classmate from Enfant de Marie whose family lived in Kenmare, had introduced Caitlin to her brother Thomas. They'd been friendly for a year now, and he called around for Caitlin at the convent on Saturdays and they'd go into town with a group of others or remain behind and walk on the lanes and the paths.

Throughout the meal the first night at the Elen, Caitlin talked incessantly about Thomas.

In a moment when I was alone with Maighread, she rolled her eyes and whispered, "I suppose we'll be having Thomas for breakfast, dinner, and supper!"

We were dressing in our room the next morning when Caitlin told us that she wanted to share something funny with us about Thomas. She wrinkled her mouth and looked at us with wide, excited eyes.

"I was throwing these little berries at him from off the tree and he was chasing me. I hid from him behind the giant willow and was sure he didn't know where I was! Then he came up from behind and grabbed me. He had gotten hold of me so hard and I fought him and I elbowed him." Caitlin's eyes grew wider, and her voice, quieter. "He looked very serious and hurt and he said, 'It's only poor Thomas, who'd never do you harm.'"

Both girls looked at each other and burst out laughing.

"Cripes!" Maighread said. "The fool!"

At this Caitlin's face fell. She colored.

"No," she said softly. "Not the fool."

Maighread tried again to engage her in conversation, but Caitlin would not speak. And I sensed very faintly the satisfaction Maighread had gotten from saying it. But she looked away, trying to dispel the moment, any satisfaction mixed with guilt that she'd hurt her sister.

But later I saw them in the hotel parlor downstairs, sitting close together on the couch, not having heard me come in behind them.

"He put his tongue in my mouth," Caitlin whispered.

Maighread took in her breath. "What did it feel like?"

"Um . . . like an eel in warm water."

They both laughed, but I sensed the strain in Maighread's laugh and Caitlin's awareness of it.

I was about to slip off when Caitlin asked, "Did you tell Mam yet? About that school in Paris?"

Maighread sighed and rolled her head. "No. I don't look forward to that. . . . I'm still not sure anyhow."

I sat on an embankment of rock while the girls walked along the strand, holding hands, Liam between them. I was tormented by the thought of Maighread going so far away alone, and into such a strange and worldly culture.

Caitlin left the two of them near the water, turned, and made her way to me, joining me.

"Thomas has asked that we stop in Kenmare before going back to Dublin. He's asked me to stay on for a week with his family. Would it be all right with you, Mammy?"

"Yes, Love," I said, though I felt a pang that she would be taken from me again so soon. "Go ahead if you like."

"He asked that you and Maighread stay as well, but Maighread says she wants to go back to Dublin. But maybe the two of you could spend one night?"

"I think so."

A mist was up on the tide, and the farther Maighread and Liam walked, the less distinctive they appeared, the waves coming in an uncanny white.

"I want to tell you something," Caitlin said. "I wanted to tell you sooner, but we didn't have many moments alone."

"What is it, Love?" I asked.

"Thomas wants to meet Daddy. He wants to ask for my hand in marriage," she said.

"Oh," I started, but before I could say another word, she interrupted me.

"We wouldn't marry this year. Next year after I finish at Enfant de Marie."

I tried to read through the blankness of her expression. "Are you happy about it? Do you want to?"

"Yes," she said.

"You don't seem happy."

She shook her head. "It isn't that."

"What is it?"

She looked at the air beyond me, struggling to articulate something. "I never looked . . . I wasn't thinking of finding a beau. Most of the other girls talk about it, but it hadn't been on my mind so much. But he came one day with his sister. A lot of girls were interested in him. But he just focused on me."

"Well, you're a lovely girl," I said.

She shook off the compliment as if it irritated her.

"You don't *have* to marry him . . . ," I said softly.

"You don't understand what I'm saying!" Her eyes spilled over with quick tears. "I *want* to marry him! I *will* marry him!"

"What's making you sad?" I asked.

"I don't know."

I put my arms around her and she looked up at me, something ancient passing between us. I understood then that she was beginning to discern the shape her life would take. She could see the shadow of it coming toward her.

"I miss my father," she said.

"Ah, Love," I said, pressing her close. "I know."

After a few moments in my arms she sighed and sat back from me.

"Things change, Love," I said. "They're meant to. And it's all right."

"Don't tell Maighread what I told you," she said. "Not yet."

"I won't."

"You know she is in love."

"Is she? I thought something. She seems pensive," I said.

"A boy named Aidan Callahan, but he fancies someone else."

"I heard the two of you talking . . . something about Maighread going to Paris?"

She looked at me hesitantly. "You'll have to speak to her about that, Mammy."

"Does this boy have something to do with why she wants to go to Paris?"

Caitlin screwed up her face. "No, I don't think so. If it were that, she'd have told me. It's a school for young ladies, anyhow."

"Well, maybe he also plans to go to Paris," I said, anxious for information.

She thought for a moment, then snorted ironically. "I don't imagine Aidan Callahan on the Continent. Frankly, Mammy, I don't know what she sees in him."

Thomas met us at the Kenmare station in a big black-and-silver automobile that shook and rumbled in place as he stored our bags in the trunk.

"This is a great lark!" Maighread laughed, delighted.

Thomas stood with his hands on his waist, arms akimbo, smiling widely as the girls admired the vehicle. His eyes kept darting to mine and away again, and I sensed his nervousness that I like him.

"I've never ridden in one of these yokes!" Caitlin cried.

"Never ridden in an automobile?" Thomas asked her. She shook her head, something passing between the two of them in the exchange of smiles.

I warmed to him immediately.

"I have," Maighread said. "Lydia Doran's father has one, but not so handsome as this one. He drove us into town one Saturday."

"Can we go for a bit of a ride around?" Caitlin asked.

From the backseat with Liam on my lap, I studied Thomas as he drove us slowly out of the town of Kenmare and onto the winding country roads. Though he was tall, he seemed no more than a boy, auburn hair and a pinkness to his skin. In the sunlight through the windscreen, the scattered whiskers on his face glinted red.

"Are you comfortable, Mrs. O'Breen?" he asked, turning obliquely.

"I am," I said.

"Don't ask if *I'm* comfortable, Mr. O'Hare!" Maighread said from her place beside me, a sarcastic lilt to her voice.

"Are *you* comfortable, Miss O'Breen?" he asked playfully, drawing out the words.

"That's the road that leads to my grandmother's house," Caitlin cried, pointing to a diverting road as we scaled a hill. Thomas halted the car, and we could see the distant turrets of the house through the trees.

"Your grandmother sold the house," I said.

"What? Why didn't you tell us?" Caitlin cried.

"Your father only told me days ago."

Two years before, Caitlin had written to her grandmother and had received no answer. She'd tried again six months or so later and had gotten a cordial but somewhat cold reply. After that she'd been uninclined to write again. And Manus did not pursue correspondence with her.

"Are the new owners in the house yet?" Maighread asked.

"I'm not sure," I said.

"Let's drive up and have a look," Caitlin said.

Thomas turned onto the road and drove to the front gates, parked, and we all got out. The gate was unlocked and the five of us wandered in. We found no one there at all. Not a groundsman or a servant. Even the gulls had abandoned the house.

Inside, windows had been left open, and drafts and light moved through the corridors. What appeared to be all the most valuable pieces of furniture had been gathered together in the main sitting room, all of an antiquated character, in the style of the armoire on Merrion Square, impervious and grotesquely elegant, festooned with cherubs and gargoyles, representing a past and darker age. Every other room was empty. Rugs had been rolled back and tapestries taken down, the place bereft of statues.

Inspired by the vastness, Liam screeched and stomped his feet. "Run after me!" he cried out to us all. Thomas engaged him in a game of chase, the two of them stirring up a riot of echoes.

We walked out onto the grounds, toppled branches and arbors thorny with undergrowth. In a clearing near the side gardens lay a vast pile of collapsed and hopelessly broken furniture, ready for burning.

"Someone broke all of this on purpose. Destroyed it," Thomas said, poking through the pieces and lifting out the detached armrest of a chair with a worn velvet backing.

All around the pile in the grass sat pieces of furniture and objects still intact, though less elegant than the ones gathered inside in the main sitting room: an open chifforobe with a water-decayed dress hanging in it, dining room chairs with faded, tapestried seats; crockery and paintings; an oval mirror on a stand tilted at an angle so it reflected the sea, whitecaps on distant waves.

"These things are likely consigned to the same fate," Thomas said.

The sun was just beginning to go down when we heard the faint strains of a concertina from the road and saw a gypsy caravan approaching. When it stopped, a big, bearded man in a gold embroidered vest descended, then peered mistrustfully in at us all through the iron bars.

I walked toward him and opened the gate, inviting him in.

"I think they're going to burn all of these things. You see, they've broken up so many of them already. But there's still a lot that's good, and you should take it."

He remained motionless a moment, his pale eyes searching mine, then nodded at me and stepped in through the gate. A wife, three daughters, and a son crept stealthily after. At first they were restrained, speaking to one another in subdued voices, but eventually they grew comfortable enough to squeal and cry out to one another at their finds. The man moved feverishly through the ruins and the cantles of what was already piled for burning, to see if there was anything worth salvaging, and managed to get out from under a broken table a tarnished, robust samovar. One of the older girls was dispatched to bring the caravan in through the gates, and they proceeded to load it up with furniture and silver and paintings, while the woman sighed rhapsodically over the find of a green velvet curtain.

Maighread and Caitlin searched through the cabinets of some of the still standing pieces. In one of the drawers, Maighread found a little box, which she kept and, examining it, wandered off.

Caitlin, who had found a candelabra, placed it on a nightstand in the grass and lit the stubs of the candles. The low breezes stretched and stirred the flames but did not extinguish them.

Thomas asked her for the matches, and he and the gypsy man lit the bonfire. As the sky darkened and the clouds raced across the moon, the tinker man sang in a long tenor, *Shall you come home again*

Michael O'Meara. Then he took up the concertina again and everyone sang "The Earl's Chair" and "The Morning Dew." The oldest tinker girls danced around the fire wrapped in shawls of Youghal lace and organza, while the youngest girl, ten or eleven years old, crawled around on all fours in the grass, letting Liam ride on her back.

Maighread stared into the flames, holding in her hands the little box she had found, while Caitlin looked pensively around her at the fallen grandeur.

Thomas came and took Caitlin's hand and they walked off together, then stood in the shadow of a pink tree. A petal wandered down onto Caitlin's shoulder and Thomas brushed it carefully away, then held her face in both hands as if it were made of something infinitely delicate and frangible.

Twenty-three

As Maighread, Liam, and I settle ourselves in the train car, I see that she has spotted someone she knows. A young man sitting across the way, engrossed in a book and oblivious of us. She looks flustered and I think this must be Aidan Callahan.

The train begins to move and he looks up and across at her and smiles. She introduces me to him, then, shifting slightly beside me, sits forward so her back is fully to me, creating the space of her own privacy. He is a handsome figure, and my heart drums with a premonition of dread. There is an edge to her earnestness. I lean my head against the window and see the two of them reflected there on the glass. He is leaning forward, smiling, with a look that says he knows how she feels about him. I close my eyes.

I hear, through the noise of the engines and the wind rushing past, strains of their conversation. They are talking about Pentecost and Haymaking, Michaelmas and Advent. Each feast still tinged with pagan connotations, suggestive of youth and coupling.

Her voice is higher pitched than usual and she is short of breath, and sensing the strain of wishing in her muscles, my head begins to ache.

"Mammy, I'm tired," Liam says and pulls at me so I settle him in my arms. Jostled by the movement of the train, he falls quickly to sleep.

The train stops in Kilkenny and Aidan Callahan rises from his seat. He does not ask Maighread for her address, but nods and says good-bye, then leaves the train.

I feel the fire of hurt spread through her. He passes outside the window and she leans past me, her lips pressed together to see if he will look up and wave, but he doesn't.

I feign oblivion to save her the pain of humiliation, but she is fierce right now against me, knowing me through. It is me she is angry with. And I allow it.

We ride the rest of the way to Dublin in silence. When I know Maighread is turned facing the other way, I steal a look at her. Droplets of sweat on her temple are as tiny as the heads of pins. She is fondling the little damascene box I'd seen her holding in Kenmare. Her fingers tighten around it and I wonder where she is, what she is imagining. I want to tell her not to think anymore of Aidan Callahan; that such passion invites tragedy. Yet how could I ever tell her such a thing?

It is later, when we get off the train and our minds are taken up with getting our bags and finding a coach, that I say to her suddenly, "You're beautiful." She hears the compassion in my voice, which she interprets as pity, and stiffens.

When we get out of the coach at Merchant's Quay, we are both surprised to see Manus come out to greet us. His eyes light at the sight of Maighread, and he reaches for her and gives her a convulsive, unpracticed hug.

"Da," she says sweetly and studies him to surmise his state of mind.

Feeling her scrutiny, he pushes a lock of hair behind his ear and smiles sheepishly at her. He has shaved and dressed nicely and seems all bumbling willingness in her presence. He lifts Liam with one arm and, with the other, clutches the bag that the driver has placed near the gate.

He looks well slept, intensely present, all tension gone from his muscles.

Maighread suppresses a smile, her eyes darting to mine as if to say, "You see how much he loves me?"

I smile back in silent acknowledgment.

"Where's Caitlin?" he asks me, a dark look coming into his eyes.

"She's staying with her friend in Kenmare. She'll come on the train in a few days."

At tea, Mrs. Flanagan brings out a golden, oblong pie, and Maighread holds court. Manus listens to everything she says, the things I've heard already, about girls I've never met but have become familiar with through her stories. He makes himself her audience for these tales and those about the foibles and eccentricities of the nuns. There is something almost childlike about his availability to her. He looks enchanted.

"Now *you* tell *me* everything," she says to him.

"I've finally finished what I've been building."

"Now will you finally take us there?"

"I'll take you all there as soon as Caitlin's back," he says.

"Take us tomorrow, Da!" Maighread cries. "You can give Caitlin her own private tour."

"All right," he says.

"What else is new?"

He shakes his head and then shrugs as if to say, "Nothing else."

"You've hardly said a word," she cries.

He looks chastised and searches himself. I sense a new struggle in him, a stronger fight to be present for her sake. He says earnestly and in a voice begging her understanding, "I spend all my time working, Love. I've forgotten how to have a conversation."

The words fill her with disappointment.

Outside the back window, robins bicker in the larch tree, and Liam mimicks their bright jabber, his voice building suddenly in volume and vehemence. Maighread starts to laugh. Manus looks at Liam and then at Maighread, and the sun comes out again in his face.

That evening as I am about to put out the upstairs lamp, I hear Maighread crying in her room. Peering in her door, I see her sitting on the edge of her bed, her face hidden in the black drift of her loosened hair. The damascene box is open on her nightstand, and inside it I see a little ivory figurine: a naked woman holding her arms open, her face lifted as if she were looking into the face of a lover. It is a piece that has been broken from a larger sculpture; an area of one leg and arm is incomplete.

Has Aidan Callahan grown necessary to her? Has she built around him a tender system of dreams and hopes? It's him, I know, that pulls at her, makes her hesitant about Paris.

She wipes her face and sighs softly. One hand lifts and brushes the silk of her new bed curtain.

The following afternoon, Manus, with Liam on his shoulders, Maighread, and I take a long walk up Baggot Street until we reach Waterloo Road, where Manus unlocks the door of the newly completed but still empty museum, set anachronistically among more residential-looking buildings.

We ascend seven flights of marble stairs until we reach the highest tier. "Come," Manus says and leads us to a door, which he unlocks. It opens outside onto the roof, where a shimmering structure vaults up before us into the sky.

"A castle!" Liam cries as he covers his eyes with his hands, the sunlight almost blinding on the walls of cut crystal, glass, and bits of amber.

I walk around the pavilion, then step a few yards back, trying to get a full picture. From a little distance it looks like the ghost of a beautifully appointed house. But stepping closer again I am aware of the intricate dialogue between translucent rock and supporting bolts of white iron.

There is a great openness to the interior. Along one wall, an arcaded gallery, all of translucent rock, set with slim Doric columns. Throughout, seashells are glazed here and there into the walls.

A curved, flying staircase, also crafted completely of translucent stone, leads to a higher tier, a balcony and more windows.

Manus walks through, opening the many windows along the lower tier, which offer excellent views out over Dublin, and on the eastern wall, down at Kingstown Harbour. I notice now windows along the domed ceiling, connected to chains, one of which Manus reaches for and works like a pulley so the panel opens, letting in soft breaking sounds of wind and the distant screeching of seabirds.

"Look here," he says, showing Maighread and Liam a drain in the floor where it slopes down in the center of the room. "If you decide to let the rain in through the windows above, it will shower down in this area, and go into the drain."

Maighread laughs. "Oh, Da! Who'd want to come up and sit in here in a deluge?"

He shrugs his shoulders. "I might be inclined to do such a thing," he says. "And I can imagine your mother doing such a thing as well."

I catch his eyes, and the look in them suffuses me with warmth.

"Yes," she says, smiling at me as well. "I can imagine her doing that."

Wrought-iron benches painted white are arranged throughout, facing off for views of the sky or, from those placed closer to the windows, down at the City.

Manus has settled himself on a bench looking toward the harbor. He leans forward, and I study the lines of his back and shoulders, his profile and his distant gaze. How many incarnations of this man have I seen? He will always be both mysterious and familiar to me, ever transforming like his god of masons and architects, Mercury.

This monument to air and light inspires reverie. Maighread walks reflectively through, unlatches one of the windows and stands with her arms crossed, gazing out. She is womanly and tall, and moves with a guarded grace. Unlike Caitlin's life, Maighread's still has not yet decided its shape.

"That boat there!" Manus cries. "That's the mercantile boat that plies between Dublin and Holland."

"That boat!" Liam echoes, standing on the bench beside Manus. "I want to go on that boat."

"We will go on a boat, Liam," Manus says. "This pavilion can be seen from the bay."

"We'll go in a boat, Mammy!" Liam cries.

"Yes, yes, Love!" I answer.

Maighread squints slightly in the breeze then gravitates toward her father and sits on the other side of him, both of their eyes set out on the sea.

"Up here I can really imagine Paris," she says, leaning against him. This morning at breakfast, Maighread spoke to us for the first time about the school in Paris; about her excitement at the idea, and about her uncertainty.

"There's the Guinness barge," Manus says, pointing, and both children look. "And over there, the Liverpool boat going out."

I wander slowly through the pavilion, running my fingers along the mirrored and mosaicked surfaces until I reach the staircase, small starfish embellishing the banister.

I ascend two or three stairs and stop. While I am in shadow, Manus and the children are lit by the descending sun that glints in Liam's fair hair and makes bright red the edge of one of his ears.

For a while it is only the wind that makes any sound, carrying in the smell of the sea and causing the chains on the open windows to shiver.

I have learned the names of all the winds but I don't think they live by any order.

Sensing my eyes on him, Liam turns and spots me on the stairs. He watches in wonder as the wind agitates my skirts. I give him a smile and he answers it by momentarily averting his eyes, then squeezing his lips together bashfully before breaking into a grin.

He turns his attention back to the boats and the water.

Both my daughters and my little son, I tell myself, will make their ways in the world.

The dark begins in the east over the Irish Sea. Ships drift in and away, and in the harbor, an anchored lightship twinkles.

ACKNOWLEDGMENTS

Thanks as always to my husband, Neil, and my daughter, Miranda, the two greatest blessings of my life.

Thanks to my agent, Regula Noetzli, for guidance and advice; and for shepherding me to my editor Doris Cooper, whose brilliant, intuitive feedback and unerring devotion have helped me to bring this book to life. I count myself among the luckiest of writers to be supported by the team at Simon and Schuster: Debbie Model, Kimberly Brissenden, Chris Lloreda, Marcia Burch, Mark Gompertz, and Trish Todd. Thank you all.

For help with translations into the Irish I wish to thank Ciaran O'Reilly, ever the sweet and steadfast friend; his mysterious brother, Brendan O'Reilly; and the very fine actor, Andrew Bennett.

I also wish to thank Claudia Bader for sharing with me her bibliography of alchemical texts. For feedback on early drafts of this novel, much thanks to my dear friends Sarah Fleming and Nancy Graham. Much gratitude to Jane Lury for invaluable feedback on the book in a later draft, and for her loving, supportive presence in my life.

And love to Carolina Conroy, magical, mystical Empress of Green.